"Harley Mazuk's WHITE WITH FISH, RED WITH MURDER is a delicious throwback to the PI stories of Hammett and Chandler, when all the dames had shapely gams. With shamus Frank Swiver on the case, no suspect goes unsuspected and no clue goes undetected. An entertaining, fun ride with colorful characters and snappy dialogue, this one's a treat! Mazuk's uncorked a real winner — good to the very last drop!"

— Alan Orloff, Agatha Award-nominated author of *Running From The Past*

"Harley Mazuk has an abiding love of wine and the hard-boiled private eye detective novel. Couple this with a sly sense of humor and an uncanny feel for the sights and sounds of San Francisco and the wine country around it shortly after the end of World War II and you have WHITE WITH FISH, RED WITH MURDER, a highly entertaining homage to the hard-boiled novels of the first half of the 20th Century."

— Con Lehane, author of *Murder at the 42nd Street Library*

"WHITE WITH FISH, RED WITH MURDER is a terrific mystery in the tradition of classic noir, a tale of deception and greed that twists and turns until its surprising end."

— Christina Kovac, author of *The Cutaway*

HARLEY MAZUK

WHITE WITH FISH
RED WITH MURDER

To

Anastasia

1

Vieux Désirs

There's promise in the air when you approach a passenger train from the platform. You can imagine it's carrying everyone you ever wanted to meet and the baggage cars are hauling your dreams.

Steam coursed through the pipes along the undersides of the cars, like blood through veins. Vera Peregrino and I strolled along the side of the Southern Pacific Cascade on a foggy, damp April afternoon in Oakland until we came to the last car. She pointed a lacquered red fingernail at *Vieux Désirs* lettered in gold paint on its side.

The invitation in my pocket read: *General Lloyd F. Thursby (U.S. Army, Ret.) requests the pleasure of your company, 1630 hours, 2 April, 1948, aboard his private railway car,* Vieux Désirs. Thursby's private varnish had a canopy over an open rear platform, marking it as a coach from an older era, but it appeared spic-and-span, with a fresh olive-green paint job.

Vera was my secretary at Old Vine Detective Agency. She was more than just my employee; we were friends, and I wanted to let her know I cared. I bought Vera some calla lilies from a flower vendor alongside the tracks. Her grateful smile showed straight white teeth between apple-red lips.

I paused alongside the track and with my thumbnail, slit the cellophane on a new deck of Pall Malls. I prefer Camels, but the Pall Mall package bears a Latin motto: *In hoc signo vinces.* My Latin's a little rusty—for all I know, it could have meant "Sign in here, Vince," but whenever I start a new case I buy Pall Malls and read the motto for good luck. I shook two out, cupped my hands, lit them, and passed one to Vera, who was gazing at me with a Mona Lisa grin.

The Southern Pacific conductor climbed down from the side door of *Vieux Désirs* as we lingered a bit. He had a wad of tobacco in his jaw and must have been waiting to spit while he'd been in the private car because he let out a stream that sluiced between the train and the platform. He saw us and touched his cap as he passed by, and I gave him a friendly nod. After he passed me, he climbed back on board the train at the next door. From that I deduced that the doors between *Vieux Désirs* and the rest of the train were locked, which I understood to be common practice among the railroads when they were hauling private cars.

My gear for the weekend was packed in a duffel bag

slung over my shoulder. I tossed it up on the landing and then held Vera's bag and gave her a hand up. Her cocktail dress was short enough that when she raised a knee to climb the steps, she revealed some thigh up around her garter. As many times as I saw it, it was inspiring, a thigh of beauty, and I gave her a wolf whistle. She held the lilies across her legs with her right hand, and used her left to grab the rail in the stairwell. When she got to the top step, she winked at me as I climbed on board.

The door into the coach off the steel landing opened into a galley. We'd gone in the service entrance. A stainless gas range dominated the layout, nestled in between shiny cabinets like a king between two rooks. Pots, pans, and cooking utensils dangled from hooks. Everything about the kitchen spoke of efficiency and careful planning. It seemed as though we could count on a good meal later tonight.

We passed through a swinging door onto a spiffy hardwood floor, mostly covered by a large and plush Persian rug. I'm no expert on Oriental carpets, but I think it was the Ardabil mosque pattern, done in dark red and a close, tight weave. It didn't take an expert to tell it was genuine, old, and expensive. There was that unmistakable *je ne sais quoi* in the way my damp, dirty brogues skimmed across the pile.

A few lights were on in the lounge; I could see burgundy wallpaper with dark wood trim. To my right were two dining tables, each with four seats, and on the left an upright piano with a light oak finish. Beyond that, a group of folks sat in the far end of the car. I led Vera partway down, until the man facing us spoke.

"Ah, you must be Frank Swiver," he said.

"I am, and this is Vera Peregrino." There were nods and greetings, and the man who had spoken rose. I strode across to shake his hand.

"Lloyd Thursby," he said. He was an older gent with gray hair and clear, alert blue eyes. He wore a camel hair topcoat draped on his shoulders like a cape, over a dark brown, well-cut suit. He stood a couple of inches taller than me, maybe six foot two, and he carried himself ramrod straight, so he appeared even taller. I had the idea he was fit and powerful for his age. "This is my majordomo," he gestured at a man standing near the rear corridor of the train car, "Fenwick." He was younger and three or four inches shorter than Thursby.

Fenwick stepped forward. "I'll take your bags, sir."

I gave him my duffel and Vera's suitcase, and when he reached out his arms to take them, his sleeves slid up, revealing thick, dark hair on the backs of his wrists and hands. He carried the luggage into the corridor, and his wrists stayed down out of his sleeves making his arms appear long and apelike.

General Thursby held out his left hand toward a dame in a chair on my right. "This is Sally DeBains." She was well dressed and well coiffed, fiftyish, and blond — though I suspected the hair color came out of a bottle.

"How do you do?" she said. She had plenty of ice on her fingers, and I clasped the hand she extended and gave it a light kiss. I thought about biting one of the rings, but she didn't strike me as a big Three Stooges fan.

"I'm well, thanks," I replied. "How do you do?" More jewelry drooped around her neck, and she obviously had gained a couple of pounds as she aged. She may have been shaking her maracas a bit lower than she used to, but she had probably been a hot number twenty years ago. For my money, she was still hot enough.

Thursby stepped back toward his chair and extended his right hand. "Over here, allow me to present Marcus Aurelius Wolff, our philosopher, and a fellow collector."

Wolff was a huge, fat man, whose bulk blocked much of the light from the window behind him. His three-piece charcoal pinstriped suit oozed polish and quality, and he held a pearl-gray hat in his lap. Although it was cool, and I still had my trench coat on, the fat man was perspiring. He beamed and drew a silk hanky out of his breast pocket, then wiped his bald head.

"An honor, sir, an honor to meet you," said Wolff.

I assured him the honor was all mine. "A collector of what?" I asked.

"Why wine, Swiver, wine, of course." Thursby laughed. "That's what brings our little group together, you know. We taste wine, we savor it, we debate about it."

"And what do you do, sir?" Wolff asked me.

"I drink it." I gave him a grin.

Thursby stepped in. "Frank is a writer working on my biography." Writer was as good as anything. General Thursby had enclosed a hand-written note with his invitation:

Swiver,

I hear you know a little about wine, but that's not the only reason I'm inviting you to my tasting. I'd like to hire you. I'll brief you about the job on the train. You can bring another operative if you like. Make it look as if you're along for the party — I don't want to tip my hand. Whether you take the case or not, I'll pay you for your time and you'll get to taste some good wines.

Thursby

That was all I knew; it wasn't much, but it was enough to get me there. I hadn't had a case for weeks, and I needed the money. He didn't want to tip his hand. I would play along.

"Miss Peregrino is my research assistant," I said. Vera smiled.

And so we circulated around the room and met

the guests, and Vera and I shook hands like a couple of politicians at the Orange County Fair.

And then as the introductions were coming to an end, I saw her, to my left, by the piano. A short black dress, low cut, raven-dark hair, emerald eyes that almost glowed, over robust cheekbones — it was Cicilia Ricci, girl of my dreams.

"And last, this is Cicilia O'Callaghan," the general went on. "Cicilia —"

"We've met." A chill ran up my spine.

"Hello, Frank. It's been a while."

"Fourteen years. You look good, Cicilia." The widow O'Callaghan, formerly Cicilia Ricci. Her hair was cut a little shorter than when I knew her — wavy on top, parted in the middle, and falling down to her shoulder blades in curls. Her dark eyebrows curved high over her big eyes in graceful roman arches. She'd been seventeen when I met her; she'd be thirty-two now. No longer a budding teenager but a woman in her prime, and more ravishing than ever, if that was possible.

"You look well too, Frank." Her voice was deep, smoky, seductive. It was Cici's normal voice.

I shook another Pall Mall out of the pack and fumbled with a box of wooden matches like a nine-year-old trying to light up in the schoolyard. "Having a little trouble, Frank?" Vera noticed. She tilted her head down and to her right, and angled an eye up at me, amused. She relieved me of the matches, struck one and held it out, steadying my hand as I lit up.

C'mon, Swiver, get a grip on yourself. You're on a case. I clenched and unclenched my fists, and turned away from Cicilia to face the general.

Vera stepped forward and sunk down onto the settee. I chose the chair on the aisle by Cicilia. "Well, ladies and gentlemen, welcome," said Thursby, returning to his seat. "It's nearly 1700 hours, and the Cascade will be departing soon. On time, I'm assured. Our tasting this evening will begin at 1900."

Fenwick had deposited our bags, crossed back through the lounge and was now coming out with a tray, which he put on the low table in front of Vera. "But for now, we have coffee, tea, and Fenwick will be opening some sparkling wine — Cava," Thursby continued.

I knew Cava from my years in Catalonia. A cork popped over my right shoulder, and Fenwick came around with glasses and a thick green bottle. I took some bubbly, as did three other guests. Thursby and Vera had tea; Cici drank coffee.

Thursby continued, "Tonight my friends, I'll be pouring a selection of wines for your enjoyment. Our theme will be comparing California wines and French wines. I have chosen the best from old world and new, and I leave it to you to decide: is one better than the other? Or are they simply different styles?"

"I'm sure it will soon be clear enough which is better," said John McQuade. He was a sour-looking gent next to Sally, who hadn't said much to me but leered at Vera during the introductions.

"Yes?" said Thursby. "Well, we'll see, won't we? Perhaps there will be some surprises. At any rate, I hope you'll find them all worthwhile. We'll be serving the wines blind, so you'll be judging them based on your impressions of what's in the glass, but without further knowledge of who made them, or where." He sipped his tea. "And for the highlight of the evening, I'm pleased to be able to pour from a magnum of the latest vintage of Ravensridge Wines Blackbird."

"That would be the '45?" asked Wolff.

"Yes, Marcus, the 1945 vintage. Many of you know the Blackbird is the rarest of California wines, bottled only in magnums — one and a half liter bottles — and I'm one of the fortunate few to whom it's allocated.

"We thank our friend, Joe Damas, the distributor, for that." He raised his teacup in a little salute to Joe, on the settee next to Vera. Joe raised his champagne saucer in reply, as smoke trailed up from the cigarette in his mouth toward his half-closed eyes.

"Pardon me, General," Vera said, "the Blackbird you're talking about, is that from the vineyard out on River Road in Sonoma?" Fenwick was just pouring for McQuade and arched an eyebrow at Vera.

General Thursby hesitated. "Yes, it is, Miss Peregrino. Do you know the wine?"

"Well, no," she answered. "I've never had the wine, but the vineyard was part of the old Fenucchi spread, right?"

Thursby blinked his blue eyes. "Yes."

"It's adjacent to my dad's ranch," said Vera with a natural smile. "I grew up next door, practically in the shadow of Blackbird Hill."

"My God. It's a small world." Thursby's eyes were fixed on Vera now. Vera was a tall attractive woman with golden-brown hair. She was an eyeful in that red dress, but Thursby wasn't ogling her the way most men do. He was studying her, concentrating on taking her in.

"I even know the legend of the Blackbird," Vera said.

McQuade rolled his eyes, but Wolff said, "Oh, do tell it, Miss Peregrino."

"Yes," said Thursby, "it's a great black falcon. That's where the Blackbird vineyard gets its name. Fog protects those old vines from the morning sun, and when the fog burns off, you'll see that black falcon watching over the vineyard, watching in silence, perched in that eucalyptus tree, high on the top of the hill above the vines."

"And no one knows where the blackbird comes from." Vera glanced my way now. Maybe she wondered what was wrong with my ear. I let go of my earlobe and released a deep breath. "No one knows what year it first appeared. But the grapes it watches over are the best in California, year after year. Zinfandel, petite sirah, Alicante, carignane—that's *nero misto*, you know? The fruit ripens slowly and late, and it is so rich, so concentrated, so dark, and so good." The room was quiet.

"Well," I interjected, breaking the spell, "if it's that good, we're in for a treat tonight."

McQuade snorted as if he didn't believe it.

"Oh, keep an open mind, Mr. McQuade," said Wolff. "A wonderful story the way you tell it, Miss Peregrino. How exciting to grow up in such a legendary place."

"And that same bird is there, every year, every day, from bud break in the spring until the last bunches are harvested—sometimes in October," said Vera. "It's true. I used to see the black falcon up there all the time when I was a little girl."

True or not, it was the sort of story that you'd want to spread around if you owned the vineyard—a legend like that could inspire the imagination, maybe drive up the price.

Then the Cascade chugged out of the station, and even though it was smooth, almost imperceptible at first, it seemed enough to shake Thursby out of his reverie. Fenwick cleared his throat.

"Well," said the general, "I foresee a late night for us, and I'm not as young as I used to be. I'm going to my cabin to rest a bit. I invite you all to make yourselves comfortable in your rooms, or avail yourselves of more tea. Thank you for joining me tonight, and I'll see you in a couple hours." He picked up a leather dispatch case that rested against his chair, turned, and headed up the corridor.

2

Night of the Honeysuckles

Vera rose and announced she wanted to go to her room. That gave me an opportunity to get out of there and compose myself before talking to Cici, so I offered to escort her.

"You're in number seven, Miss Peregrino," said Fenwick. "And you're in one," he told me. The first cabin we came to had a 9 under a half-moon of three stars. I assumed that would be Thursby's. We passed eight, and I dropped Vera at her room, telling her I'd come for her at seven.

"Nineteen hundred hours." She saluted, mocking the general's voice.

At the far end of the car, from the galley and the lounge, were a toilet and shower room and cabin number one. It had a sitting area, which could be converted into a single bed. There was a good-sized window, covered by venetian blinds, closed, and burgundy curtains, drawn open. It had a connecting door on the side of compartment two.

An envelope on the bed had my name on it. I unpacked my duffel, opened the blinds, and sat down watching the backyards of Oakland glide by while I slit the envelope flap.

It was from Thursby. Inside was a check made out to Old Vine Detective Agency for $150, signed by Nick Fenwick, and a note from the general. I recognized his handwriting from the note that accompanied my invitation.

Swiver,

Thanks for coming. Enclosed is a check for your retainer. Let me know when that runs out.

Two things — first, there are some tensions among the guests. I can still take care of myself, but I wouldn't mind having someone I can depend on to watch my back. And second, the police are doing nothing in the O'Callaghan killing. They closed the case as an accidental poisoning. I'm sure it's murder, but I need some kind of proof. I want you to find it. Rusty O'Callaghan was my friend.

I suggest you commence your investigation with the widow.

Thursby

My stomach knotted up, and a dull garnet haze came between my eyes and the paper after I read the words *"killing . . . murder."* I hadn't known Rusty O'Callaghan, but I knew of him, and I thought he was a lucky guy who had it all. He had money, good looks, and wit. He had Cici.

And I had Vera. A few hours ago, we'd met in the office on Post Street to go to the train in Oakland together. We had a couple of glasses of cabernet together, and one thing led to another, as it often did for us. And after we'd made love, she whispered in my ear, "I love you, Frank."

"It'll be exciting to go along as an op, not just a secretary," she said. Vera's scarlet cocktail dress was folded neatly over the back of one of my client chairs; my suit was hung up, but the rest of my clothes were all over the floor, and we both lounged naked, face-to-face, legs intertwined, on the old leather davenport that I had alongside one wall. Not entirely naked, she still wore her red, high-heeled shoes, and I had my fedora on the back of my head. The light coming through the office window fell on the downy yellow hair on her upper thighs. Vera was about five eight. Her height and long legs made her appear slender and elegant, like a fashion model or a rich girl. Yet from another angle or in a different outfit she might look like an athlete who rode a bike to work, or a sinewy, but healthy, farmer's daughter. She had golden brown hair that fell across her shoulders just far enough to cover her breasts if she ever decided to do a Lady Godiva act. But now her hair had fallen back to the sides and she lay there, breasts revealed, in all her wanton beauty.

I wanted to say, "I love you too, Vera," but for some reason, I didn't. I couldn't because something felt different from that time I had been in love, in love with Cici.

I splashed a little water on my face at the washbasin, and started to shave.

I remembered when Rusty O'Callaghan had died. I'd even clipped the story from the *Examiner* at the time. It was only a couple of months ago. He'd died at home one morning, the apparent victim of a bizarre poisoning.

Then, in the mirror over the sink, I saw the connecting door to compartment two start to open. I thought I'd checked the lock, but maybe not—someone was coming in. Everything was close in the small train cabin. I turned and was about to shoulder the door hard, but a whiff of scent in the air made me stop myself. Cicilia O'Callaghan came into the compartment quickly and closed the door behind her.

"Hello, Frank." Her voice was deep, with a dry whispery note. It was the kind of voice that an actress might use for a passionate love scene. It was the kind of voice that would make the actor play the sap for her.

"Hi ya, doll. Still using the same perfume as the old

days?"

"Night of the Honeysuckles, Frank. It's been a long time. I'm surprised you remembered."

There are some things a man doesn't forget, like the feeling I had when you threw me over for Rusty. "Yeah, it brings back old times." My voice sounded hollow to me. Cici had slipped into my room without shoes. Minus her high heels, she was about five feet four inches — of trouble. Of all the compartments in the general's private varnish, she had to have the one next to mine.

"Thank God you're here tonight, Frank. I need help."

I didn't know what to say to that. So I said nothing and drank in Cicilia with my eyes. After fourteen years, they were thirsty eyes and she was as refreshing as a splash of Vouvray, and more intoxicating too. Her skin had a healthy golden-olive glow, as if she'd been in the sun. Her black dress was simple and elegant, but un-widow-like. The low cut only emphasized her ripe and voluptuous breasts. With my height advantage in the small compartment, I was practically forced to eyeball her cleavage.

She followed my gaze. "You like what you see, Frank?"

"You know I always did, Cici. Who wouldn't?"

"Rusty, for one. He couldn't have cared less." She sighed. "It's nice to be noticed again." The train rocked, and Cici bounced against me.

"Oh, yeah. Rusty O'Callaghan. Tough break about your husband. A poison mushroom omelet? You were there, weren't you?"

"Yeah. I'd thought they were chanterelles." She blinked her eyes. "Well, at least it didn't happen at the restaurant."

"I can see how that might be bad for business, poisoning the diners." Rusty O'Callaghan had opened the popular restaurant, *Chez Cici*, where he'd installed Cicilia, his new wife, as chef.

"You say you need help, doll?" Night of the Honeysuckles seemed to be entangled in the waves of her hair, just under my nose. My mind drifted back to those nights fourteen years ago, when Cici would finish her waitressing shift at John's Grill and we'd leave together and hurry over to my single room.

In '33, I was a recent Berkeley grad, trying to crack into a teaching job. I happened into John's one night, wondering if I could afford a sandwich and a beer. The beer was only a nickel, but I paid with a piece of my heart.

Cicilia Ricci had been a waitress there. She was about eighteen then, maybe seventeen and a half, when I met her, and she was the stuff young men dream about. Petite, with dark-brown, almost ebony hair, she had emerald eyes. You know the color of the sea off Monterey sometimes when the sunlight angles across it? Her eyes were that kind of sparkling green that had their own light, and when I gazed into them, they lured me deep into their sea-green abyss. I'd kept coming back to John's, to sit at one of Cicilia's tables, but I wasn't coming back for the food. I watched Cici move around the tables, we talked, she winked at me, or licked her lips, and a burning would start deep down inside me.

Ronald "Rusty" O'Callaghan had been a rumrunner in southern California in the 1920s who had blown into town late in 1933 when Repeal dried things up for him. He started showing up at John's Grill. O'Callaghan would dig into a twenty-four-ounce T-bone and drink a half-pint of Scotch whisky. He gave Cicilia rides in his Packard. He told her tales of gun-battles off the Catalina coast, of punching a shark in the nose while clinging to a floating wooden crate of gin, and of paying off the LA cops, while outsmarting the G-men. He carried a thick roll of banknotes and laughed loudly. Rusty O'Callaghan, a man of action who had an air of danger about him, brought excitement into the restaurant. Cicilia Ricci must have felt that excitement, and felt it was all for her.

I'd despised Rusty O'Callaghan when he took Cicilia out of John's, and I'd envied him when he married her. That was in '34, the last time I'd seen either of them, and the first time I had that empty ache inside. Rusty O'Callaghan sure was a lucky guy, and I'd drawn a losing hand. Now O'Callaghan was dead. A police spokesman had termed the death "suspicious, but presumably accidental." And

I'd lived to read about it.

I was bitter about being dumped, but that passion I'd felt for Cicilia never quit burning inside me. There's been a little pilot light on these last fourteen years.

"**I** need money, Frank," she said. "I'm a poor widow now, you know. Thursby owes me, but he won't pay up."

"Poor? I hear *Chez Cici* does good business."

"Sure, Chez Cici does good, but doing good in the restaurant business just pays the bills. Owning one restaurant means working fifty-two weeks a year, and if you're good, it's a living, but that's about all. It's not enough. What I've got to do is expand. I want to open a branch in Sausalito."

"So how's the general owe you, doll? Did he run up a tab?" I breathed in the scent of honeysuckles warmed by body heat, maybe a little garlic and oil too, from all those hours in the kitchen, and a definite, undeniable undercurrent of muskiness, rising up from her center. It was making my head spin, but I sucked it in like a man struggling in the water takes air when he's at the surface.

"Hardly," she said. "Look, I found these in Rusty's desk."

Cicilia carried a little black bag on a thin strap over her shoulder, and she reached in and extracted a fistful of papers, half sheets, and some even smaller — the size of currency. She handed them to me as she spoke. "Gambling debts, Frank. They're promissory notes for gambling debts."

I flipped through them. Five hundred here, $1000 on another, $700, $2400. The same scrawl at the bottom of each one might have been "Lloyd Thursby." It might have been the same hand that had signed the notes I'd received.

Cici kept talking, filling me in as I glanced through the IOUs. "Rusty used to go over to Thursby's place four or five nights a week, around ten or eleven, and sit with the general and play cards for hours."

"Looks like Rusty was a lucky guy."

"Hah! Lucky?" She turned, sauntered over to the window, and peered out. "You couldn't prove it by me. I never even knew he was winning, Frank. The soft-headed bum never brought home a nickel. He just took the general's paper."

"You show these to Thursby?" I followed her.

"Not yet. I just found them. But you can show them to Thursby. You can make him pay me. Thursby threatened me and had his goon throw me out."

"His goon?"

"Fenwick." Cici turned back to me. "That hairy wine-steward." Fenwick—I didn't like the picture in my mind of him with his paws on Cici, giving her the bum's rush. Something told me the apeman and I weren't going to get along.

I felt a tug at my trousers. I'd been reviewing the notes Cici had given me and musing over Fenwick. When I glanced at her again, I saw her black dress on the floor in a circle around her feet. She was squatting down in front of me, her butt on the seat, while her fingers worked at my fly.

"Jesus, doll. What do you think you're doing?"

"Oh, Frank. I can't help it. It's been so long, Frank. I'm so hot. I want you to make me feel like a woman again."

It'd been a long time all right. Fourteen years is a long time. Did Cicilia think she could just walk out of my life without so much as a fare-thee-well, then sashay back in fourteen years later and pick up where she'd left off? Now she rose to her feet, her green eyes flashing and locked on mine. Reaching behind her back, Cici undid the clasp on her black bra. She slipped it off, tossed it across the compartment, and shook her shoulders. The IOUs wafted to the floor as I cupped each breast with a hand and plunged my face down into their softness.

Maybe you've walked with danger and laughed and said, "Let's go; you can't beat me." Maybe you know what it's like to go without something for years, like maybe you were a boozer who lived through Prohibition without getting a drink. Then all of a sudden after all those years you can have it again, and it's better than ever. If so, I guess

I don't have to tell you what I felt, lying with Cici across the Pullman bed of my compartment. And if you haven't done anything like that, maybe you wouldn't understand the feeling I'm talking about anyhow.

I checked my watch, and it was almost seven. It's not that I didn't know where the time had gone. It's more like I didn't know where *I* had been. Wherever it was, I liked it there, and I didn't want to come back.

"Okay, Cici, I'll take your case. I'll talk to Thursby."

"Be careful, Frank. He's dangerous."

"I laugh at danger."

"I knew I could count on you. I'll give you ten percent of whatever you collect."

"Twenty-five dollars a day, doll. Plus expenses." She knew she could count on me. Hell, Cici could have seduced Mohandas Gandhi into donning a suit and tie, and he would have eaten filet mignon to please her.

"Right now, we've got to get dressed," I said. "It's seven o'clock." I yanked her off the bed to her feet and reeling her in, planted a long kiss on her lips. "There's wine out there to taste." I sent her on her way to her compartment with a smack on the butt. That bitterness from fourteen years ago—it wasn't completely gone, but Cici had sweetened me up a little.

I had two clients, and two jobs to do. I needed the work bad, but could I give Cici what she wanted and help Thursby too?

3

A Slug through the Pump

Cici slipped through the connecting door back to her compartment. After a couple of moments, I wondered if she had really been there at all. Maybe it had been a dream. The plush on the wine-red seat had a dark stain, and I touched it. Wet. Well, I'd had dreams like that before, and Cicilia had played a starring role in some of them.

I glanced around the room. On the floor were the promissory notes made out to Rusty O'Callaghan, signed "Lloyd Thursby." I hadn't had those when I left town. The scent of honeysuckles still lingered, and that wasn't my aftershave I smelled, therefore, it had been Cicilia.

I cleaned up quickly and dressed, trying to regain my focus. I was uneasy working for Cici, but I wasn't quite sure why. All right, perhaps I did know why — Vera. What I'd done with Cici didn't bother me. It had been swell. But it would likely hurt Vera if she knew. She had no claims on me, nor I on her, but she had some expectations, and I knew right away I'd failed to live up to them. Only a few hours ago, I'd bought her those calla lilies. Only a half-hour ago, I'd been thinking about telling Vera I loved her. Now that I'd seen Cici again, my world with Vera had been shaken.

I shrugged it off. I had to watch Thursby's back. I wasn't entirely comfortable working for the general without having talked to him about the case, but I expected that to straighten itself out. At any rate, it felt good to be working after so many bad months, and I had Thursby's check warming my pocket.

I angled my shoulders through the compartment door and stepped into the corridor. The train was moving along at a good clip now, and I loped along the hallway like a sailor who'd found his sea legs.

Stopping at number seven, I rapped a couple of times with my knuckles and called "Vera," but she didn't answer. I was surprised that she would have gone ahead without me, but it was after seven, so I was late. Vera liked her wine as much as I did and probably didn't want them to start without her. Resolving to make it up to her, I rolled back into motion with the train and continued on my course for the lounge.

"I purchased the '45 *Bourgognes* in some depth," the fat man was declaiming from a seat by the window. Vera was already there. Her golden hair, and her bare shoulders and arms were bright spots, picking up light from the little wall lamps around the curtained lounge. I gave her a friendly wink. She jerked her head away.

"I understand, Marcus, that you found prices low," said Joe Damas, a lightweight guy, tough and wiry, maybe about five eight, Vera's height. He had olive skin and short, curly black hair. A cigarette drooped from his lips, and he squinted as the smoke curled up to his eyes.

"Indeed I did, Joe, indeed I did. I was fortunate to have American dollars. Not only was the franc weak after the war, but many of these estates and domains needed cash. One might say I was in the right place at the right time."

"I hear you made a real killing." Hints of an accent tinted Joe's English, but I couldn't place it.

Marcus Wolff never hesitated. "There was benefit all around, Joe, I assure you. I obtained some great wines. The producers of those wines realized what they needed too. Money to rebuild, money to buy barrels, money to live until the next harvest. Indeed, although I certainly enriched my cellar—I don't deny that, no sir, not for a moment I don't—my French friends had some very real needs. Many fulfilled them, thanks to our little exchange."

"So you might say, Marcus," said Sally DeBains, "that you were doing our French friends quite a favor."

"Well, Madame DeBains," Wolff said, "I am too humble to express it quite that way myself, but, if you wish to . . ."

"You're a living, breathing Marshall Plan, ain't you?" said Mrs. DeBains. "So very generous."

"You're too kind, Madame DeBains, too kind," the fat man said.

At this point, John McQuade spoke up. "Well, Wolff, if those '45 Burgundies are as good as you say, I would very much like to try some."

"Alas, Mr. McQuade, I wish it were possible." Wolff steepled his fingers and glanced heavenward. "But I wouldn't think of opening any now. They're far too young. It would be a crime to open them now, sir, yes, a crime."

Someone muttered something that sounded like "generous" under his breath and followed it with a snicker. Wolff's bulbous head snapped around, but rather than rejoin that, he beamed magnanimously and used the opportunity to acknowledge my arrival in the lounge.

"Aha! Joe, Madame DeBains. Here's our writer friend, Mr. Swiver. Forgive me, sir. We were engaged in an enjoyable discussion of our favorite subject, wine." He hoisted his bulk out of the easy chair and extended a fat pink hand on a wrist as thick as my calf to wave me to a seat.

"Don't let me interrupt, Mr. Wolff." I sat by Vera, leaned in and said in a low tone, "Hey, sweetheart. Sorry I was late. You look like a million bucks, you know?"

"Don't give me your line, you bastard," she whispered without looking at me. She jabbed at me with an elbow and moved away to a seat between Damas and Wolff. Cicilia O'Callaghan slinked in, a smoldering ember in black. Her hair and makeup were perfect. She settled into the seat Vera had left. I felt lightheaded at her nearness; but one thing was certain, I had to hide my feelings for Cici from Vera.

"Are you a connoisseur of the grape too?" asked Mrs. DeBains.

"Hardly, Mrs. DeBains, though I do enjoy pulling a cork now and then," I said. "Pardon me, but are you *the* Sally DeBains, of Noir Côtes DeBains?"

"Yes."

"I've been a big fan of your pinot noir for years."

The old dame grasped my hand and surprised me with a grip like a lumberjack's. "Ah, well then you *are* a connoisseur, Mr. Swiver." She laughed.

And so we went around the room making small talk. John McQuade turned out to be a pretty well-known wine critic. He was the author of a monthly newsletter, *From the Spitbucket*. I'd heard of it, but didn't read it. I preferred to spend my discretionary income on a couple of nice bottles of grenache, or an issue of *Argosy*.

During these pleasantries, Fenwick had been popping in and out of the kitchen, getting things ready for the dinner. But General Thursby had not yet made an appearance. So the next time Fenwick popped out, with a tray of roasted pecans, I said, "Say, where is General Thursby anyway?

It's nearly seven thirty. I could use a glass of wine."

"He's still in his compartment, sir," said Fenwick.

"Well, shouldn't you call him?"

"I'm sure he'll be out presently, sir."

"Come, come, Fenwick," said Wolff. "This is unusual. General Thursby is usually very prompt. When he says '1900 hours' you can set your watch by it. If your watch went to nineteen. Ahem. Aha, ha, ha, ha. 'He who laughs best today will also laugh last.' Nietzsche. Why don't you go check on him, Fenwick? We're all assembled here. Your dinner is ready, isn't it?"

"Well, yeah, but . . ." said Fenwick.

"Well, then, why risk burning anything?" said Wolff. "Go ahead, Fenwick, go ahead. Summon your boss."

The steward scowled. "Very good, Mr. Wolff." He headed into the corridor.

"Maybe he's fallen asleep. Taking a little nap or something," Wolff rambled on. "The gentle rocking of the train, eh? I daresay we'll all sleep like babes tonight."

"Tell us again what you're writing for the general," McQuade said to me.

"Well, I'm working on a biography. Thursby's military career, the war, and all. Vera is my research assistant."

"How charming," said McQuade, staring hard at her. "Must take all the drudgery out of research, having so lovely an assistant." My research assistant was quiet. I thought she was being a little hard on me for being five or ten minutes late. Maybe something else was eating her.

Just then Fenwick reappeared from the corridor. "The general doesn't answer my knock, and the door to his compartment is locked."

"Well, I hope he's all right," said Sally DeBains. "Can't we check on him? Do you have a key?"

"No, General Thursby had the only keys. He must have dozed off or something."

"How about the connecting door, Fenwick?" asked Wolff. "Who's in number eight?"

"Number eight is mine, Mr. Wolff," said Fenwick. "The general likes me to bunk close by, in case he needs anything. I suppose we could try the door from eight."

"Let me come with you," I said.

Now, the apeman gave me a scowl, but he didn't object when I followed him back into the corridor. I tried the door when we passed number nine, but it was nothing doing. Fenwick plucked out a key from a pants pocket under his apron and unlocked the door to eight. The cabin was tidy with a smoky odor that I didn't immediately place. Fenwick tried the connecting door and the handle turned. He tapped on it, cracked it open, and called through, "General? General Thursby? It's seven thirty, sir." There was no answer, but a little more of that smell seemed to waft in. It was the smell of gunsmoke.

"Let's go, Fenwick." I brushed past him into number nine.

Some broken bottle glass crunched under my feet. The compartment's outside window was broken. Train noise and cool air rushed in. The table was on its side as was the chair. General Thursby was sprawled on his back, a broken-off crystal stem clutched in his hand. An overturned bottle rolled back and forth on the floor as the train rocked. I picked up the intact bottle when it rolled against my foot and set it on the sink—a '45 DeBains pinot noir.

A big red splotch bloomed in the center of Lloyd Thursby's white shirt. I didn't need a taste to know it wasn't the pinot.

4

He Would Have Wanted It That Way

The smell of gunfire still hung in the room, despite the draft from the window, as the others filed in behind Fenwick and me.

"He was a good friend."

"A great warrior."

"He will be missed."

"Damn," said Fenwick. "The bottle of '45 Blackbird Noir that we were going to feature tonight is gone!"

"Stop the train! Call the police!" cried Spitbucket McQuade. He reached toward the emergency cord.

"Hold on, McQuade." I stopped his arm. "I'm a detective. I'll handle this."

"A dick, eh? I thought you said you were a writer, or something," said Mrs. DeBains.

"That was just cover, sister, but there's no need for that now. Vera, go up front, sweetheart. See if you can raise the conductor; bring him back here."

She appeared defiant for a moment and said nothing, but then she started out. Fenwick said, "Hold on. You'll need this key."

"You have a key to the Southern Pacific cars?" I asked.

"No, the Southern Pacific's open. It's the key to our private car. I keep it locked. Got a deadbolt that needs a key on both sides." He withdrew a small ring of keys from his vest pocket and held one out to Vera. He seemed to be gazing off somewhere else as he pressed it into her hand.

It was good to see Vera take the keys and go into action. Whatever had been bothering her, at least I could depend on her now. Too bad Thursby hadn't been able to depend on me. *"I wouldn't mind having someone I can depend on to watch my back,"* he'd said. Yeah, well, a fine job I'd done of that. True, he hadn't taken it in the back. It seemed as if Thursby had been face-to-face with his killer. But it was no use worrying about that. I could give the money back. Or I could start earning it.

"Fenwick," I said, "when did you see the general last?"

"Not since he went to his compartment, shamus." Of course, Fenwick knew my job. He'd signed the check. "He told me he didn't want to be disturbed until the tasting. I had plenty to do anyhow, fixing dinner, getting the wines ready."

"I say, Fenwick, you know this sort of thing really

shakes a person up." It was Wolff wiping his forehead with his hankie. "Don't you suppose we could open a bottle and have a drink? I mean, a murder, after all."

"Now hold on, there, Mr. Wolff . . ."

"I could do with one myself," said Mrs. DeBains. "How long have we been on this train?"

"He's right, Fenwick. Let's go on with the tasting," said Damas.

"General Thursby would have wanted it that way." McQuade straightened his tie as I turned his arm loose.

Fenwick hesitated, but then shrugged. "All right. I guess there's no harm in drinking the first flight. Anyhow, I've already got 'em breathing." I glanced again at Thursby sprawled out in his compartment. Fenwick was talking about the wines, not his boss.

He stepped out and squeezed past guests in the corridor, turning to go to the lounge. "This way, folks." As the others followed, Vera came down through the galley with the conductor in tow. He was the one I'd seen on the platform in Oakland. He still had a big bulge in his right cheek.

"In here." Vera pointed into compartment nine. The conductor looked us both up and down and came in to where I was still standing with the general's body.

"Oh, my." He started working the bulge in his cheek.

"We've had a shooting here," I said. The conductor glanced around the room trying to absorb the scene, and his eyes bugged out as if he'd swallowed that chew. Then he stared at me and backed up. "Wait a minute. It's not me. I'm a private dick on a case. General Thursby's been shot. We don't know who did it. Has anybody from your cars been back here?"

"Oh, no. Not possible. Your door's been locked. I checked it myself before we left Oakland." A little tobacco juice escaped, and trickled toward his chin, but he caught it with his tongue.

"Could anyone have gone in or out from the platform at any of the stops? Martinez? Sacramento?"

"Could of. Didn't." He appeared to need to spit. It probably wouldn't have made any difference if he did. Clean up was going to be a bitch with the blood and wine.

"How d'you know?" I asked.

"Get out at each station. Put the steps down; help folks in and out. When the engineer starts her up, I look back to make sure nobody's being dragged. Ain't nobody been in or out of this car. I can swear to that."

"Where are we now?"

The conductor consulted his watch from his vest pocket. "Let's see. It's comin' up on seven forty-five. We already left Sacramento. Next stop is Chico at nine ten if we're on time."

"We need some law," I said. "We've got a murder on your train."

"I'll tell the engineer. You're getting off in Chico." He

was gone quicker than a talking white rabbit with a very important date.

The conductor hurried off to see the engineer, or to spit. I stayed behind in compartment nine a few minutes and scanned again for clues. None jumped out at me. I poked around at the broken bottle glass and found a large piece, with the label still sticking to it like a wet leaf sticks to your shoe. It was another '45 DeBains Pinot Noir, same as the unbroken bottle I had found. I tucked the intact bottle into my jacket pocket for now, deciding to take it along.

I also checked through the general's pockets. His wallet had four crisp hundred-dollar bills with consecutive numbers, and a hundred-odd bucks more in smaller bills.

On the floor beside the body was a torn piece of paper. It was most of the top of a page of *From the Spitbucket*, the May-June '48 edition. The headline read "Ravensridge Blackbird Noir: How does it measure up to the great wines of France?" There were dark stains on the paper that could have been red wine, or could have been blood.

Aside from that, I found the usual change, pocketknife, fountain pen, and a ring of keys. I didn't see any guns in the room or any weapon on Thursby's body. There were two cartridge shells on the floor, so I was looking for an automatic as the murder weapon or a killer who emptied the cylinders of his revolver. The wound in the chest was bad, perhaps from a large caliber gun like a .45, and at close range. I couldn't do much of anything for old Thursby now. I didn't want to touch the doorknob on the inside of the compartment, so I exited Thursby's through the connecting door, into number eight, then out to the corridor. After detouring to my room to drop off the '45 Noir Côtes DeBains, I rejoined the rest of the group.

5

Cicilia Tells a Story

I like a wine tasting well enough. Mostly I like a wine drinking. A tasting will often start off quiet, maybe even a little strained, until everybody gets a few ounces down the gullet, and then somebody swirls his wine right up over the rim of the glass and onto his white shirt. After that, things start to loosen up a bit. But I've never been to a wine tasting quite as strained at the beginning as this one was. That's how it goes when somebody shoots the host.

The tables were rearranged end to end along the center of the car so we could all sit together. Vera was next to McQuade opposite Wolff at one end. I decided to let her watch the two gents. I'd keep my private eye on Cicilia, Sally DeBains, and Joe Damas. I parked myself next to Mrs. DeBains, opposite Damas. The eighth seat was vacant. Fenwick had a bottle in a brown paper bag in his hand and was going around the room pouring. There were six glasses at each place arranged in an inverted U-shape on white placemats. The lights danced with the motion of the train, and the crystal sparkled. It was all quite elegant.

"Flight one," said Fenwick, "is called 'A Tribute to Rusty.' It consists of three red wines from Bordeaux, and three cabernet sauvignon wines from California, all served blind."

"'Tribute to Rusty?' What the hell do you mean by that, Fenwick?" demanded Cicilia.

"That's what General Thursby wanted to begin with," he said. "It's a tribute to his friend and to all the great tastings the late Mr. O'Callaghan staged at his restaurant."

"Well, I like that. His restaurant? You mean *Chez Cici*? Everybody knows that's *my* restaurant." The emerald fire in Cici's eyes out-sparkled the crystal.

"Hmmm. Perhaps General Thursby thought you were just the cook, Mrs. O'Callaghan," said McQuade.

"Just the cook!" She leaned forward and looked around Vera at McQuade. "What do you know, you little creep? Anyhow, I arrange all the tastings. I pick the themes and the wines. I select the foods to accompany them. I am *Chez Cici*."

"*Chez Cici, c'est moi*, eh?" chuckled Damas.

Cicilia lifted the first glass that Fenwick had poured for her, gave it a swirl, and dipping her nose into the bowl of the glass, inhaled hard. Then she drained it all in one gulp, swirled it in her cheeks and swallowed. "Bah. French.

Weak, and what it gives away in backbone, it more than makes up for in lack of fruit."

I took a sip. I agreed with the French part. McQuade piped up, "Bravo, my dear. Your palate is on track. Clearly it is French. A St. Emilion I think. But where you see flaws, I see elegance, finesse. I wonder why you're missing that."

"A St. Emilion is it, McQuade? Why don't you tell us which one? You can identify Bordeaux by the chateau and vintage, can't you?" McQuade's expression turned sour as he peered down into his glass. "Anyhow," Cici continued. "Rusty didn't know anything about wine. He drank Scotch mostly, sometimes gin or beer." She knocked back a second glass of wine. "This is better. California cabernet, no doubt. Some eucalyptus, but the main difference is good ripe fruit."

I tasted number two. The eucalyptus was there all right. Fourteen years ago, Cici knew how to use her talented tongue. Now she'd developed an accomplished palate.

Things calmed down a little. My fellow guests swirled, sniffed, and sipped in relative silence for a while, working their ways through flight one. The Cascade rattled on north.

"My friends," Wolff said after some time had passed. "Let's raise a glass to our dear host, the man who made all this possible for us, General Thursby. I say, Fenwick, I'm sure you're as shaken up by this as the rest of us. Why don't you join us?"

The apeman scowled again, his thick brows a continuous dark line across his forehead. But as the others murmured their agreement and encouragement, he ambled over to the empty place at Vera's table, poured a glass from the first bottle, and held it in front of himself.

Big Wolff lifted his bulk up out of his seat and held up his glass toward the center of the lounge. The long stem disappeared under his fat fingers. "To Lloyd Thursby: general, wine collector, friend," he said, and the others echoed, "To Thursby." Fenwick's eyes had that faraway dreaminess again. He downed his wine and threw the empty glass across the room. Sally DeBains drank and then threw her glass against the same wall. Wolff followed suit. Vera drained her wine, glared at me, and hurled her glass too. That Vera. She throws like a girl, and her glass came more toward my head than toward the back wall. I winked at her, drank, and tossed mine. Fenwick ambled off into the galley and soon reappeared with a whiskbroom and dustpan dangling from his long arms. He started to clean up the glass shards. The rest of us resumed drinking flight one.

We drank in silence for a while. By the fourth wine of the flight, one of Sally DeBains' Alexander Valley cabernets, a contented calm came over the group. The snide remarks ceased.

"I like this one," said Vera. It was a good young wine,

perhaps the best of that flight so far, vibrant with fruit and alive, and I wished Fenwick had poured me a bigger taste.

The fifth wine tasted French and expensive. It was dark garnet and had a rich, powerful nose of cedar and tobacco. I'm not saying it was better than four, but it sure was complex. But it was still too young, and finished with a tannic bite. This was hard work!

The last wine of the flight seemed older, and I wondered if it were a pre-war French wine. It was big, profound, and ripe. "Woo!" I said. "What's this? A '29 Latour?"

"No." I might have expected that from one of the experts, but it was Vera. "Sniff it, Frank. You get that eucalyptus? A touch of *yerba buena*? This is Californian. Napa maybe. Smooth isn't it?" She loved it, and it showed.

"Well, my friends, let's see what they are, shall we?" Wolff wrapped his pudgy paws around the bottle in the bag labeled with a "#1." It turned out to be a 1946 St. Emilion, a Beausejour to be specific. Most of them didn't think much of it, but McQuade praised its finesse. The best I could have said for it was "austere," but I kept clammed. Cicilia had been right about number two being from California. It turned out to be a Charles Krug Cabernet from 1945.

And so it went, with Wolff pulling off the bags, reading the labels out, then passing the bottles around to see if anyone wanted seconds. Vera helped herself to a few more snorts. I hoped she remembered we were working. Finally, the fat man asked everyone what was his or her favorite, and we progressed around the room like that. Well, you would hardly have remembered poor Thursby was lying in the first compartment down the hall with two slugs through the pump. Everybody was having a jolly time. Until he came around to me. Old spoil-the-fun Frank.

I reared up and began to pontificate, pacing in the lounge, my wine stem in my fingers. "Well, I'll tell you. I liked number six, the '43 Inglenook. It was profound and intense, and it was a big wine. There were none better."

"Hell, Swiver," said McQuade. "It might taste okay now, but how about in ten years? Will it last?"

"No." I inverted the bottle over my glass and pouring the last drops in. "It will not last. That's the end of it. All gone." This cracked 'em up, led by Wolff and his hearty fat man's laugh, and Mrs. DeBains, who had quite a hoot too.

"These wines aren't what get me," I pressed on. "It's that we're sitting here like a real civilized gang, when we're not. One of us, one of *you*, that is," and I pointed a finger in the air for emphasis, "bumped off the host, and that's hardly civilized. You're laughing and carrying on like you don't care. Why? I thought you were his friends."

"You always were the life of the party, Frank." Cici grinned, and this brought on another round of chuckles, though a little more self-conscious this time, to everyone except Fenwick. The dark-visaged man had cleaned up the broken glass and was hovering in the kitchen door, grim-faced with a dustpan dangling from one hand and a whiskbroom from the other.

"Just a minute, Mr. Swiver," said Sally DeBains. "How do you know it was one of us?"

"Fenwick keeps the door of the private car locked, Mrs. DeBains. Nick, did you give the key to anyone?"

"Not until your gal went to fetch the conductor. Nobody else has been in here since we left Oakland."

"And you all probably heard the conductor say no one got on or off our car at the stations along the way."

"Okay, then," I said. "Who's glad to see Thursby dead?" Things got quiet. Damas looked down. Cicilia crossed her arms. Wolff cleared his throat and dabbed at his lips with a big linen hankie.

"Well, sir . . ." he began, "you can hardly blame us for trying to make the best of a bad situation, a very bad situation, indeed. We're not amused by the general's death. On the contrary, I'm, well, actually, I'm quite broken up. But 'Is life not a thousand times too short for us to bore ourselves?' Nietzsche again." He tried to make his round face long, but he wasn't very good at it. "Why, I've known Lloyd Thursby for years. Since before the war, oh, must be thirteen or fourteen years now. He was like a brother to me, you know."

"That's a laugh," said Damas.

Wolff seemed stunned by this. "Why, Joe, how could you say that? I'm shocked, I . . ."

"Come on, Marcus," Damas said. He removed the cigarette from the corner of his mouth and pointed at the fat man with it. "Brothers? You two were barely cordial. You wanted some of the Blackbird wine. Thursby refused to sell you any."

"My dear fellow, we were rival collectors, to be sure, but friendly rivals, friendly in every way," Wolff insisted.

"Marcus, remember how you stormed out of the auction tasting at my place the last time you tried to buy the Blackbird Noir from Thursby?" said Cicilia. "Was that a friendly scene? How much did you offer him? Wasn't it $300 for a case of six magnums of the 1943 Blackbird?"

"My dear Cici," Wolff started to purr.

"I'm not your dear Cici, fats."

Wolff kept his voice steady. "Mrs. O'Callaghan, you know I'm a collector, and the Blackbird Noir is the rarest of American wines, the greatest prize."

"Now that was a scene that might have interested you, Frank," she said. "I have a private room upstairs at Cici's. It's for special events, and this was a charity auction for the Earthquake Survivors' Fund. We have it every year."

"Cicilia, I hardly think Mr. Swiver cares to hear about—"

"Let her tell it, Wolff," I said.

"We were upstairs, about two dozen of us, mostly

men, some with their young girls by their sides. The room was well lit, and the jewelry glittered. I prepared a pre-auction dinner, and they had paid twenty-five dollars each for my food and a tasting of selected bottles from some of the cellars being auctioned off. There were Latours and La Tache, top whites and reds from all across pre-war Europe, and of course there was the Blackbird, and I created a menu that was more than a match for the best of them. I started them off with seared rare tuna, on a bed of artichokes, carrots, and potatoes, topped with *ali oli*."

"I remember it well. It was all delicious, Cici," said Sally DeBains.

"Thanks, Sally." Cici carried on with her story. "General Thursby was at the head of the table, and Marcus Aurelius Wolff, the philosopher, was by his side. Now, Frank, everybody here knows that Marcus has the best cellar, the largest and the finest collection of wine in San Francisco. Whatever Marcus wants in the wine world, Marcus gets. That's how he built up his cellar."

"I am a determined bidder when a wine I want goes on the block," the philosopher said.

"I hear sometimes it's more than determination," said McQuade. "Intimidation might be more accurate." He sounded bitter.

Wolff stared hard at the critic. "Well, I can't help it if I have more cash than some of the bidders, can I?" McQuade withered a bit.

Cici stood up and pushed in her chair. She selected one of her glasses from the tasting and paced up and down on the Oriental rug, steady on her black high heels as she plunged ahead with her story. "There's always been one exception. There's one thing missing from Wolff's cellar that keeps it from being perfect—Ravensridge Blackbird Noir."

"Well," I said, "if you always get what you want, Mr. Wolff, why don't you go to the store and get some?"

"Because you can't, Frank," said Cici. "It's just not that easy. Joe here is the distributor. He sells it only to restaurants, the finest restaurants in the country, of course. I probably get the largest allocation. You can come and buy a bottle with dinner at *Chez Cici*, but I open it for you, and the bottle stays on the premises."

"As sole distributor, that's one of the conditions I must insist upon," said Damas. "In fact, if I didn't, the owner of Ravensridge would cut me off."

"Who is the owner of Ravensridge?" I asked.

"Ahh, that's another condition, Frank," said Cici. "Only Joe and the owner know that. It's supposed to be a partnership. I've heard it's a few orthodontists from the City who grow wine as a hobby. But whoever it is, it's a bigger secret than the Manhattan Project. There's one other thing—only one private individual has any in his cellar. That was Lloyd Thursby. And he had plenty, year after year."

"How'd that happen, Joe?" I said.

Damas pondered that for a few ticks. "I'm not at liberty to discuss that, Swiver. You'd have a better chance of getting it out of old Thursby."

Cici rejoined her tale after the interruption. "And so there they were, Frank, sitting side by side. A great feast, but our friend Wolff wasn't eating. Now Marcus comes to *Chez Cici* at least twice a week, and he eats like Diamond Jim Brady. If you couldn't tell from looking at him, well, take it from me; our philosopher friend has a hearty appetite. But maybe he don't like tuna, you think. Well, I brought out the roasted veal, with prosciutto and sage. Ah, the aroma of the sage—it was heavenly! But still Wolff, he hardly touched a thing. At least he drank well, along with the rest of the old men. The bottles were passed around the tables, and all the young girls seemed very gay, and the old men beamed and talked about how lovely and supple the wines were. There was true enthusiasm, and I think, the warm friendship that too much wine causes.

"I was working, but I was enjoying myself too, and I had just ordered the kitchen to put the black raspberry crème brulees under the broiler. I opened a bottle of '41 Blackbird Noir for the guests. We were pouring that, and I noticed Wolff was turning red, redder, and crimson. I thought he must have had something caught in his throat. Suddenly he rose up to his feet, and seemed to sway left and right, as he towered over Thursby. 'I said $300, man,' he shouted. 'Three-hundred American. You'll not sell them to me for that? Why that's more than the '29 Latour has fetched, more than the double nought Lafite.'" I didn't know Cici did impersonations, but she'd puffed up like Wolff, and now she waddled like a penguin.

"And Thursby patted his mouth with his napkin and shook his head no. 'Very well,' says Wolff. 'You're robbing me, but I must have them. I will make it $350, sir, and that's my final offer.' Then the magnum of the Blackbird that was being passed came to Thursby, and he poured a few ounces in his glass. He took a sip, swished it around in his mouth, savored it, and swallowed. And again he said, 'No, Marcus, no.'"

I was listening carefully to Cicilia and trying to keep an eye on the big man. He squirmed in his chair like maybe his shorts were too tight, but he kept his face calm, looking down at his glass occasionally, agitating his wine, and drinking steadily. With his bulk, I doubted the small amount we'd had thus far would have had much effect on him.

"Well, Wolff was livid. Sally, you were there. You could see the smoke coming out of his ears, couldn't you? And all of a sudden the stem of the wineglass he was holding just snaps in his fat hand, and there's the bowl, still full of wine sitting on top of his fist. And Wolff sets it down on the table and bends closer to the general and says something more quietly. I didn't hear it, but now

Thursby's hot. He pulls his napkin out of his collar and stands up to the philosopher so they're belly-to-belly and chest-to-chest, and he leans his face close to Wolff's. 'Is that a threat, Marcus? Is that a threat?' And Wolff says, 'I don't make idle threats, General.' Wolff bumped Thursby with his belly and spun around and strode out of the restaurant.

Cici's story was over. She finished the glass of wine she'd been carrying while she talked, and she sat back down. The room was quiet, except for the rattling of the Cascade as it steamed north. Then she spoke again. "Say, is there any wine left in that, Frank?" Cici reached over to me for bottle number five, a lovely '34 La Mission Haut-Brion.

"Speaking of wine, Wolff, old boy," McQuade said, "wasn't that a large bottle I saw you with in the corridor this evening?"

"What were you doing in the corridor with a bottle of wine, Wolff?" I asked.

"Sir, a bottle of wine didn't kill Lloyd Thursby," said Wolff. "He was shot through the heart, by God. Perhaps you should be asking who was in the corridor with a gun."

"Wolff, it appears that somebody stole a magnum of the Blackbird, possibly at the time of the murder. You were in the corridor, possibly at the time of the murder, possibly with a magnum. Can you explain it?"

"Bah, this is ridiculous. What if I did have a bottle?

I'm a wine collector. This is a wine tasting. What could be more natural?"

"Well, what were you doing in the corridor?"

"Taking the air, blast it." Wolff was raising his voice now. "It's a bit claustrophobic in the cabin, as nice as it is, for a man of my size."

"Taking the air!" Sally DeBains hooted. "Be careful, he'll outbid us all for it!"

"At any rate," Wolff continued, "it was not that much later that I saw someone in the corridor . . . with a gun."

6

Frisking Sally

It was so quiet you could hear a train rattle. No one spoke for several seconds, and I listened to the pleasant clickety-clackety sound of our car riding over the rails, and I felt the rhythm of it as we swayed and rolled.

"Well, old sport?" Damas arched an eyebrow. "Are you going to drop the other shoe?"

"Very well, Joe," said Wolff. "I saw Madame DeBains. She apparently was coming out of cabin nine. At any rate, she was coming toward me in the corridor from that end, and my compartment is number six. It was nearly seven o'clock, and I had decided to come to the lounge here for the tasting. I don't believe she saw me, as she kept glancing back the other way over her shoulder. I stepped back into my room to let her pass and closed the door all but a crack. She was carrying a small pistol in her hand. Just as she came about even with my room, she stopped, and considered the gun she was holding. Then she glanced up and down the hall. She proceeded to hitch up her skirt, revealing quite a bit of her leg, if I do say so, and tucked the revolver into a small holster on her thigh."

"Say, what's the idea of looking at my legs, Wolff?"

"My dear, I am a collector—not just of wine, but of all beautiful things."

Smooth. I would have to remember that line. "Let's see the gat, Mrs. DeBains," I said

"I beg your pardon." She laid a hand to her breast.

"Don't make him take it away from you, lady. He will you know." This was from Vera, and though it was to the point, not entirely helpful.

Still DeBains hesitated. I added, "I will, you know," and finally the dame stood up, planted her right leg out front, and hoisted her skirt. Then, when it was up just above her knees, she stopped.

"Well, come and get it, dick. I'm not giving everyone a free show. And be careful not to snag my nylons. They're a new pair."

I stepped next to her and bent to one knee. From my low vantage point, I saw that Joe Damas had a heater under the table in his left hand, and it was pointed at me. I maintained my poker face and carried on with the frisk of the DeBains dame. I put my hands around her leg, just above the knee. Then I slid one up each side of her thigh, over the tops of the stockings. Bingo. Warm flesh, cold steel. It was indeed tucked into a holster, worn on the outside of the thigh. I felt to see if the safety was on. Satisfied that it was, I drew the gun up to clear the top of the leather, and extracted it. DeBains didn't flinch.

Now I wanted to get out of Joe's line of fire and behind him if I could. Rising, I produced a snub-nosed Smith & Wesson .32 revolver. I ambled around the table to the other side. I felt foolish but obligated to smell the gun to see if it had been fired recently, so I did.

Mrs. DeBains seemed amused by my discomfort. "What do you think, Mr. Swiver? Does it smell like it's been used recently?"

"This is not the murder weapon," I announced. "It hasn't been fired tonight, and besides, it's not likely a small caliber gun like this would have caused Thursby's wounds, even at close range."

"Say, not bad, peeper," DeBains said. "What else could you tell from down there?"

"Frank's good with his hands, Mrs. DeBains," Vera said. "He knows his way around under a woman's dress." She glanced at Cici. Hadn't I been circumspect with Cici — at least in public? I wondered what was bothering Vera. Whatever it was, the wine wasn't making things any better.

"I can tell, sweetheart," DeBains shot back.

"Well, Mrs. DeBains?" I said. "What were you doing in the corridor with your roscoe drawn?"

She thought for a second. "Well, I may as well tell you.

I went to see General Thursby. You see, he owned some property I want. Some vineyard property, as a matter of fact, and I was going to make him an offer for it."

"Did you?"

"It would have been a waste of breath," she said. "When I entered, he was already dead." Vera gasped and raised the back of her hand up to her mouth. The others were mainly quiet, but no one was falling asleep.

"I guess when I saw him sprawled out like that, I instinctively drew my heater." She bent her knees and leveled an imaginary gun in front of her. "But I didn't stay to look around; I backed out quick. I probably was in the general's compartment less than half a minute. I must have been halfway down the hall before I realized my gun was still in my hand."

"You went out through the door into the corridor?" I said.

"Yeah, why?"

"Well," I said, "someone locked the door from the inside. That's the way Fenwick and I found it."

Now it was DeBains's turn to gasp. "You mean the killer was still in cabin nine when I was?"

"Could have been," I said, "but there aren't many hiding places."

She plopped down hard into her chair. "Oh, my!"

I was now standing just behind Joe Damas's left shoulder. Everyone's eyes were on DeBains. I grabbed

Joe's left forearm, yanked it up around behind him, and relieved him of a small, blue Beretta automatic. In a flash, I had popped out the magazine, and ejected a round from the chamber.

"Very nice, Joe. But I've always thought of these Beretta .25s as ladies' guns."

"Well, what kind of a rod would you expect a nance to be packing?" DeBains hooted her laugh again, but with no humor in it.

For a swarthy guy, Joe was turning quite livid. "You had no right to take that from me!" he screamed.

"You were pointing it at me. That gives me the right."

"I was covering you, you fool. I was pointing it at Sally DeBains." He pointed at her across the room.

That made me think while I sniffed the barrel. "Thanks, Joe. That won't be necessary anymore. Vera and I will look out for each other."

"I think I'll look out for myself," said Vera, and took another drink. I had no idea what was eating her. Vera and I had shared many bottles of wine, and she'd never acted like this before. Maybe she was jealous of Cici. But I couldn't recall ever mentioning that the two of us had a past. How would she know?

"Has Joe's gun been fired, Mr. Swiver?" asked Wolff. I sniffed it.

"No," I said. "Smells like wine, actually."

"Pass it over here, and I'll see if I can identify the wine

and the vintage for you." It was McQuade.

"You mean you can tell me that from a sniff?"

"Perhaps. I usually smell the aromas in a glass, but if I can help . . ."

I gave the gun to McQuade, who waved the barrel around underneath his nose. He sniffed several little short snorts, then a big long inhalation, filling his lungs. He closed his eyes and continued to hold the little automatic under his nose. He opened his eyes. "This is very interesting. It's a complex nose—very distinct black raspberry, cherry, vanilla, clove, gun oil, of course, and something rather foul. Perhaps you shouldn't carry it tucked into your trousers, Joe." He was playing to the room. "At any rate, I might not be able to identify the wine with any certainty, except that I recall this aroma. Something I've had within the last week or so, I believe. The clove is the telltale element." He opened his eyes and fixed them on Sally DeBains. "Sally, I do believe it's one of yours—your pinot noir. 1945, I think."

I was skeptical about the parlor trick, but he pulled it off with such confidence, you had to consider it. What if he were right? What did that mean—'45 Noir Côtes DeBains Pinot? That matched the bottles in Thursby's compartment.

McQuade passed the Beretta back to me for my collection and wiped his hands with a hanky, complaining that now everything would probably smell like gun oil for the rest of the evening. Then he cleared his throat in the silence that followed. "Thank you for that, Mr. Swiver. By the way, I'm sure we're all glad to have a detective on board. But exactly what *are* you doing here? I don't recall the general ever inviting you to any events in the past."

Fenwick was still hanging around. He knew why Vera and I were there. If I gave the rest of them a story, he could shoot holes in it. Besides, I didn't see that a lie would be to my advantage. So I leveled with them.

"General Thursby wanted to hire me. As it happens, we never had a chance to discuss the exact terms of my employment."

"I can tell you more about that." It was the apeman.

"Fenwick," said Cicilia, "these bottles are empty, and I'm getting thirsty. What else have you got?"

"There's another flight coming," he sneered. "But listen, Swiver, I was there last week when Mrs. O'Callaghan paid the boss a visit. I couldn't help but overhear . . ."

"Couldn't help it? You were probably listening at the keyhole, you hairy creep!" Cici sprang out of her chair and lunged for Fenwick. I was already standing, and I grabbed her arms from behind and lifted her petite frame off the floor and away from the steward.

"Turn me loose, Frank. I'll teach this jerk . . ."

"Take it easy, doll. Let's hear what he's got to say. Then we'll all have another round."

"Well, well, well, Frank," said Vera. "Second time

tonight you've got her in your arms."

Cici stopped squirming, and we both turned to Vera. Vera couldn't have known what happened in my compartment, and that was the only other time I'd touched Cici. "Never mind for now, Frank," Vera said. "Let's hear what Fenwick has to say."

"Well, like I was sayin'," he continued, "Mrs. O'Callaghan come to the house one afternoon last week. It was before I'd sent the invitations, so last Thursday, maybe. I was cleaning in the billiard room, which is right next door to the library, and the boss had left the doors open. I overheard the O'Callaghan broad tryin' to put the touch on the general for some lettuce. I didn't catch all the details, but Thursby turned her down. She wasn't too happy. They argued."

"I'm a businesswoman, you big ape." Cicilia struggled some more, and I had to tighten my grip on her arms. "I made him a business proposition. That don't mean anything."

"You know, Rusty O'Callaghan was the general's pal." Fenwick's eyes were heavy-lidded, and he seemed to be kind of dreamy. "He used to come over to the house late, three, maybe four nights a week. Rusty and the boss would sit up until one or two in the morning playin' cards. Rusty listened to the general's war stories, and he told the boss stories about Prohibition and runnin' hooch off Catalina."

"'Rusty' this and 'Rusty' that," said Cici. "Sounds like

you were pretty chummy with him, Fenwick."

"He was a regular guy, not like most of the general's friends." Fenwick's eyes moved around the room, taking in each guest in turn, except Vera and me. "He always had a kind word or a cigar or something for me. Made me feel like, you know, like I was somebody, not a piece of the furniture."

Wolff was staring down over his belly at his shoes. DeBains straightened her seams. McQuade had his nose in a glass. No one could look Fenwick in the eye, except Vera, who was staring at him.

"Anyhow, the point is, they started arguing about Rusty."

"That's ridiculous." Cicilia quit kicking and squirming and spoke in a calm tone. "I'm trying to raise some cash to expand *Chez Cici*. I'm going to open a branch in Sausalito, if you must know. I asked Thursby for a loan of twenty-five grand. As a matter of fact, I offered to stake my cellar as collateral. I've got more than 1500 cases, you know. Anyhow, he refused. I guess I got a little hot. But it was about jack, not about Rusty."

"I couldn't hear everything, but I definitely heard them two yellin' back and forth about Rusty O'Callaghan." Fenwick pointed across the room at Cici with a finger on the end of a hairy hand and wrist. "Thursby was real fond of him, you know. Rusty was sort of like the son the general never had, I think."

"That's all very well, Fenwick." I turned Cici loose. "You say you heard them arguing about O'Callaghan. Cicilia says it was about money. But what are you getting at?" I rounded the table, keeping between the apeman and Cici. "I thought you were going to tell us why Thursby hired me."

"I'm getting to that, shamus. The next day, I'm sending out the invitations to this party. Thursby calls me in and says to add one more to the list—you. He says he needs a private dick. He saw your ad in the *Yellow Pages*, and he figured with a business name like 'Old Vine Detective Agency,' maybe you knew something about wine. 'See if you can get him to come on the train next Friday,' he says. 'I'll write a note for you to enclose with the invitation. Rusty O'Callaghan was murdered, and if the police won't do anything about it, I will.'"

That was like what Thursby had mentioned in the note: "*. . . the police are doing nothing in the O'Callaghan killing.*"

"All right, but what's that got to do with Cicilia arguing with your boss last week?" I spread my hands palms up.

"Frank, you big sap," said Vera. "Don't you see? General Thursby knew your little chippy blipped-off her husband. He wants you to prove it."

7

In Which I Go through Vera's Drawers

isten, Fenwick," I said. "We could probably all use a drink." I knew I could. "Why don't you get the next flight ready? I suggest we pair up and search the rooms. I've already disarmed two of you birds. But those two guns weren't fired. We're looking for a gun that was used . . . tonight. Let's meet back here in fifteen minutes."

I told Vera to stick with Fenwick and to search compartments three and four after he uncorked the wine. Other than that, I let them choose their own partners, and I didn't care if they paired up with their friends, or with the one they trusted least so they could keep an eye on each other. Either way was likely to produce something instructive.

"Who are you going with, Frank?" Vera asked.

"I'll take Mrs. O'Callaghan," I said. "We'll look in seven and eight."

Vera said nothing but did a sharp turn on her heel and strode off to join Fenwick in the galley.

Number eight was Fenwick's. It was spartan, neat and tidy. The bed was made, and you could bounce a silver dollar off the tight sheets. I searched through the drawers while Cicilia lingered in the middle of the floor.

"So what's the story, doll?" I wasn't looking at her when I spoke. I couldn't.

"What story?"

"The true story, not the line you spun me about the IOUs."

"That is true, Frank. Rusty was at Thursby's, night after night, gambling while I worked in the kitchen at *Chez Cici* and closed up the joint."

"So what's this about a loan?" I asked. "Why put up your cellar for collateral if he already owes you twenty-five gees?"

"I tried to collect on the debt, but I didn't have the paper with me. Thursby said he didn't owe Rusty anything, that the big sap lost thousands to him. He said I couldn't prove otherwise. So I asked for a loan. Couldn't hurt to try."

"You went to try to get the money he owed Rusty, but you didn't take the IOUs with you?"

"I didn't even know about them then. I just knew that Rusty once told me he was carrying Thursby on a gambling debt, and that if we ever needed dough, we could tap the general for plenty. I happened to find the notes the other day when I was cleaning out some of Rusty's old things. I don't think he ever intended to try to collect. He liked the old man, and just enjoyed sitting up with him."

"Yeah, I think I would have liked the old guy too. This place is clean." The drawers had underwear and a couple of changes of clothes, neatly folded and stacked. It was about right for what a guy would pack for a long weekend—a utilitarian guy who was used to traveling light, living on what he could wrap in a bindle. "Let's check number seven."

Rather than going out into the corridor, I stepped to the connecting door between seven and eight. I unlocked it on Fenwick's side and it opened. Vera hadn't locked her side. I stepped through, and Cicilia followed.

It was just a little room like the others, but it was alive with Vera Peregrino. A calla lily beckoned from the neck of an empty bottle on the nightstand; Vera's cologne, Vineyard Mornings, wafted in the air. What a sweetheart. I knew she had nothing to do with the killing of Thursby, but I went through the motions. That meant going through the drawers.

"So, did you kill him?" I was glancing around the compartment, not at Cici.

"Are you crazy, Frank? How could I? I was hauling your ass in the sack."

"Not Thursby, doll. Rusty. Did you murder your husband?"

"How can you even say that?"

I stopped searching, turned around, and dove into the green depths of her eyes. "Don't play innocent, Cicilia. It doesn't work for you. There was always something about you, something different. It's what drove me wild fourteen years ago, and it's something I recalled tonight. You're danger."

"Frank, we still have seven or eight minutes until we have to be back." She wrapped her arms around my neck and pressed her breasts up against me. The motion of the train caused us to rock together. She kissed me, hard and long, and I let her. Danger could come in a very nice package.

She wanted more than the kiss, but I held her at arm's length. "C'mon, Cici, this is Vera's cabin. She's already sore. She seems to know about us. Maybe we made a mistake."

"Why? How did we make a mistake?"

I wasn't so sure I had, but I had another feeling—I didn't want to hurt Vera. "We're not the same people we were fourteen years ago. And there's Vera—"

"I'll make you forget about Vera."

But I turned away from her and bent to check the bottom drawer. Cicilia wrapped her arms around me from behind and ran her hands down over my stomach. The bottom drawer was clean. I shut it and moved up to the middle drawer. Cici blew warm breath on the back of my neck. A pair of jeans, a white blouse, a cotton dress, a pullover sweater. Cicilia nibbled my ear lobe and then stuck her tongue in my ear. She moved her hands down the front of my pants.

"Find anything, Frank?"

"Not yet. How about you?"

"I think I'm getting warm," she said.

"I sure as hell am." Then I slid the middle drawer shut and yanked open the top drawer. The smell of Vineyard Mornings was gone. Something else hung in the air now, but I ignored it and plunged on with my search. I had to finish this and get out of here before I lost control. Socks, change of underwear, extra nylons, garter belt, more panties, a .45 automatic. I closed the drawer. Vera didn't have any .45 automatics. I opened the drawer again and it was still there.

"Uh-oh. I think I found a weapon," I said.

Cicilia had her hand down the front of my trousers now. "So did I."

I lifted the .45, a pair of Vera's underpants dangling from the barrel. I sniffed it but I really didn't need to. It had been fired recently, and the aroma was so strong I realized that's what I'd smelled when I'd first opened the drawer. I drew back from Cici's touch.

"Well, well," said Cicilia.

"This isn't Vera's, Cici." I knew Vera well enough to know she wasn't a killer.

"What's it doing in here, I wonder?" Cici said.

"Someone must be trying to frame her."

"Why?"

"I don't know, but I know Vera." I wrapped the gun in my handkerchief and dropped it in my jacket pocket. "Thursby supposedly packed a pair of army automatics. Fenwick can probably identify it if this is one of them." Things weren't making sense to me.

We were back in the lounge. I had been hoping to talk to Vera about the gun before the others came back, but no such luck. She and Fenwick were the last two to return.

"All right," I began. "We'll be in Chico soon, and the law will be here. It'll be out of my hands. Let's get some drinks and see what we can figure out before then. First of all, who else is carrying a gun?"

Fenwick was circling around the tables, pouring the first bottle of flight two. Wolff raised his huge bulk and drew a pearl-handled Colt revolver out of the waistband of his trousers.

"Look, here's my gun. It's not been fired. I'm sure you can verify that."

It was a big .45-caliber double-action piece, the sort that could have made the wounds in Thursby's chest, but it hadn't been fired. "Okay, Wolff, thanks." I laid it on the table with the other guns. "Who checked out Mr. Wolff's compartment?"

Damas and McQuade had paired up. Joe gave the report in his accented English. I still couldn't place his accent. It was non-specific, an accent that dripped like a case of the clap but one that didn't test positive for the gonococcus germ. "We searched Sally DeBains' room, and it was clean. We also checked out Wolff's compartment. Two things turned up, both pretty disturbing. First of all, a letter." He held out a sheet of paper.

"Now wait just a moment, sir," Wolff said. "That letter is mine, and a man's correspondence, well, it's private, by God."

"Wolff, we've got a body in there. Getting to the bottom of the murder is more important than your privacy." I grabbed the sheet from Joe Damas. "By the way, this first wine is just delicious."

"I assure you, sir, my letter has no bearing on the unfortunate events that have spoiled our trip. But reading it here to the group would be very distressing to me. I do agree, by the way, about the wine. Fabulous nose, smooth on the palate, polished, round on the finish."

"It's a burgundy, that's certain," said McQuade. "Chambertin, I'd venture, pre-war."

I tried another taste and sloshed it around in my mouth. McQuade was good. "Mmmm. Just delicious. Anyhow, there's no need to read it aloud; this isn't a trial. We're not entering it in to evidence. I'll just see—" It was handwritten in black ink, on good stationary, headed *31 January 1948, Buenos Aires*. It was from a friend of Wolff's who said Europe was too hot for him now; he had moved to Argentina, where he'd settled and planted vineyards. He was inviting Wolff to visit for his first harvest. The letter was signed "Willi."

"So?" I looked at Damas.

"Willi," he said.

"Who's Willi?" I asked.

"Oh, Willi is just a friend of mine, from Europe. Before the war. We spent some time together in Paris." Wolff said "Willi" so that it sounded like "Villi." I didn't like it.

Damas stood and slid a blue box out of his side pocket. He withdrew a short, thick cigarette, placed it between his lips and lit up. "'Villi' is Wilhelm Canaris. Admiral Wilhelm Canaris, of the Third Reich."

"Ridiculous," snorted Wolff and pounded his fist on the table.

"Canaris?" I said. "I thought he was dead."

"Sure." Damas held the cigarette and circled his hand while blowing out smoke. "A lot of the Nazis want you to think they're dead, Swiver. That's how they stay alive."

"No, no, this Willi was no Nazi," said Wolff. "He was just a friend of mine."

I drank a mouthful of wine number two, and swirled it around in my mouth. Another good red, though it was hard-pressed to keep up with the first one in this flight.

"Are you going to see Willi?" I asked.

"In Argentina? Why, yes, of course," said Wolff. "'A friend whose hopes we cannot satisfy is a friend we would rather have as an enemy.' Friedrich Nietzsche said that. I wouldn't want Willi as an enemy."

"You know, of course, Swiver, our Herr Wolff had friends in high places in Hitler's Germany. During the war, they say he traveled freely in Europe," said Sally DeBains.

"These are rumors and innuendos that have plagued me for years." Wolff planted his knuckles on the table and rose to his feet, leaning forward. "As a businessman and a wine merchant, I traveled extensively in the capitals of the great wine-making nations in the '30s. Rome, Paris, Madrid, yes, even Berlin. Of course, I had friends everywhere. But I assure you, these friendships never influenced my patriotism. I'm an American, sir. I bleed red, white, and blue. Besides, what do my old business acquaintances have to do with this sad affair of tonight, I ask you?"

On the other side of the table, Damas paced back and forth behind McQuade, Vera, and Cici, who had remained seated. "And I'll answer that for you," said Damas. "General Thursby was retired from active duty, sure. But I believe he was keeping a hand in intelligence work. Tracking down Nazis in hiding. You know, with the OSS? So maybe he was squeezing Wolff here about his Axis connections."

"Oh, this is absurd, sir. Too far-fetched," said Wolff. "If General Thursby was looking in my closet for Nazis, he was wasting his time."

"Well, just thinking out loud here, Wolff," I said. "It seems you had the opportunity. John McQuade saw you in the corridor around the time of the murder. Now we hear you may have had the motive too — General Thursby may have been investigating you for ties to the Nazis."

"Motive?" Wolff replied. "Why, sir, don't be ridiculous. Most of the people in this room had more of a motive to kill Lloyd Thursby than I did. The general and I were old friends. I didn't want him dead. No, by God. I only wanted to buy the Blackbird."

"Oh, yes. There was one more thing, Mr. Swiver." McQuade fumbled down under the table and brought up a magnum of wine. "Here is the missing bottle of the 1945 Ravensridge Blackbird Noir. We found it in Marcus Wolff's cabin."

8

The Blackbird

McQuade handed me the bottle, and I considered it at arm's length to see what I could glean from it. It was an eye-catching bottle, dark green with a gold label and gold wax over the top of the neck. The label had black lettering "Blackbird Noir" and "Ravensridge Wines" on the right, and a pulp artist's drawing of a rather sinister black bird along the left side. The feathers on the bird's chest resembled the scales of a serpent. "How do you explain this, Wolff?" I asked.

"Explain it? Hell, Frank," said Vera, "let's open it."

"Now hold on just a minute, my friends," said Wolff. "We're still on flight two here."

"Yeah," said DeBains, "but if we stay on flight two much longer, we'll be in Chico, and the law will come, and who knows if we'll get to drink this beauty." She plunked an empty glass down on the table next to the bottle.

"This is the bottle the General planned to serve

tonight," said Fenwick. "It's the 1945 vintage."

"I don't see how he could have planned to serve it. He gave it to me!" cried Wolff.

"He gave it to you?" I said. "Let's see, I seem to remember, when you were out in the corridor with this bottle, you were just 'taking the air,' right? I'd like to hear the rest of the story, Mr. Wolff. Fenwick, why don't you do the honors on this?" I held the big bottle out to the hirsute steward.

For a man of his bulk, Wolff was quick. He shoved his chair back and sprang to his feet between us. "You will not!" He snatched the bottle from me. But Fenwick wrapped his arm around the philosopher's neck.

Wolff seemed to consider tossing the steward off, or sitting and crushing him, but after a pause, he handed the bottle back to me. "All right, all right, here." He relaxed and Fenwick released him. I passed the magnum to Nick. "Open it if you must," Wolff continued. "I suppose I do owe you all an explanation. Very well." He knocked back the contents of flight two, wine three, which I was sipping. It was another spectacular wine. Wolff breathed deeply. "You all know me, friends. You know me for my hospitality. I'm a collector, and it's true that my greatest unfulfilled desire is to possess the Blackbird. It's also true, as Mrs. O'Callaghan so stirringly related, that Lloyd Thursby and I have had words over the Blackbird in the past. Heated words, to be sure, but nothing more than words. Despite those words, you all know I was a friend to General Thursby, no less a friend than any of you. If I were not his friend, would he have invited me along tonight? I weep for General Thursby." He held his glass of number four aloft. "I honor General Thursby." A couple of voices mumbled, "General Thursby," and the philosopher drank.

"Well," he continued, "hope springs eternal, as they say." His eyes beamed, and he grinned. "I came aboard tonight with a good bit of money, determined to make the general another offer. Cicilia told you how I offered $350, and how Thursby turned me down. $350 for a case of six magnums, nearly sixty dollars each, sir, an unheard of sum for a California wine and in any event, most generous. Well, this evening, I called on General Thursby in cabin nine, where I found him alive and well."

"Yeah," said Vera, "but how was he doing when you left?"

"Our meeting was quite cordial, by God. I made my offer plainly — $400 for a case of six magnums of the Blackbird. And General Thursby, well . . . he said, 'Yes.'"

"He agreed to sell you the Blackbird?" asked Cicilia.

"Indeed he did. He surprised even me. I drew out my bankroll, and I peeled off four new hundred-dollar bills. Thursby demurred. He didn't have a case of the Blackbird with him, but he suggested I pick it up at his home when we returned to San Francisco. I agreed, and said, 'General, take the money now. Keep it as a token of my good faith.' And to that, he replied, 'Well, then, Marcus, I want you to have this, as a gift . . . as a token of my good faith.' He fetched out a bottle of the Blackbird, the very bottle you see here." At this point, Fenwick had returned with the bottle, open now, and a ship's decanter.

"Come on, Wolff," I said. "A few weeks ago you made Thursby a huge offer for the Blackbird and he refused in front of witnesses. Now you're saying that in private he gave you a bottle as a gift? Isn't it more likely that you shot him and pilfered the wine? Where's your bill of sale? Where's your receipt?"

"Where's the gun I shot him with? My God, sir, it's absurd. Find yourself another suspect." He slugged down the rest of his number four, and slammed the glass back down on the table.

"Well," McQuade muttered, "you really should obtain a bill of sale if you buy rare wine at this time of night. No witnesses."

"All right, Wolff. Let's let that percolate for a while," I said. "After all, your gun's not the murder weapon. Does anyone else have anything? Anybody have any shooting irons they need to check?"

McQuade cleared his throat. "Very well. I have a gun too." He fumbled inside his suit coat and drew out a Luger. "It's from the war. I appropriated it from a German officer. Rhone Valley campaign. I captured him in a vineyard of the highest quality."

"I'm sure. So why does a critic need to carry a piece?" I took the pistol from him, and began checking it out.

"Well, Wolff, Damas, and Mrs. Debains were all armed. You might just as well ask why does a wine collector, or a distributor, or a vintner need to carry a roscoe."

"Right now, I'm asking you." It was the most dangerous wine tasting I'd ever attended. These folks liked wine, sure, but they liked guns too. A swell combination.

McQuade turned away and raised a hand to his chin as he spoke. "I've been receiving threats lately. People don't seem to be able to take a little honest criticism."

"Honest criticism? Vicious bile is more like it," said Vera. "I've read some of his stuff, Frank. I've mucked better shit out of our barn."

"What gives you the right to slander my work?" said McQuade. "As a matter of fact, Miss Peregrino, what in hell is your role here, anyhow? I mean, we all know Swiver's a dick, not a writer. So you're no research assistant. What are you, his date?"

"I'm an operative," snapped Vera, "with Old Vine Detective Agency."

"Oh, I see, an operative," McQuade said. "By the way, Miss Peregrino, there's a winery in the Russian River Valley, Peregrine Vineyards. They make some particularly noxious plonk. I believe the owner's name is Peregrino, Angelo Peregrino or something like that. You wouldn't be related, would you?"

"Angelo and Louisa Peregrino are my parents." Vera's dress may have been scarlet, but it was nothing compared to the fire in her eyes.

"I see." McQuade raised his nose a bit higher up in the air at that. "So, tell me what a critic should say about 'Peregrine Chablis.' Or 'Peregrine Burgundy' for that matter?"

"Well, you might say the chablis is flabby, and over cropped," said Vera, "or that the burgundy lacks backbone and depth. That'd be wine criticism, you dumb mug, and there's a difference between that and what you wrote."

"Don't tell me how to do my job," said McQuade. "I was tasting fine wine while you were still eating pablum."

I stepped between them. "All right, you two. Let's get back to the game. McQuade's Luger hasn't been fired either. So far, that's Mrs. DeBains, Mr. Wolff, Mr. Damas, and Spitbucket McQuade who've checked their guns. Anybody else?"

Vera, Fenwick, and Cicilia shook their heads, or said they were unarmed. "How about you, shamus?" asked Damas.

"No, I'm not carrying." I removed my suit jacket and folded it over the back of my chair. I was warm enough in my vest, and now they could all see I had no shoulder holster. "Fine. Now, the search of the rooms. Who else besides Damas and McQuade has something to report?"

It turned out that Wolff and DeBains had partnered but found nothing to report in cabins one and two, mine and Cicilia's. Vera and Fenwick had rummaged through the compartments of Joe Damas and Spitbucket McQuade.

"Joe's room passed inspection," said Vera, "though I don't care for his cologne." Damas glowered at her but kept clammed. "The critic's room, number three, yielded some interesting results. Show 'em, Nick."

Fenwick had given everyone a new crystal stem and decanted the Blackbird. Now he was going around the little group, pouring the '45 Blackbird into the new glasses. He put down the decanter and retrieved some papers from inside his monkey jacket. "We found this." He unfolded the papers and handed them to me.

It was two pages of typewritten wine tasting notes. They had been crumpled up then flattened and folded. The top of the first page was torn off. It was dated May–June 1948.

"What is this, Vera?"

"It's the next issue of McQuade's newsletter, *From the Spitbucket*."

"Give me that. It's my galley proofs." McQuade lunged toward me, but I moved the papers back away from him.

"Don't worry," I told him. "I'll buy a subscription. Why is this important, Vera?"

"Two things, Frank—first, put it with the stained paper from the floor by the body." I flattened the *Spitbucket* out on the table. Then I lined up the piece of paper from the floor of Thursby's room along the top.

"It's a match."

"That's what I expected," she said. "The second thing is the lead story. It's a vertical tasting of Ravensridge wines from the Blackbird vineyard."

"What's a vertical?" I asked. I could picture a wine taster ending up horizontal.

"That's multiple vintages of the same wine, Mr. Swiver," said McQuade. "For this tasting, I report on ten wines from the Blackbird vineyard dating back to 1933, tasted blind, with a couple of grand cru Burgundies thrown in for comparison."

"How could you get all those wines, when Wolff can't even get one bottle?" I said.

"Well, the distributor was able to arrange it for me."

"Joe Damas arranged the tasting?"

"Yes, that's right," said McQuade.

"So," I said, "what's your verdict?"

He snorted. "Well, my next issue should lay to rest once and for all the notion that any American vineyard can challenge the grand crus of France. The Burgundies were clearly better. Ravensridge is the most overrated of American wines, deserving none of its reputation. I suspect that most of those who place the Blackbird on a pedestal have heard about it, but never tasted it. If they had tried it, they certainly wouldn't seek it out, not at half the price."

"By God, sir, you couldn't be more wrong," cried Wolff. "There are overrated wines around the world, wines that trade on their names and their past glories, or appeal to snobs because of their scarcity. But the Blackbird, why, sir, it's a *rara avis* indeed. A wine of beauty and a joy forever. I may not have owned it before tonight." Wolff had a wistfulness in his eyes, and a catch in his voice as he saw Fenwick pour the last of it into Vera's glass. "Alas, I do not own any once again, but by God, sir, I've tasted it often enough, thanks to Lloyd Thursby's kindness. There's not a vintage of it made that couldn't hold its own among the world's finest reds. Nay, sir, it would surpass them."

Wolff's words of homage to the Blackbird hung in the air, until Vera broke the silence. "How about you and the widow, Frank?" she asked. "Did you get any searching done?"

"Yeah, we did our job. Fenwick's room was clean. I'm afraid I found something in number seven, Vera." I picked up my jacket and removed the handkerchief with the .45 pistol from my pocket and laid it on the table. I unfolded the edges of the hankie. "This is the murder weapon."

As everyone considered the Colt semi-automatic, the Cascade slowed to a stop. We had arrived in Chico.

9

Rara Avis

That's General Thursby's pistol, a Colt .45 automatic, model 1911, U.S. military issue," said Fenwick. "Where did you find it?"

"It was in one of your drawers, blondie," said Cici. I watched Vera.

"That's impossible," Vera protested, wide-eyed. "I never saw it before."

"It's true, sweetheart," I said. "Was anyone in your room?"

"Someone's coming," Fenwick alerted us.

There were footsteps in the corridor, and in a moment, the Southern Pacific conductor joined us.

"Okay, folks, we're shifting you to a side track here, and we're going to uncouple your coach. I called the Chico police. Won't be long." He slurred his words and smelled as if he'd been having a little tasting of his own with a bottle of Four Roses. "Thanks for choosing Southern

Pacific." He touched the bill of his cap and headed back the way he came.

I looked at the large glass of wine Fenwick had poured me. I had a couple of glasses from flight two, still untouched, and if they were anything like the first four, I didn't want to waste them. But the Blackbird's presence drew my eye.

The center of the wine in the glass was opaque and blacker than the slag in a coal miner's britches. The color changed in a gradient from black at the core to garnet at the rim, and the garnet rim was bright, almost glowing like a corona.

With the private coach uncoupled, the electricity was off in the lounge, and Fenwick had turned on the gas lamps. The reflection of the flickering lights danced across the surface of the dark liquid. I swirled the long stem and stuck my nose down into the deep bowl.

It was as if someone had hit me in the face with a blackberry pie. But it was more than just that. Chocolate, tobacco, licorice, black raspberries, eucalyptus too, all heady and alcoholic. The sensation was that I could take a bite of the aroma and chew it. I closed my eyes and savored the symphony of smells.

That was a mistake. When I opened them again, there were only seven of us in the lounge. "Who's gone?"

"Damas, Frank," said Vera. "He's taking a powder."

"Or he may have gone to the little boy's room,"

suggested Mrs. DeBains.

I was out of my chair in a second and headed down the corridor. Sure enough, the door was open and Joe was on his way down the steel steps. I grabbed with one arm and got a handful of the collars from his suit coat and shirt. It was enough to stop him until I had a firm grip of his left arm.

"So, Joe, you trying to fade on us?" I said.

"I have to get back to San Francisco," he whined. "I'm going to check the schedule here at the station."

"Not now, you're not. We'll have some law first. Then we can see about who goes back to town." I dragged him back up into the train car. It was only then that I noticed a bloody handkerchief wrapped around his right hand. "What happened to your hand?"

"Shaving accident. Take your hands off me, you hired thug."

I turned him loose and gave him a shove along the corridor. When we got back to the lounge, I told him to sit, and I removed the bloody hanky from his hand.

"My God, Joe, what happened to you?" asked Wolff. Despite the hard words earlier, the old guy seemed concerned for Damas. It was the first time that night I'd noticed anyone passing a kind or unselfish remark.

"It's nothing." Joe shrugged.

"I'll get the first aid kit," said Fenwick.

Vera set to work on the cuts after Fenwick brought in

the kit. When she'd cleaned up Joe's paw, it didn't look too bad, and then she probed in the web between Damas's thumb and index finger with some tweezers. "It's a piece of glass, Frank."

It was a thick piece, and bottle green. "You were in Thursby's cabin too, weren't you?" I said.

"No, absolutely not. I broke a bottle of toilette water freshening up in my room."

"We didn't find any broken glass in your cabin," said Vera.

"It's no good, Joe. That piece of glass is from the mess in Thursby's room. You cut your hand in there . . ."

"No! Nonsense!" he said.

"Swiver," Fenwick boomed out. "I saw Mr. Damas come out of the general's quarters." Mother of mercy. Am I the only one who didn't go to Thursby's room tonight?

"Oh, all right, damn you. I did go to see Thursby," said Joe. "But I didn't kill him; I swear it."

"Why'd you go see him, Joe?" I said.

"Business."

"Your business is our business now. Spill."

He examined some of the faces in the room. He didn't see any sympathy.

"Very well." He savored a long drink of his wine. "For years, I've been distributor of Ravensridge Wines—sole distributor. But recently, the principal partner in Wine Partners' Trust . . ."

"The San Francisco orthodontists?"

"Yeah, the orthodontists. Humph," he snorted. "Well the principal partner informed me my services would no longer be needed. He was going to create a mailing list and sell the entire production by subscription."

"That's preposterous," said McQuade. "No one will buy wines by mail. Why, you need a reputable wine merchant, you need wholesalers, men who know the trade, advertising."

"Seems like you've done all right for Ravensridge, Joe. Why would the owners make a change like that?" I asked.

"Why? Simple supply and demand," he said. "Ravensridge can build a mailing list practically by word of mouth. Then they allocate the product to the list members. They can sell the entire production to collectors. And besides, they'll double their profits. Look, I buy from the winery at five dollars for each magnum. I sell them to restaurants for ten dollars."

"I can get twenty-five dollars at retail," Cicilia contributed.

"But by going direct to the consumer," Joe continued, "Ravensridge can charge ten dollars per magnum and make both their profit and mine too. This black bird lays golden eggs. There are plenty of eggs to go around, but Ravensridge wants *all* the eggs."

"Ten dollars for each bottle?" Vera whistled. She finished wrapping a bandage around Joe's hand, and cut the end. "Why, Dad sells his jugs for only fifty cents apiece."

McQuade rolled his eyes. "Your father's chablis would be robbery at half that figure."

"Anyhow, the point is," Damas continued, "Ravensridge is my most prestigious and most profitable client. If I lose their trade, I can't stay in business. I decided I had to go talk to Thursby. I had to make him see our common interest. So I visited his cabin.

"I understand your problem about the distribution, Joe," I said, "but why go to General Thursby about it? How did you expect him to help you?"

He gave me a look reserved for hopelessly slow children.

"*Mon dieu*, don't you see? Thursby owned the Blackbird Vineyard."

10

Delgado's Law

My God," said Wolff. "I always thought of General Thursby as a fellow collector, but the proprietor of Ravensridge? I never imagined it."

"Owner of the Blackbird Vineyard . . . gee . . . it kind of made him our neighbor," said Vera. "I never imagined it either."

Fenwick and Damas, of course, knew about Thursby's ownership. I hadn't, and it seemed to be a genuine surprise to Wolff and Vera too. Cicilia crossed her legs and picked at a thread on her dress, as if she didn't much care who owned the damned vineyard. It was a little harder reading Sally DeBains and Spitbucket McQuade. The dame maintained her poker face; I couldn't tell what cards she might be holding. She had paid a call on Thursby to make him an offer on some vineyard property though. Could it have been the Blackbird? McQuade was shifty and didn't meet my eye.

"I hear sirens," said Fenwick. "The buttons'll be here any second."

"Well, there's still time to buy a drink." Vera raised her glass of the '45 Blackbird and knocked back a good, solid slug. It made sense to me, so I did the same.

We heard a couple of car doors close and two sets of flatfeet coming our way. Then one more car door slammed. The uniforms came in first. Behind them was a dick in a brown suit. If his suit had been white, he would have looked a little like a refrigerator.

"I'm Lieutenant Delgado, chief of detectives in this burg," said the fridge. "You got a stiff on board?"

I told him he should peek in number nine. "Who're you?" he snarled at me.

I told him I was Frank Swiver, a shamus from San Francisco. "Lemme see your private ticket," he snapped.

I showed him the facsimile of my PI license. He examined it and tossed it back to me. He didn't seem too impressed. Maybe he'd seen one before. "Hey, Click and Clack," he called to the two uniforms, "go check out number nine." The flatties turned and headed down the corridor.

"Tell me about it, Swiver," Delgado said.

So I started to tell him the story, how General Thursby was alive at five o'clock when we left Oakland, but dead by seven thirty when we entered his compartment. "Did you touch anything?" the lieutenant barked.

"The door knobs, before we knew Thursby was dead. I picked up a bottle that was rolling around on the floor, and the shell casings. I stepped in the wine, or the blood."

"Don't you know better than to dance the fandango at a crime scene? Where'd you get that license?"

"Monkey Ward's catalog, Lieutenant. Didn't I see you in line at the five and dime for your tin star?" He stepped forward, and I thought he was going to belt me, but just then Click returned.

"They had a shooting all right, Lieutenant. Old gent, got it through the ticker. 'S blood all over. I think Al is going to puke."

"Oh, for Christ's sake," Delgado said. "Get him the hell outside. I don't want him to throw up on my murder. Call for the photographer and the print man. Then get a meat wagon over here." Click scurried away, and Delgado grinned at me. "Listen, shamus, I can play nice. But don't crack wise with me if you want to keep your teeth, okay?" He shook a balled up fist under my chin. Then he drew it back and glanced around. "Say, there's a lot of wine here. What gives?"

Cicilia, in her black outfit, gave him a very deadpan "We were having a wake." Delgado did a double take at her, but she stared him down.

The lieutenant told me to show him the body. The

whole bloody mess was still there. Delgado asked me the deceased party's name, and wrote it in a spiral notebook with the stub of a pencil. In a little while, a couple of lab guys, one with a camera, arrived. It was getting crowded in number nine, but even Kezar Stadium would have been crowded with Delgado in it. He told the photographer to take pictures of everything. He told the print man where to dust. Then he returned to the lounge and started taking names of the guests.

I told Delgado that no one else had been in our coach since we'd departed Oakland, and none of us had left the train, so one of those present was the killer.

"Maybe General Thursby killed himself," Delgado said.

"A good trick if he did," I said. "There were two cartridges. It looks like there were two shots close together. But since they were both in the heart, it's not likely Thursby was alive when the second one was fired."

"We'll see what the lab says." I was feeling thirsty again, but Delgado's bulk was between my last inch of Blackbird and me.

He grabbed a glass of my wine from flight two and drank. He made a sour face. "Geez, this is awful. What'd you pay for it?"

McQuade had been continuing to swirl, sniff, and sip from his place at the table. Now he drank from his number five glass. "My God, Lieutenant, this is a Musigny! It's glorious."

Wolff plucked the bag off bottle number five. "Astounding," he said holding it up. "The '45 Comte de Vogue, a great Musigny."

"Screw your Count de Bogus, I say. Smells like cow shit. And I know." Lieutenant Delgado grinned. "I was raised on a dairy farm." He drained the rest of my Musigny, just to make sure he didn't like it. "Let's see," he thought aloud, "we got the body. Now I need the murder weapon. Any ideas, Swiver?"

The arsenal I'd collected was lying on the table in plain view: DeBains's .32, Damas's .25, McQuade's Luger, Wolff's Colt revolver, and General Thursby's pistol.

"None of them have been fired," I said, "except the .45 automatic." Delgado's eyes widened.

"General Thursby's pistol," said Fenwick.

"Shot with his own gun, eh?" Delgado checked the safety and the chamber then slid out the clip. He held it up to his nose. "Could have been fired recently," he considered, peering into the chamber.

"See what the lab says," I suggested.

"Where'd you find this?" Delgado asked.

"Well, Lieutenant, we paired off and searched the compartments about forty-five minutes ago. The gun was in a drawer in number seven."

"And who's bunking in number seven?"

"Seven is mine," said Vera. "But I didn't have any gun in my drawers. Tell him, Frank."

"Lieutenant, Miss Peregrino is my operative. She didn't have a gun . . ."

"You say you found it in her room?" he said.

"Yes, but—"

"Looks like she borrowed one," said Delgado. "Why'd you do it, sister?"

"Do what?" she said.

"Why'd you pop General Thursby?"

"That's crazy," Vera said. "I didn't shoot anyone. I never saw that gun before."

Damas had been sitting quiet, smoking, since the law arrived. Now he piped up, "When I opened my door to come to the lounge for the tasting, I saw Miss Peregrino in the corridor. It was about the time of the shooting."

"Why you ungrateful little fairy." She rose. "I just helped you with your cut hand . . ."

"Watch it, sister." Delgado held out an arm like the limb of a redwood between Joe and Vera to keep them apart.

"Listen, Delgado," I said, "Vera and I are on a case. We were working for General Thursby."

"Look, pal, I got a body in there. This could be the weapon that he was plugged with. It was found in the frail's room. And now I got an eyewitness who places her on the scene at the right time. You got anything else for me?"

"I got nothing . . . yet—nothing definite. That's the

point." I put my hands on Vera's shoulders and sat her down. Then I stepped between Delgado and her. "We still need a motive." I took out my Pall Malls and offered him one.

He accepted a smoke but tucked it behind his ear, then rubbed his chin. He needed a shave. "I'll tell you how I operate, shamus. I don't like to waste any time on a homicide. I like to clear cases fast, before the trail goes cold. We got everything we need right here: the killer, the murder weapon . . . Why sit around and play with our thumbs? I'll get the motive out of her when I take her downtown."

"Don't be ridiculous, Lieutenant. The killer could be anyone in the room," I said.

"Then how do you know it's not blondie?" said Delgado. "Were you with her all night since the train left the city?"

"He was with me," said Cicilia.

I wish Cici had kept her mouth shut. Now that she'd piped up, I couldn't lie. Vera was getting squeezed. She shifted in her seat and put a tense but gentle hand on my hip. When I looked at her, she whispered, "Do something." But what? I didn't see how I could reason with Delgado. I didn't see how any one could.

"See, so you don't know that." He jabbed a thick finger in my chest. "Anyhow, I got a hunch about this one. Nine times out of ten I make a move on my hunch, it pays off. I usually get a full confession when I put the suspect under the lights. Don't worry about no motive," said Delgado. "She'll start to sing. Now stand aside."

"Delgado, you're making a mistake," I said. Cold air blew into the car. I felt a chill.

"No more warnings, bub." He held his fist up under my chin.

"Frank," Vera raised a hand to her throat. "No! Don't let him take me." Delgado brushed me back with his forearm, stuck a rough paw under Vera's armpit. She reached around for something to cling to, but he yanked her to her feet. He twisted her arms behind her, whipped out his handcuffs, and slapped them on Vera's wrists. She started to shake.

"Take it easy, Lieutenant." I pushed in between them.

"Don't interfere, shamus, or I'll take you along too." He brushed me off like I was a fly. I didn't mind that. I'd take a beating for Vera.

"Please," she said. "Help me, Frank. Stop him." She turned to Delgado and started to scream, "No. I didn't kill anyone! It's not my gun." Then he tapped her on the jaw with a beefy fist. Vera's teeth clacked together, and she shut up. I grabbed his fist, and he gave me a shot to the sternum with the other one, and I went over backward. He was a cop, a 250-pound cop, and I was a pacifist. I couldn't fight him. But it makes a guy feel pretty low to do nothing while a muscle-bound thug drags his secretary away.

"You're under arrest for murder, sister," the lieutenant said. "Let's you and me go for a ride."

He dragged Vera past me. She planted a foot and bent over me. "You set me up, didn't you, you bastard!"

"No! Vera—"

"If I didn't have these cuffs on, Frank—" I wanted her to know I'd find a way to save her. But then Delgado yanked her arm, and one of those red four-inch heels broke, and he pulled her out limping. I had failed General Thursby, but that was nothing. Now I had failed Vera too.

Lieutenant Delgado had taken off with Vera in his car, and eventually the two uniforms that he had called "Click and Clack" herded the rest of us downtown to their clubhouse. It was on the ground floor of the Chico New Municipal building, just up Main Street at West Fifth. There were two dicks in the detective room. One was tall and lanky, and shook his limp sandy hair back off his face. He wore a blue suit. The other had curly black hair, and had his jacket off, but was perspiring anyhow. He was overweight, though not nearly as large as Wolff was. I saw no sign of Delgado or Vera. I tried to find out where she was, but Sandy said, "We'll ask the questions." I wondered if he had thought of that himself.

We waited around on chairs and a bench, and Sandy

and Curly alternated calling Damas, DeBains, Fenwick, Wolff, McQuade, and Cicilia one at a time into an office with a glass window for interrogation. I sat with them, trying to guess which one was a killer.

A uniformed cop was in the room with the detectives working a typewriter, while Sandy or Curly asked the questions. The door was shut, and the building was so well built that I couldn't even hear the sound of the typewriter keys inside the little room.

After they each signed their statements, my fellow travelers were free to go. It was as easy as that. The southbound train was due in Chico at three thirty in the morning, about six hours after we'd arrived. I imagined Joe, Sally, Apeman, Marcus Wolff, Spitbucket McQuade, and the widow O'Callaghan were all on that train by now. Sandy and Curly called me last. I missed that train.

When my turn with Sandy and Curly came around, I made my statement, and I stuck to the truth, but not the whole truth. I didn't tell everything. For instance, I said I couldn't tell them why Thursby had hired me. I left out the visit from Cicilia and the fact that I was working for her too. And I didn't say anything about how I'd failed Vera and the shame I'd felt, watching Delgado slap the cuffs on Vera and haul her out of the train.

When we were done, I signed my statement and

requested to see Vera.

"Who's Vera?" asked Curly.

"The Peregrino broad. The dame Delgado has in the cooler downstairs," said Sandy. "Did you see him bring her in? What an eyeful! That Delgado. Sure took his time driving over here from the station, y'know?" He winked at Curly. "You say she works for you, peeper? Okay, I can take you down to see her."

I followed Sandy to the lock-up, which was in the basement of the New Municipal Building, and he called for a matron. A woman, who reminded me a little of Curly but with a darker mustache, came along.

"Visitor for that blonde from the train," announced Sandy.

"Sign the book," said the matron. I wrote "T.S. Eliot." Then she opened a barred door and steered me into the ladies' cellblock.

There were two parallel hallways, and we moved down the one on the right. I braced myself for the catcalls and humiliation of walking the gantlet of a woman's jail, but the cells were empty. About two-thirds of the way down the hall, we came to a cell with a figure under a blanket on the cot.

The matron ran her nightstick across the bars. "Somebody to see you, honey." Then, turning to me, she continued, "I'll be sitting down there." She pointed with her stick. "I don't care what you two talk about, Mr. Eliot, but don't pass her anything, and don't touch, get it?"

I told her I had it, and she walked back up the hall to a wooden chair with a fan back and parked herself.

Vera rolled out of the bed and eased on over to the bars. They had taken her red party dress and given her a blue denim work shirt and a pair of dungarees. The jeans were too big and Vera held them up at the waist with her left hand. The light was in the aisle over me, and it cast a shadow of bars, light and dark, across her face. "So what do you want, you bastard?"

She didn't sound happy to see me, and her eyes were puffy. I guessed she needed some sleep. "I want to help you get out, sweetheart," I said.

"You're the one who got me in here, you dumb cluck."

"Listen, Vera, what could I do? I know you didn't kill Thursby, but I found the gun in your drawer. I had to turn it over. It's the murder weapon. I sure as hell didn't know Delgado was going to snap the bracelets on you."

"Delgado! Jesus, Frank. You know what Delgado did? He got lost on his way from the train station, that's what. He drove out of town, and parked by the river. Then he climbed in the back seat with me while I had my hands cuffed behind me." She shivered. "He tried to kiss me. I bit him. He slapped me, and started to play with my tits. I kicked him in the balls. Hard." Her nostrils flared, and the veins in her lean arms protruded. "When he got his color back, he slugged me in the face a couple of times, then climbed in front and drove me down here. He said if I'd been smart, I would have come across for him. Then everything would have been okay, he said." Vera swallowed hard, and wrapped her arms across her chest, shrinking into herself. She bit her lip, and blinked. "Do you think the fat slob would have let me go, if I'd put out?" she whispered.

"Don't trust him." My mind began to race through what had happened tonight. No woman should have to endure crap like that bastard Delgado dealt Vera. But Vera wasn't any woman. She was my secretary. If I had known on the train what I knew now, I think I would have clocked him. I couldn't go back and change what I'd done, or make up for what I'd failed to do for Vera. But it was my responsibility to spring her, and I wouldn't fail at that. "Listen, sweetheart, I can get you out. First of all, I can say you were with me when Thursby . . ."

"Don't give me that, Frank. I came back to your room to pick you up for the wine tasting. I saw you in there with the O'Callaghan skirt." She started to cry. "It was only yesterday I told you I loved you. I've been such a fool, damn it. I'll never trust you again."

Well, she *had* seen us. At least I hadn't lied to her about Cici and myself. "Vera, I'm sorry." I was close to the bars now, and she lashed out at my face. I reared back, but she still managed to scratch my cheek. She was fast.

"Hey, none of that," the matron yelled. "Five more

minutes."

"Look, kid," I said, "I know you're sore at me. But the surest way to get you out of here is to find the real killer. And that's what I'm going to do. It might take a few days. I've got to get back to San Francisco first."

"Frank, call my brother Lorenzo. He's a lawyer in LA. Try to get his help."

"Will do, sweetheart. Soon as I get back." I told her I'd stick around until the next train, and when the stores opened, I could go get her some things.

I didn't figure I was likely to get a kiss goodbye with Vera so sore, so I just gave her a little wink, a salute, and turned to go.

"Frank . . ." she began. I stopped. "Frank, there's something about Fenwick . . . something wrong."

"What is it, honey?"

"I don't know. I can't place my finger on it. Be careful, all right? I just have a feeling he's not what he seems to be. I don't know."

"Don't worry, sweetheart. I'll check him out."

11

Chico

I f you ever find yourself in Chico before dawn, and you're hungry, you could do a lot worse than the Chico Terminal Diner, across from the station. It's a very streamlined affair, with chrome outside, and a neon sign that buzzes.

The only other patron was a man in a black topcoat and a derby hat who was hunched over the counter. I picked out a red vinyl booth and slid into it. The air was steamy, moist, and comforting, and I smelled bacon and coffee. I spotted a young redhead behind the counter in a white dress with a black apron at the waist. She scowled at me, and I gave her my most charming smile in return. I'd been up all night, and it probably wasn't too charming at 5 a.m., but it was enough to get her to come around the counter with a coffee pot.

She plunked down a thick cup and saucer. The cup was off-white and said, "Chico Terminal Diner," in black script. "Coffee?" she asked. I nodded. She poured. Her first name, Arbutus, was embroidered in the same black script above her left breast, which tested the strength of the cotton fabric. Either Arbutus had grown some since starting work at the Terminal Diner, or her mom was washing the uniform in water that was too hot.

"Cream?"

"No thanks."

"You know what you want?"

It occurred to me right about then that what I wanted was to rip Arbutus's dress open and see those great tits, which I imagined were topped off with puffy pink nipples. I wanted to bury my face in them and rub them with my unshaven cheeks. I wanted to see the soft, titian hair that curled down below her belly and see if it was steamy, moist, and comforting down there, as steamy and moist and comforting as the inside of the Chico Terminal Diner.

Being a stranger in town, I didn't know how well that would go over. "I'll have two eggs, sunny side up, toast, side of spuds, order of bacon," I said. She called it in over her shoulder, licked the tip of her pencil, and wrote on a little green check pad. Then she turned and strutted back toward the kitchen, swinging her hips. The coffee was strong and good, and it helped me fight the fatigue that was coming on.

I finished my first cup of coffee and looked for Arbutus. She was just heading over with my breakfast in one hand, and the coffee pot in the other. She had opened the top button of her dress, exposing a hint of cleavage. Arbutus served my plate and then bent over to refill my cup, exposing a little bit more. She had a splash of freckles below her neck, and her slip was black.

"You open all night here?"

"Yeah," she said.

"You on the night shift?"

"That's right. And my dogs are really barking now. Sam doesn't let us sit down if there's customers."

"Sam the owner?"

"He's the night manager and the breakfast cook. He's back there now."

She turned again and sauntered away, swinging her rear end. Her rear bumpers looked as good as the ones in front. I dug into the chow.

Sam at the Terminal Diner made good home fries. No, not just good home fries, great home fries. I smoked a Pall Mall, finished a second refill on the coffee, and called for my check. When Arbutus came over with it, the top two buttons of her dress were undone. She plopped her green pad down in front of me, leaned an elbow on the table, letting the top flap of her dress hang down, and started adding up my bill. I blew some smoke her way, and straightened for a better view.

"Say, I have to get back to the City," I said. "When's the next rattler south to Oakland, Red?"

"What's your hurry, mister? Don'cha wanna see anything while you're in Chico?"

I winked at her. "I'll bet there's some swell things to see. But I have to get back to San Francisco."

"The Cascade only comes through once a day in each direction, and you've missed the southbound," she said. "But there's a local after lunch. Makes all the stops but it'll get you to Oakland in time for a late dinner."

"That's great. Now I just have to find somewhere to spend a few hours. The station's not much."

"Chico's not much. Hey, you want to come with me? I get off in about ten minutes."

"You think your folks would like that?"

"Are you kidding? I'm eighteen. I've got my own apartment, you know."

"Swell," I said.

"Just don't call me 'Red,' all right? My name's Arbutus, and I figure you know that." She looked playful, and pointed at the embroidered script. "I saw you eyeing my chest."

12

Chief Bidwell

Arbutus took me to a corner bodega in her neighborhood that opened early, and I bought a bottle of rosé. Something about her hair made me think pink. We crossed the street to an old Victorian house where she had a one-room walkup on the second floor, and we drank together.

We talked, and I told her I was a private dick on a case, and that I wanted to barber with the police chief before I blew town.

"That'd be Uncle Biddy," she said.

"Who?" I asked.

"Chief Bidwell. He's my uncle. He goes in to work about nine. I think I can get you in to see him." She swallowed half her rosé. "This stuff goes down real easy, don't it? You may fill my glass again, shamus." So I did.

Chico was a small town. Still, it was a lucky break that my waitress was related to the chief of police. There was nothing I could do until later in the morning when the chief came in. So we finished that bottle, which was an Italian Swiss Colony, and everything you could ask for in a rosé. Then I must have napped for a couple of hours.

Anyhow, the next thing I remember was Arbutus shaking me and the morning's light streaming in through the thin lace curtains in her bay window.

"Hey, wake up, old man."

"Mmmm. Must have dozed off. What time is it?"

"Nine thirty. I let you sleep a couple hours."

"You must be tired too, working all night."

"I'll catch some shuteye after I take you over to see Uncle Biddy." Arbutus paraded between the window and me to her closet. The morning sun lit her body from behind and her hair was the color of cayenne pepper. She grabbed a clean gray sweatshirt, and tugged it over her head. Then she slipped into underpants and a pair of blue jeans. "C'mon, pin your diapers on."

I was slower than Arbutus, but I took some fresh clothes out of my duffel bag and made myself presentable.

"You look like that movie actor, you know?" Arbutus said.

"What movie actor?"

"You know, that guy who was in *Out of the Past* last year."

"Well, Kirk Douglas was in that, and Robert Mitchum."

"Yeah, you look like Robert Mitchum. You move like

him too. He's very dreamy." I think Mitchum was quite a few years younger than I was, so I interpreted that as a compliment.

It was sunny but still chilly in Chico. We stopped at a drug store, and I bought some things I hoped would help keep Vera comfortable, like some wool socks. "Is there a bakery around here?"

"Not close by. Sam makes good pies at the diner," she said.

"Can he make one with a hacksaw in it for me?" We strolled toward the New Municipal Building, and shared a kiss before going in. The sergeant at the desk knew Arbutus. She asked him if Uncle Biddy was in yet, and he waved us in with a jerk of his head.

"You wait here a second while I talk to him." She was back out pretty quick and said, "You can go in. Listen, I'm tired. I'm gonna go back to my room and saw wood. So long, Frank."

"So long, Red."

She gave me a sharp right to the gut, and a playful smirk. "I told you not to call me that, you big lug. Big dreamy lug."

Chief Bidwell was a serious-looking older gent. If I was Bob Mitchum, then he was Walter Brennan. His office was neat and his desktop uncluttered. Dark wood panels absorbed a lot of the light coming in through the tall windows behind him. "Sit down.

Mr. Swiver, is it? You're that private operative up on the train from the bay last night, isn't that right? My niece says I should talk to you."

I told him his information was good and that he had a fine niece. "Oh, Arbutus. She's a real hell-raiser, she is. Couldn't get along at home. She moved out last fall, took a room of her own. She dropped out of high school. Darn shame, but there's no telling her. She has a good heart though. What's on your mind, Mr. Swiver? You didn't come to talk about my niece, did you?"

"No, Chief, I didn't. I came to tell you that you have an innocent girl under glass downstairs."

"Oh, you must mean the Peregrino girl. Well, Lieutenant Delgado seems to think he's got the right person."

"I had the impression that Lieutenant Delgado doesn't think much at all."

"Now that's kind of harsh, son. Delgado's my best detective. He believes he can lean on the girl a little and she'll sing."

I told Chief Bidwell that Delgado tried to lean on Vera last night, not in the interrogation room, but in the back seat of his car, down by the river. He shook his head and glanced out the window. "Is that the truth, son?"

"Well, she says she bit him on the mouth, when he

tried to force himself on her. Maybe you'll see some marks on him."

Now we made eye contact, and the chief held it for half a minute. He leaned in over his desk and held down a button on a little brown box. "Sergeant, send Lieutenant Delgado in here."

"He's gone home, Chief," squawked the box.

Bidwell released the button. "Want me to call him in?"

I wondered for a moment what I'd do if I saw the big bum again. Probably bust my hand on him. Nothing that would do Vera any good. I shook my head no.

"Does Miss Peregrino want to file a complaint?"

"No, Chief, there's no need for that. Miss Peregrino just wants to go home to San Francisco."

"That's all then," he said into the box. Then to me, "I can't allow that, Mr. Swiver. She has to be arraigned. The judge will set bail, but I don't reckon it'll be low, seeing as how this is a capital case."

"We're on the nut, Chief. We can't scrape together much for bail. But you know, this shouldn't even be a Chico case. We're from San Francisco. General Thursby was murdered somewhere between Oakland and Sacramento."

"Yes, well, it's too bad you didn't find the body a little sooner then. And where were the Southern Pacific bulls?"

I told him we hadn't seen any railway cops. "Maybe because the murder occurred in a private car."

"Well, it was their train; they should have been on the

job. Anyhow, we won't oppose a change of venue, but you're going to need to get her a lawyer to file for one. Bail, a lawyer, either way or both, you need to raise some cash."

His words were sensible, even fair. I realized I'd be wasting my breath and his time to keep pressing him. "All right," I said. "I'm going to head back this afternoon, and I'll see what I can do. Are you going to protect Vera from Delgado?"

"I hate to hear what you said about my lieutenant." He looked down. He shook his head. "Police work's changed since I started. But Delgado should know better. He has a wife and two kids. I'll have him in for a talk and see what he says. I'll tell you one thing. He'll never pull a stunt like that again on my force. Son, you go back to San Francisco with an easy mind. Miss Peregrino will be safe in my jail."

I thanked him and hustled downstairs to see Vera. Her left eye was black this morning, and the right one was puffy and half-closed. She wasn't exactly glad to see me, but she accepted the things I'd brought. I told her what Chief Bidwell had said.

"Frank, I'm worried about my cat. I left her enough food for the weekend, but I figured I'd be back in town Monday. Could you take care of her?"

I told her I was on the case, and I'd probably spring her by Monday, but if not, I'd feed the cat. "I'm heading back to town after lunch. I'll clear you. Don't lose heart, kid."

"Frank, I got news for you. You're not the world's best detective. If I have to depend on you . . ."

"I said I'll get you out, baby, and I will. Duck soup. Eggs in the coffee. Meanwhile, if you run into any trouble with anybody here, ask for Chief Bidwell. He seems like a pretty square guy."

I said so long, and ambled out into the late morning sun in Chico. It was nearly noon. I had a train to catch.

13

Chardonnay

The local had me back in Oakland in five and a half hours. I rode on the east side of the train, snapped the brim of my hat down over my eyes, and slept. Counting the two hours I'd had at Arbutus's place, I'd managed nearly a full night's rest by the time we arrived. It was approaching dusk; some snap was in the air, and the lights of San Francisco sparkled at me with their excitement. I figured I could still do some work.

By the time I had crossed the bay, it was seven thirty. I dined on chow mein at a place on Jackson then I ambled over to Powell and climbed on a cable car down to Union Square. From there I hiked to my office in the Rose Building on Post Street.

I often came in at odd hours, due to the nature of PI work. The night porter, an old boozehound named Tom, was on duty in the lobby and rode me up to the seventh floor in the elevator. "Gimme a call when you're ready to go, Mr. Swiver."

I tipped him four bits, which I figured he'd consume in beer before I needed him again.

I let myself in, switched on some lights, and rifled through Vera's desk in the reception area, hunting for her personal phone book. When I found it, I settled in at my desk and got on the blower to her brother, Lorenzo Peregrino, the Los Angeles attorney. Lorenzo was eating a late dinner and seemed a bit inconvenienced. I told him his sister was in stir. He seemed more interested in getting back to his lasagna, but I kept him on the horn until he promised to go up to Chico in person for the arraignment Monday. I don't know. Vera was my secretary. If you're a private dick and your secretary gets in a jam, you have to do something. You get her out. It doesn't matter what it takes, or how much time. She's your secretary, and you have to do something. Lawyers must operate on a different code.

"One thing, Swiver."

"Yes?"

"It's going to take some money," he said.

"I'd better get your family rate."

"I'm talking about the bail. I don't know how they do things in Chiclet, but down here bail in a murder case is gonna be at least ten grand, probably more."

"Chico. Call me when you have a figure." I gave him my office number and my home phone, and I hung up.

My next call was to Vera's folks. Louisa Peregrino answered, and I gave her the bad news. I told her I had spoken to Lorenzo, and he was on the case.

"Mrs. Peregrino, the reason I'm calling is about bail money."

"We don't have much," she said, "but what we've got I will give for Vera. And I'll light a fire under Lorenzo's fat *posteriore*."

"If we need big money, can we count on you to put up the ranch for bond?" The line went quiet, and I thought that maybe I'd lost the connection. "Mrs. Peregrino?"

"Mr. Swiver, you'd better find the real killer and get my daughter out."

"What's the matter? Your land must be worth pretty good money."

"My land is Angelo's land. Of course, I would do it. But I'm not so sure about Angelo. The land is something special to him, how you say . . . *molto prezioso* . . . very precious."

"More precious than his daughter?"

"I'll do what I can for my Vera. But my advice to you is to find the killer." She hung up.

I turned out the lights and locked up. On the way out, I asked Tommy for an empty box. He had a case of Lucky Lager deposit bottles, and we emptied it out. I tucked the empty box under my arm and sauntered back to Union Square.

I boarded a Mason Street car and rode up to North Beach. I hopped off at Greenwich Street and strolled east toward Telegraph Hill where Vera had a three-room walkup in the shadow of Coit Tower.

I climbed the stairs and let myself in with her key. When I switched on the light, a big golden longhaired cat ambled out in front of me, lay down, and rolled from side to side, meowing. Her name was Chardonnay. I rubbed her belly and talked to her a few minutes in a soothing tone. Then I moved to the kitchen and hunted up some cat food and other things Chardonnay might need. I placed her in the beer case. It made a good cat carrier. It was sturdy enough to hold the weight of twenty-four full bottles, and already had holes in the sides.

My flop was an apartment on Haight Street, south of the Panhandle, so I walked over to Washington Square Park and splurged on a hack.

It was nearly ten thirty when I got home. I was pleased with what I'd accomplished with the Peregrinos and the cat. Now all I wanted was to stand under the shower for a while. I set the "case of Chardonnay" down on the floor and opened the lids to let her climb out and get to know the apartment. I tossed my suit jacket over a chair, kicked off my brogues, and undid my tie. Out in the kitchen, I found a bowl in the unwashed pile, rinsed it, and filled it with cat food. Chardonnay crept out of her box.

I walked down the hall, and into the bathroom, where

I turned on the shower. I sniffed a familiar scent in the air, which at first reminded me I'd have to fix a litter box for Chardonnay. Then I opened the bedroom door. There was the scent again, only stronger — Night of the Honeysuckles. I switched on the light, and there was Cicilia O'Callaghan, waiting on my bed.

14

It's a Dirty Business

Well," I said, "I see you're no longer in mourning." Cici was stretched across the bed in a red satin chemise, trimmed in sheer lace. It wasn't much of a garment; I've seen bigger outfits in the toddlers' department. At any rate it left little to the imagination. What was it about this dame that she could make me forget about the blonde in the lockup in Chico?

"I had to see you, Frank. I was so hot riding back to town on the train. Then I couldn't concentrate all day at the restaurant."

"How'd you get in, anyhow?"

"Your super. He's a nice man. He didn't want your poor sister Cici down from Santa Rosa to have to wait in the lobby." Good old George. He was a retired coalminer from West Virginia with black lungs but a heart of gold.

"Listen, doll, right now I need to take a shower. Keep your motor running, I'll be right back, okay?" I slipped out of my pants and shirt, eased my undershirt over my head, and grabbed a bath towel. "See you soon."

In the misted-up bathroom, I hung up my towel and dropped my shorts. I was just climbing into the tub under the hot water when the door opened. You guessed it—Cici again—wrapped in my spare towel.

"Let me lather you up, Frank." She dropped her towel and climbed in after me. "I'll clean you off from stem to stern. Hmmm, think I'll start with your stem."

She knelt down in the tub in front of me. My back was to the showerhead, and I closed my eyes and let the hot water soothe my neck and back. Cicilia Ricci, the girl I had remembered for fourteen years. Now she was Cicilia O'Callaghan, the woman of my dreams, and she was with me. Was she really mine now, after all these years? If she was, what else mattered?

Sunday morning, I woke up early. I had been a paperboy for the *Chronicle* for nine years when I was a kid, and since then, I'd always awakened around six. I had dreamt of Vera, but I felt the images of the dream slipping away like ripples in a pond, even as I tried to recall them.

Sure, Vera was my secretary, but she meant a lot to me too. We'd known each other for nearly three years, and our relationship had grown from employer-secretary to friendship. The dream was about that friendship. Business was slow, and we knocked off early and rented bicycles in Golden Gate Park. Okay, it was like a date—friendship with a dollop of romance—we were seeing each other outside of work. Vera, with her long strong thighs, was a natural, and she pedaled into Sutro Forest while I tried to keep up. The trail became narrower and narrower and then climbed steeply into the woods, and I pedaled as hard as I could but I was losing her. Then I caught the cuff of my trousers in the bicycle chain, and toppled over, spilling our picnic basket. Apples rolled away. I lay in the lupine and called out to her. She came back and crawled after the rolling apples while I lay there. Then she cut my cuff off and bent over and kissed me. At which point, I either woke up, or the rest of the dream slipped away.

Cici was asleep, on her back. Her mouth was slightly open, and her breathing was quiet. I could slip away too.

I rinsed again in the shower, just to wash the sleep away, and dressed quietly in a light pink shirt and charcoal slacks. I fed Chardonnay, ground some coffee beans, and put java on to percolate. Then I donned a purple corduroy sport coat and set out on a quest for a fresh loaf of sourdough bread.

Cici was still asleep when I returned. I lifted the covers and made a mental map of the topography—the hills of her breasts, the valley between. Then I ate buttered toast and drank coffee alone, and by then it was time to leave for eight o'clock mass.

The morning was quiet and foggy, but the church bells were ringing the hour as I turned on to Masonic Avenue where I attended St. Agnes' parish church. I arrived just as the pastor, Father Gallagher, followed by two altar boys, was proceeding to the altar. I had another quick rinse with the holy water, genuflected, and slipped into a pew on the left-hand side, clipping the brim of my fedora to the seat back. The church had some middle-aged, blue-collar men, some families, a growing number of Mexicans and Filipinos who lived in the Haight district, and a number of young women alone. They were war widows. I smiled and nodded at some of the gals I'd seen before.

Don't worry; I'm not going to preach to you. Some folks go to church because their faith is strong. Mine's weak; I go in spite of it.

I was born a Catholic, and I accompanied my folks to church every Sunday when I was a boy. When I left home for college, I started to lapse, and by the time I'd graduated, I hadn't been in a church for three years. That was fourteen or fifteen years ago, around the time I was seeing a girl name Cicilia Ricci. When she married Rusty, I took it hard. I kicked around for a while, trying to get work and enough to eat during the Depression. When I could, I bought a drink instead of a meal.

Today was Low Sunday, the Sunday after Easter. Father Gallagher zipped through the beginning of the liturgy. We were all standing as he stepped up to the pulpit to read the gospel. This week, it was according to St. John.

At that time, when it was late that same day, the first of the week, though the doors where the disciples gathered had been closed for fear of the Jews, Jesus came and stood in the midst and said to them, 'Peace be to you!'

Peace. I had this nagging feeling about Vera's arrest. I kept trying to reason it out, to explain to myself what had happened. Delgado didn't have anything on her. Maybe if I'd opposed Delgado with a little force, if I hadn't made it so easy for him, I'd have protected Vera better. Meanwhile, Father Gallagher was going on with the reading.

When he had said this, He breathed upon them, and said to them, 'Receive the Holy Spirit; whose sins you shall forgive, they are forgiven them; and whose sins you shall retain, they are retained.' Now Thomas, one of the Twelve, called the Twin, was not with them when Jesus came.

In 1936, an old college friend dragged me to a meeting in Berkeley where I heard about the Abe Lincoln Brigade in Spain. He was joining up, and he offered to pay my way over to Spain if I'd come with him.

Well, my Spanish was pretty decent, and I didn't have anything here holding me back, so off I went. My buddy and I spent a year and a half in Spain, and I saw things I wish I'd never seen. I couldn't make sense of it all, but I knew I didn't want to see anything like the Spanish Civil War again.

I was still down and out when I got back, and when I could, I'd get a meal and a flop at a House of Hospitality on Portrero. Sometimes I picked up a free paper they had there, the *Catholic Worker*. Then Dorothy Day came to Berkeley to speak. I went to hear her and that's when I realized what was eating me. I was a pacifist. *Pax Domini sit semper vobiscum.* And since then, I've made it a point never to miss Sunday mass.

And after eight days, His disciples were again inside, and Thomas with them. Jesus came, the doors being closed, and stood in their midst, and said, 'Peace be to you!'

Peace! I had bought peace hook, line, and sinker. And now, what had I done to Vera in the name of peace? What had I failed to do to protect her?

Then He said to Thomas, 'Bring here your finger, and see My hands; and bring here your hand, and put it into My side; and be not unbelieving, but believing.' Thomas answered and said to Him, 'My Lord and my God!'

Two passages stood out, as if John was talking to me, and I thought, what is he trying to say? The first thing was the line, "whose sins you shall forgive, they are forgiven them; and whose sins you shall retain, they are retained." And the other was the little story about St. Thomas, called "the Twin." I started wondering about that and turning over the reappearance of Cici in my life, and the murder case in the light of today's scripture.

Father Gallagher gave the sermon. I was hoping he'd say something that would give me some new insight, but somehow, he related the whole darn thing to his usual tirade about the "dangers and the spread of atheistic communism." I tuned that out.

I dropped a buck in the basket when it came around, but I didn't go to communion. Having been out of town yesterday, I hadn't had a chance to go to confession, and besides, I'd had breakfast. I stayed in the pew and reflected on Vera sitting in that jail cell and what I was going to do about it.

After communion, it wasn't long until I heard "*Dominus vobiscum.*"

The altar boys squeaked, "*Et cum spiritu tuo.*"

"*Ite, missa est,*" Father Gallagher intoned.

"*Deo gratias,*" was the response, and the eight o'clock mass was over. It was only about 8:40 a.m. They deposited God back in his little sanctuary on the altar and locked him up. Next performance at nine.

I shook the priest's hand on the way out and said, "Morning, padre." Then I paused and said, "Father, why do you think John calls Thomas 'the twin'?"

"Didymus."

"How's that, padre?"

"Didymus," said Father Gallagher. "That's the Greek word St. John uses. Means 'twin.'"

"I wonder why he mentions that, Father."

Father Gallagher shrugged. "Thomas must have had a twin brother. Nice to see you here, Frank." He turned and extended his hand toward the lady behind me, so I donned my hat and moved away. Fog still curled around the tops of St. Agnes' bell tower. It was time to focus on how I was going to catch Thursby's killer and get Vera out of jail. I marched back to my place.

Cicilia was gone. She had eaten some of the bread and had drunk coffee, and she'd left me a note on the kitchen table.

Frank,

Thanks for having me last night. I really needed to be with you. I'd forgotten how you and I were made for each other.

Please come to Chez Cici tonight for dinner. Come late.
Until then,

Love,

Cici

A late dinner suited me fine. I had plenty to do. I had another cup of coffee and then headed down to my car.

My heap was a straight-eight '35 Pontiac Business Coupe two-passenger model. Pontiac called it the "Improved Eight" if you want the full name, though they didn't say what had been wrong with the old eight-cylinder engine. The '35 cost about $700 new, and I picked it up for a song in 1942 from a fellow who'd been drafted. The straight-eight engine gave me some power on the hills, and the body was in good shape, painted dark gray on the top with pearl gray sides. I'm talking about the car body, not the guy who'd been drafted.

My first call that morning was going to be on Nick Fenwick, so I followed Masonic north from Haight toward the residence of the late General Thursby.

15

Drinking out of the Same Bottle

I had Thursby's address from the invitation to the tasting, and had no trouble finding a parking space on the street near his house on Maple Street in Presidio Heights. The wind from the bay was sweeping across the hill, and the fog was lifting. I thought it might be a fine Sunday.

General Thursby's place was a corner house, set back a few feet behind a low garden wall at the sidewalk. I entered through the gate, crossed to the steps in a couple of strides, and climbed up onto a little porch. There was a large black knocker on the door in the shape of a falcon with a thick ring in its beak. I knocked. Nothing happened. I knocked some more with the same result.

I went back down the stairs and around the corner. I found a service entrance and a garage. I couldn't get into the garage, but through the garage door window, I could see a long, black Buick convertible within. A terra cotta planter hung through a black metal band between the garage door and the side door, and a few pansies curled over the edge staring down at me. I tried the bell on the service door.

This time, hairy-armed Fenwick in a white T-shirt opened the door. "Oh, it's you."

"Nick, I'd like to talk with you. Can I come in?"

"What's there to say, shamus? The boss is dead. He don't care no more who killed Rusty O'Callaghan. I liked Rusty. I liked him a lot. You can keep the advance. But I don't figure I should slip you any more spinach to find out what we already know. His wife scrambled something in the eggs that chilled him."

"I'm also interested in who croaked your boss."

"Well, I guess that's a matter for the johns. Nobody's payin' you to snoop into it, right?" He started to shut the door, but I slipped my foot in.

"Look, the law has my secretary in the cooler up in Chico. I'm not going to let it go until I get her out."

Fenwick poked his head into the door opening. His eyes flashed something new, something I hadn't seen before—caring? Humanity? "They're still holding Vera?"

"It's gone pretty rough on her."

He backed off the door. "Come on in."

It was dark inside, but rather than flipping the light switch, Fenwick drew up the blinds and let in the morning glare. We were in a high-ceilinged, eat-in kitchen, bigger than some apartments. I felt the heat emanating from a steam radiator beneath the windows. A big six-burner gas range dominated one wall, around a corner from an old icebox and a large modern refrigerator. In the center of the floor was a white table and chairs for four. A lamp with a metal shade hung down over the table. A door was open to a pantry that would have made a fair-sized flop for a family in Chinatown.

"It don't seem right they should try to pin this on Vera. What do you want to know?"

He crossed to the kitchen table and straddled the back of one of the wood frame chairs. Gesturing for me to take a seat opposite, he unrolled a pack of Luckies from his T-shirt sleeve, shook one out, and extracted it from the deck with his lips. He slid the pack over to me.

"Well, the night of the killing, what did you see?"

"I told you that on the train."

"Yeah." I lit up a Lucky and blew out a cloud of smoke. *Ah, yes, it's toasted.* "But there was a lot of confusion. Everybody was talking. Most of 'em were at cross-purposes. You know that. I'd like to hear what you have to say without anybody interrupting you."

"Well, I spent my time in the galley, you know. Dinner for eight, it don't cook itself, and the wine don't get up and pull its own corks. I was pretty busy."

"Did you take any breaks? Did you go to your room?"

"Just after the train got rollin', I had to go to the can," he said. "I'd been holding it since I got on board, 'cause I didn't want to flush in the station."

"You're a class act, Fenwick. Did you see anyone?"

"When I came out I saw Vera. She asked me for an empty bottle, to put flowers in."

"You ever see Miss Peregrino before?" I asked.

"Naw. Only when she came on the train." He blew smoke. "But I noticed her well enough then. Long gams coming out of that red dress. Who wouldn't notice her?"

"All right. Anything else?"

"I just returned to the galley, and stayed in there until dinner was almost ready. It was warm in the kitchen, and I came out for a smoke break and a stretch. That's when I saw Joe Damas lurch out of the boss's compartment, kind of funny, holding one arm. I could see he was bleeding."

"Didn't you go to see what had happened?"

"No," he said.

"Why not?"

"I was going to, but just then the timer for the oven sounded. Makes a little *ding-ding*. I had to go back to the kitchen. I didn't want to burn the meat."

"When was this that you saw Damas?" I asked.

"Lemme think." He pressed his thumb and fingertips to his chin and slid them together. "Must have been after we left Davis, I guess. Just before seven."

That was very close to what I figured must have been

the time of death, though we hadn't discovered the body for another half hour or so. "So I guess you knew that Thursby owned the Blackbird vineyard."

There seemed to be a sudden change in the light angling in from the kitchen windows. Now it cast shadows across Fenwick's eyes, giving his face that dark visage again. "I knew."

"General Thursby knew, Damas knew, and you knew. Anybody else?"

"The poor sap who sold him the vineyard knew."

"Oh, yeah. Fenucchi or something like that, right?"

"Yeah, Fenucchi," he said.

"But I hear he's dead."

Fenwick turned away. "May as well have a drink if you're going to sit here and keep chinning." He got up and went into the pantry and came back with two glass tumblers, like you might see in a European cafe, and an open bottle of Louis Martini Barbera. Fenwick filled each glass about three-quarters of the way, which finished the bottle.

I drank some of the Martini. It was rough and might have been better with a plate of *spaghetti alla Bolognese*, but it was a good drink on a Sunday morning. I remember my dad and my uncle used to open a bottle of Louis Martini after mass. They'd sit around the kitchen table with tumblers like these and discuss the merits of the sermon. Some weeks it would require a second bottle to sort out the fine points of the theology.

"How did you like that wine, Swiver?"

"This Louis Martini?"

"Shit, no. The Blackbird the other night."

"I have to admit, it was . . . decadent, ethereal. It was a wine epiphany." He gave me a quizzical expression, arching a dark, bushy eyebrow. "It was magnificent, Fenwick, the best I've ever had."

"Me and the general, we made that wine. Since the war, when I signed on here with Thursby, he's been taking me up there in the fall. We crush the grapes; we ferment them; we barrel the juice. I'm assistant winemaker too."

"When did Thursby buy the Blackbird?"

"I don't know," he said. Sometimes his voice slipped into a dreamy monotone, as if he were in a trance. It had that quality now. "I didn't meet him until after the war."

"You keep the general's cellar here, right?"

"Yeah."

"So what vintages of the Blackbird do you have?"

He thought for a beat. "Goes back to '33. Maybe there are a few bottles of '32 or earlier lying around." He winked. "Nobody to make wine for '42 and '43 with the war going on. I think the General sold off the grapes or the juice. Then the '44, it just rested in the barrels longer. We bottled that vintage at the same time as we made the '45."

"You in the Army during the war?" I asked him, and I helped myself to another Lucky Strike. *L.S.M.F.T. Lucky*

Strike Means Fine Tobacco.

"Artillery," he said.

"Drafted?"

"No, I joined up during the Depression. It was that or the CCC."

"Tell me about Rusty O'Callaghan," I said.

"He's dead. It wasn't no accident, you know."

"How do you know that?"

Fenwick raised his eyebrows at that. Then he scowled and turned his head away. "Listen, I don't *know* it, see. But I'll tell you what: I know mushrooms. What's the twist say? 'I thought they were chanterelles,' or something like that. We saw it in the newspaper when O'Callaghan croaked. It's like I told the boss. You don't need to be no expert to recognize chanterelles. You won't mistake them for anything else. Ain't no poison mushrooms look anything like chanterelles." He drank some of his wine.

"Anyhow, the general took it hard. He really liked O'Callaghan. Then, just when he was probably forgetting about it, the O'Callaghan dame shows up here asking for a handout."

"A loan," I said.

"Yeah. She asked him for twenty-five grand. I overheard the whole thing. I was in the billiard room, polishing the cue balls or something, and they were in the general's office, the library. Mrs. O'Callaghan offered to put up the cellar at her restaurant as collateral. Well, that visit set Thursby off. He told her he wasn't giving her the dough because she'd killed her husband, and he told her he'd hire a private dick to prove it if he had to. After she's gone, that's when he tells me to hire you." He jabbed a finger toward me. "He told me if the cops weren't gonna do anything, he would."

"Cicilia says her husband played cards with the general."

"That's right. He'd be here three or four nights a week, sometimes 'til early in the morning."

"She says Thursby lost. A lot. Rusty took his paper but never tried to collect."

"Lemme tell you something," said Fenwick. "They played for money, sure, but they didn't care about the money. Thursby just loved the company. He loved to swap stories with O'Callaghan. I think Rusty was like a son to the old guy. And O'Callaghan was a right gee. He liked General Thursby. Anyhow, my guess is that the money just changed hands back and forth. If General Thursby lost for a few nights, he'd win it back. And O'Callaghan, he might have been a gambler, but he was a typical Irishman, you know. When he drank too much, he lost. And when he lost, he drank too much. I figure they were about even, or maybe O'Callaghan was down a little. Probably less than a c-note."

I drank and considered what Fenwick was telling me. When we were drinking out of the same bottle, he seemed like a reasonable sort.

"Where's *Vieux Desirs*, Fenwick?"

"Where you saw it last. Still on the siding in Chico. I locked it up as good as I could."

"And what are you going to do?" I asked.

"About *Vieux Desirs*? Nothing."

"No, what are *you* going to do? I don't suppose you can stay here forever."

"Ah, I don't know." He took a drink. "General Thursby was a bachelor. He don't have no family — he was an only child and his parents are long dead. Thursby's lawyer called last night. I'm still on the payroll. He wants me to stay on and take care of the place until they read the will and settle the estate. Then I guess I'll find a new job and move on. Hell, I never should have quit the Army."

"Who do you think drilled your boss?"

"I don't know."

"Who had a reason?" I said.

"Maybe you weren't listening on the train, shamus. Seems to me like most of them did, right? Let's see, one, the boss hired you to pin the O'Callaghan killing on Cicilia. She just might resent him for that. Two, there's you."

"Me?"

"Sure. Maybe the O'Callaghan dame got to you, Swiver, paid you to do the job. Maybe you're looking for someone to pin it on."

"I'm not a hired gun."

He held his palms up. "Hey, I'm just sayin'. Better watch yourself." We stared at each other. Fenwick drank.

"Three, what about Vera? Neither of us think it's her, but now it turns out the Peregrinos and the boss had neighboring land. Maybe she had some old score."

"What about you?" I said.

"Naw. I'm not a hired gun either. Let's see, then there's DeBains. She wants the Blackbird vineyard. The General didn't want to sell. She's quick on the trigger, you know. Five, McQuade's an ass, doesn't like Ravensridge wine."

"That's no reason to kill a man. I've had bad bottles, but I don't go after the winemaker."

"Yeah, but McQuade's a critic, and a mean one. They could have argued. You think Thursby likes reading that bullshit about his wine? Maybe he tried to shoot McQuade, but the critic was faster." He paused and we both had a drink. Fenwick drained his Louis Martini, and I wasn't far behind.

"Ah, what the hell." He pushed back from the table. "Sunday's a day of rest, right?" He turned to the counter by the sink, to a large bottle, a magnum of Blackbird Noir. "I opened this yesterday when I come home," he said, bringing the bottle over to the table, "but I only had one glass with my dinner. Somehow, I didn't feel like drinking it. See how you like the '39 compared to the '45 we had on the train the other night." He filled his glass, but I stopped him from pouring for me until I could drain off the rest of my barbera.

"What was I saying? Oh, yeah. Hell of a group, ain't they? All his so-called friends. Now we come to Damas." He held up his fingers. "How many's that?"

"Four."

"I thought it was more."

"I'm not counting Vera and myself."

"All right, four." He shrugged it off. "The general was cutting Damas out of the distribution chain. That would ruin Joe. He already lost the DeBains account last year."

"Why?" I asked. I had finished my Louis Martini, and Fenwick poured me a glass of the 1939 Blackbird. We'd called it a red wine, and it paid tribute to that concept with a little garnet around the edges. But for the most part, it was black, with a deep black core that absorbed the sunlight in the kitchen.

"Why'd Damas lose the DeBains account? You'd have to ask Joe or Sally DeBains. I don't know. But I've heard . . . well, not all the wines Damas sells taste the same out of the bottle as they did at the winery."

"What do you mean?"

"I mean Joe might have been doing something to increase his profits," Fenwick said. "I don't know what. Maybe he's stepping on the wine to stretch it. Or maybe he's counterfeiting. Counterfeiting ain't just for currency you know. What's to stop somebody gluing an expensive label on a cheap jug wine? Anyhow, whatever Joe was doin', Sally got wind of it and fired him. I wouldn't turn my back on Damas. He's a fairy, I think, but he's plenty tough. I heard he was with the French underground during the war."

So that's where he got that accent. I sniffed the '39 Blackbird. The bouquet was incredibly complex. I smelled smoky meat, raisins, molasses, eucalyptus, and the hot earth of Russian River's slopes. I tasted a mouthful. It was a mouthful all right. A few more years' bottle age than the 1945 we'd had the other night sure didn't diminish the power of this beauty. It oozed black fruit — plums, currants, blackberries — and wild, gamy meat, smoky leather, and earth. It was an enormous wine, full of glycerin, lush and self-indulgent, smooth on the palate with grippy tannins on the finish. Would someone kill for this?

"Well, that's everybody except Wolff," I said.

"Wolff, yeah. And if I had to choose, I'd guess it was him. All the years I've been here, he's been after the general for some of this wine. Thursby always denied him. Then Friday night, Wolff ends up with a magnum of Blackbird in his bunk. I can't buy it that suddenly the boss sells him some."

"Did Thursby usually carry much cash?"

"Depends on where we were going," said Fenwick. "He might have had those four c-notes with him. I don't know. I bring the checkbook, not the cash."

"So why do you like Wolff for the killing?"

"Well, the philosopher wanted the wine. That much we know. And what'd he say the other night? When he wants something, he gets it. He's big and fat, but inside he's hard. A real tough guy. Then there's the Nazi connection."

"Oh, yeah," I said. "That letter from Willi. Well, it stinks, but just because he's got Kraut friends . . . I don't know. The war's over, you know?"

"Not for everybody. See, there's still war criminals out there. There are Nazis on the run, Nazis in hiding. Look, Swiver, you ever hear of Bill Donovan?"

"I heard of a Bill Donovan in Spain, I think, when I was there. I believe he was an observer, or something, for the American government."

"Well, I don't know about that," said Fenwick. "This is General Donovan, Wild Bill Donovan. An Army guy, but he's in some kind of intelligence work now. Then there's another wine writer that Thursby knew, guy named Schoonmaker. Now this guy's good. Not a dope like McQuade. He knows California wine. Anyhow, he meets General Thursby up in Sonoma in '46. Frank Schoonmaker, I think he was a spy during the war. About a month or so later he comes to San Francisco with General Donovan. They get together with the boss for dinner. Now General Thursby was officially retired, but I think Donovan gave him a job."

"How do you know that?"

"They don't tell me things, see, but the general would

ask me to go for stuff. A book at the library. Call somebody on the phone. Drive him to meet someone. It wasn't just normal stuff that an old pensioner does. He was working on something. He was doing research. I don't know if he was tryin' to pin something on Wolff, or maybe he was just going to use Wolff to get a lead on some of his old Nazi buddies down in Argentina. But I do know he was working on something, something that involved Wolff. So what I'm thinkin' is maybe Wolff got wind of it. Or maybe Thursby had Wolff in a squeeze, see, no way out. Either way, Wolff knows Thursby's working alone, so he figures if he kills the general, the heat is off. He pops him on the train. With all those other folks there, maybe he figures he can get away with it, that the cops will pin the murder on somebody else."

The '39 Blackbird, on top of the barbera was making me feel a little dull. I decided I'd had enough of Fenwick's theorizing for now. I got the name and address of the lawyer handling Thursby's will and wrote it in my notebook. Then I asked Fenwick if he'd sell me a bottle of the Blackbird.

He loosened into a tentative grin at that request. "What the hell." His smile broadened as the idea sank in. "I could let you have a bottle of the '44 for a ten-spot. It's a little mellower than this." I figured I should get it for five dollars, the same cost as Damas paid, but like the man said, what the hell.

I had the bottle under my arm and had a hand on the doorknob. Fenwick was slumped over the chair with a fresh smoke in his lips and his gaze on a tumbler of the black wine in front of him. The shadows of his eye sockets were as black as the wine.

"By the way, Fenwick. I'm curious about the timer in the kitchen. How is it that you heard the little *ding-ding* of the timer, but you didn't hear a couple shots from a big gun like a .45? How could you hear that little timer when none of us heard the gunshots that killed Thursby?"

He gazed up at me. He appeared savage and hairy again, and the light from the windows hit his eyes now and gave an animal-like reflection. Then he gained some sort of control, and he grinned slightly. "Artillery."

"Artillery?"

"Yeah. I told you I was in the artillery. Well, you know we had earplugs. And when a whole battery starts blasting it's deafening. Hell of a lot louder than a train. But we could still hear if a call came squawkin' on the radio, or something like that. We wouldn't hear a nearby gunshot. The artillery noise would cover it up. But we'd hear a different type of sound like a voice or a buzzer. I figure same thing happened. Nobody heard the shots because the train noise smothered 'em. But a little bell—it's a different pitch or something. It stands out." He looked back down at his drink. "Anyhow, I heard it."

16

The Road to Damascus

The sun was out now, and the day had warmed up a bit while I was in Thursby's kitchen with Fenwick. I climbed back in the Pontiac and rolled down the windows. A little fresh air would do me some good.

So would some coffee. I turned north on Leavenworth and headed toward the Wharf, where I knew of a café open Sunday mornings. I parked on Beach and sauntered up to the piers.

I sat by the window with my java and tried to visualize what might have happened on *Vieux Desirs* the other night. A dead general, broken glass and wine all over the floor, and a murder weapon in with some underwear two doors down? What possible scripts would play out that way and explain those facts?

The counterman gave me a refill on the coffee. I had asked Fenwick for a list of the addresses he had used to send out the invitations for the wine tasting, and I studied it while I sipped my second cup. Joe Damas had an address on Magnolia, in the Marina district. That was close by, so I figured I'd call on him next.

The coffee was the boost I needed. I was all cranked up and ready to go as I hoofed it back to my heap. The Blackbird was singing. I felt better than new. Soon I was rolling west on Bay Street. I turned south on Laguna, and then turned again onto Magnolia.

The address for Damas was an apartment building. It appeared clean and respectable from the outside. In the vestibule was an intercom panel. Each buzzer had a name next to it. I found one marked "Damas, J" and I leaned on it. The vestibule was clean and respectable. None of the mailboxes was busted. Each mailbox had a name and apartment number. Somebody buzzed me in.

Joe was in 3-C. I boarded a small self-service elevator at the back of the lobby. The inside of the elevator was clean and respectable; however, when I got to the third floor there was an unrespectable smell. An immigrant family's Sunday cabbage dinner?

The red and gold carpet was well worn, but looked to have been vacuumed recently. At any rate, it was clean and respectable, more than I could say for the wallpaper.

As I walked along the hallway, a door opened. Joe Damas poked his head out.

"Hello, Joe. Can we talk?"

He frowned. "Yeah, okay. Give me a minute first."

He slipped back in and closed the door. I waited a second and thought I heard talking. I put my ear to his door. Two voices, *kemo sabe*. Men. Not speaking English. Maybe French. The conversation stopped. After a few moments, the door opened. "Let's get it over with," Joe muttered. "Come on in."

As I was about to step in, I heard the next door down the hall open. I entered slowly, lingering in the hall long enough to see a thin man in a gray suit and fedora poke his head and shoulder out of the door and peer up the hall. It was a young face. When he saw me, he snapped the brim of his hat down and stepped out, closing the door behind him. He placed a cigarette in his mouth and, with his head down, paused to light it. I stepped in.

Damas's apartment had a clean, modern look. Everything was neat and tidy, except for a couple of champagne flutes and an ashtray full of butts on the cocktail table. The apartment had an Eastern exposure and a lot of light streamed in through tall windows. The dregs in the flutes were golden in the sunlight.

Joe wore a white cotton dress shirt, open at the collar, and high-waisted gray flannel trousers. He wore black socks, no shoes, and he appeared lean and trim as he moved quietly through the short hall into the living room.

"Sit." Joe folded himself down onto a low leather davenport. I parked myself on a matching leather chair at a right angle to the couch. A pack of Gauloises lay on the cocktail table. Joe helped himself to one and tossed the flat blue box to me.

"Your hand doesn't look too bad." I lit up. Taking my first draw on the French cigarette, I realized how good Luckies were.

"Oh, this." He held it up, waving his cigarette. The hand had only a couple of flesh-colored bandages between the thumb and index finger, running from the back around to the palm. It wasn't nearly as dramatic as it had been with the bloody handkerchief wrapped around it Friday night. "It'll be okay"

"Good. Well, you were just going to tell me how it happened when Delgado came in and broke up our little party. You cut your hand when you were in Thursby's room. How?"

"Ah, *merde*. Well, I'd rather tell you than the law. Like I said on the train, Thursby was going to cut me off as distributor of Ravensridge. I couldn't afford that. So I go to his room to try to make a deal. We argue. I draw my Beretta, but I was just blustering—I wouldn't have shot him. I want to shake him up, do something dramatic, you know? So I swing the gun and smash one of the bottles he had on his table. Well, the broken glass cuts my hand. So I don't think I made a very forceful impression." He grinned. "Anyhow, you know I'm telling you the truth because my gun wasn't fired."

"Sure, you didn't fire your gun. But somebody fired

Thursby's .45."

"Not me."

"No? Maybe when he saw you waving your gun, he drew on you. You struggled. Maybe that's when the bottle broke. Then you got the gun away from the old man and drilled him."

"No, no, Swiver, that's not how it was. I swear it. I broke the bottle. It was a clumsy move. I was cut and bleeding. I pulled out my handkerchief, wrapped it on my hand, and left."

"Joe, you said Thursby was going to cut you off. You say you visited his compartment to make a deal. What sort of a deal?"

"Well, I had some information I thought the general would like to have. Understand me now; the war is over, yes? But are all the Nazis dead or captured? No. Well, I came to San Francisco in the summer of '43 . . ."

"Where are you from, Joe?" I asked. "Syria?"

"My father was from Syria. From Damascus, *Damas* in French. I was born in Marseilles. My mother was French. Her name was 'Moreau,' but she called me 'Damas' for my father. Why do you ask?"

"Just curious. What did you do during the war?"

"Hah. Well, the Army didn't take me because I was *homosexuel*." He said it the French way. "I should have joined the Legion. I knew Legionnaires who were *tantouse*. Hell, I slept with enough of them. But," he shrugged and blew smoke out through his nostrils, "I made my way north, to Lyons, and found a Resistance unit there."

"What did you do in the Resistance?"

"I have a talent with documents. If someone needed a ration card, I could make it. Eventually, I did birth certificates and papers for false identities. I learned to do passports."

"You were a forger?"

"*Oui*. I did this for three years. I became quite good at it. At the end, I was preparing many sets of papers for American and British pilots. They were shot down at night, and if the Resistance found them before the *Boches*, I made papers for them, and we would try to get them to Switzerland or to Spain. It was hard with the Americans. They don't know any French. You can dress an American pilot in old French clothes, but he still looks American. The papers had to be so good that the Gestapo don't even glance twice at these airmen."

"You did it for three years? That would have been until '42 or '43. Then what happened?"

He sighed. "Let me open another bottle of the Taittinger." He was up and on his way to the kitchen before I could say anything. I didn't like that much. I figured there must be a back door off the kitchen and that the young man I'd seen in the hall had come out of Joe's place. With Joe, I didn't know if he'd come back with a bottle of Champagne or his roscoe in his hand. I didn't even know if he would come back.

But he returned. Joe floated back into the room, relaxed, almost smiling, with a fresh bottle of Champagne and a clean flute for me. At home he seemed more at ease, more graceful on his feet and more self-confident than he had been on the train. He began again where he'd left off as he worked the cork.

"In December of '42 I had some trouble with a woman. She had certain expectations of me, you know? Expectations I was not prepared to meet. When I didn't, she went to the Gestapo. She gave them hundreds of ration cards from my studio. They picked me up. It was very bad for me. They kept me for about three weeks in Lyons, and when they decided they couldn't get any names out of me, I think they were going to send me east to a camp. Well, that would have been the end for me."

By this time, he had popped the cork and poured two fresh glasses. He slid one across the cocktail table to me and lit another smoke for himself. He continued with his story. "If I was going to get away, I had to make my move while I was still in France. Fortunately, there was a guard, just a boy really. A blond, Aryan, Hitler youth. He had soft, light hair on his cheeks. I don't think he'd ever shaved. Well, I made love to him. Then that night he left the cell door open for me, and I escaped. I traveled south, then west and over the Pyrenees into Spain. From there to Lisbon, and then America."

"It must have been very hard."

He shrugged and grinned again. "I had excellent papers."

We drank our Champagne. It was *brut*, but after the way the Gauloise had burned my tongue and throat, it was like honey. "At any rate," Joe continued, "I came to San Francisco. Now, I had always liked wine, and I figured I knew a little about it. I set myself up in business, working with some of the family wineries up north of the bay. Eventually, I met the general, Sally DeBains, the whole crowd." He waved his cigarette in a circle when he said "the whole crowd," but most of the time he let it hang from his lips. The end bobbed up and down while he talked, and he squinted as the smoke drifted up in front of his eyes.

"After the war, it was natural for me to travel to France," he said, "and begin to add French wines to my portfolio. Well, the night before my first buying trip to France, General Thursby, he takes me aside at *Chez Cici*. He tells me there are some Americans who are still fighting the war against the fascists. He tells me he is one of them; he is a Nazi hunter. He says he will pay me if I gather information for him. So for the last two years, when I go to France, I talk to old friends-people in Lyons, friends from the Resistance who survived the war. I bring Thursby information. I don't know what he does with my intelligence or who he is working with, but he pays very well. Now I know General Thursby would love to pin something on our fat friend, Wolff."

"Why?"

"Why? Where were you on December 7, 1941, Swiver?"

"When the Japs attacked? I was here in the City. I had just come out of Sunday mass when I heard the news. Everybody remembers where they were that morning."

"Well," he said, "Marcus Aurelius Wolff had gone to France in November of '41 and had been tasting wine in Bourgogne, then in Alsace. Tasting and buying wine. Then he crossed by train into the Reich. On December 7, he was in Berlin."

"Wasn't he repatriated? I thought enemy nationals were exchanged when war was declared."

"Most of them were, but for some reason, not Wolff. He slipped out of sight at times. At other times he appeared in Berlin, Rome, Madrid, or Vienna. He continued to travel in occupied Europe. He moved around as he pleased. This is why Thursby never trusted him.

"In 1944, Wolff was in Paris when the Americans rolled in. He still had his American passport, so . . . here he is." Joe shrugged again. "Wolff says he had many friends in Europe. He says he's loyal to the United States, and that he never did anything illegal. Nor did he give aid or comfort to the enemy. He's just a businessman — a successful businessman, and one, apparently, who does not see, or does not care what is going on around him, as long as he makes his profit." Joe rubbed the thumb and fingers of his left hand together.

The sun had passed south around the corner, and was no longer streaming in through the east windows. The Champagne in my glass was no longer golden, but held the pale light of an early spring day. I noticed then how chilly Joe kept his apartment.

"The last few years here in San Francisco, Wolff has moved in the same circle with General Thursby," Damas said. "Can you think of any reason that Thursby should deny Wolff or anyone the Blackbird? *Mais non!* Thursby was playing a game with him. He had set his hook and was trying to reel him in, trying to land this big fish, this leviathan. Thursby felt certain that Wolff had been a Nazi spy or a collaborator. All he needed was proof. Well, that was my deal. I was going to offer Thursby the proof he needed."

"You can prove that Wolff was a spy for the Third Reich?" I said.

"Ah, well, my friend, it is not so simple, but, yes, that was the essence of it. Continued distribution rights to Ravensridge wines for me, Wolff's head served up in a *bouillabaisse* for General Thursby."

Wolff's bulbous head, bobbing in a fish stew was not an appetizing picture. I drained off my glass.

"You see," Joe continued, "I was just in France last November. There is a certain *auberge* outside of Avignon where I often stop when I am in the Rhone region. The patron, he is an old friend, you know? He is, oh, how do you say in English? He is not *tantouse* himself, but he . . . he—"

"He accepts." I let it hang. I wasn't so sure I accepted.

"*Oui*," said Joe. "That is it. Well, he knows I live in America now and travel to buy wine in France. So one night we're talking, and he told me that during the war, a certain American, a very fat American, stayed there. He was visiting in Chateauneuf-du-Pape, buying wine. One day he drove out in his car like usual. But instead of coming back in the evening with the boot full of wine, like usual, he came back after lunch empty-handed. Empty-handed and very angry. He stomped off to the village post office, where, my friend supposes, he telephoned.

"The next morning, two Gestapo, they join the fat man in the morning and ride off. When they come back that afternoon, the fat man has *beaucoup* Chateauneuf-du-Pape. He and the Gestapo are all smiling. They have a long dinner at the auberge, and open three or four bottles of the best wine. These were pre-war wines, the finest old vintages by Bouchet, a *vigneron* in a village a few miles from the *auberge*."

Joe refilled the glasses. The Taittinger was disappearing, like the eastern light. "Well, my friend says Bouchet, an old man, had been very drunk when our fat man came to call. Now most of the *vignerons*, they had their oldest, best bottles hidden away in secret cellars to keep them from the Germans. The war years, they were not so good, those vintages. Those, they sell to the Germans. But this man, with the wine in his belly, he had the courage, the drunkard's courage, to refuse to sell the fat man *any* year's wine. Not just the best old bottles but the current vintage too.

"Well, you know how some collectors are," he continued, "when they want a wine, they don't take no for an answer." That was beginning to sound familiar. "So my friend thinks the next day our fat man returns with his two Gestapo thugs. The old man, Bouchet, that was the last time anyone saw him. And Wolff returns to the *auberge* with his wine."

I could guess what happened to the old man, and the story gave me a chill. I had seen too many little dramas like that acted out in my years in Spain. Of course, it wasn't the Gestapo. It was the *Guardia Civil,* or sometimes it was the POUM militia, or the Nationalist Army, or even the Republican Army. But there was always a helpless old man, too often drunk, and many times his old wife, or worse, his young daughter.

"You know this fat American was Wolff?" I gazed out the window at the cool sky.

"*Certainement* it was Wolff! Who else? How many fat American wine collectors traveled with German officers during the war?" Joe drew on his cigarette. "Wait, I have a photograph of Wolff." He opened a large folding wallet and withdrew a snapshot. He slid it over the cocktail table to me. There were Thursby, Wolff, and Joe Damas at a table in some posh restaurant. They seemed to be having a good time.

"I was going to take this photograph of Wolff with me on the next trip to France," said Joe. "I was planning to show the picture to my friend, the patron of the inn. And I understand Bouchet had a daughter, who saw the fat man, who lived. Maybe I find her, show the picture to Mademoiselle Bouchet. They will identify the man — the guest at the *auberge* back in '43, the fat man who came to buy wine. Maybe they will sign a statement.

"I was going to tell the general I could deliver this to him, if he kept me on as distributor. Now, I don't know. I can still get the sworn statement in May when I go, but what will I do with it?"

He paused, finished his wine. "At any rate, you can be sure it was Wolff." He had another smoke and offered me one, but I declined. I had enough of a bad taste in my mouth.

I stood up. The bottle of Taittinger was coming to an end. Time for the last question. "Joe, I hear Sally DeBains quit using you as a distributor last year. You say Thursby was about to drop you too. What's the problem? Why are you losing your clients?"

"Ah, DeBains. She knows nothing, the cow. Let her go.

I am building my portfolio with new clients all the time."
Joe rubbed the palm of his hand across his short wiry hair.

"Like who?"

"I'm concentrating more on imports. I go to France twice a year, you know? I no longer distribute Noir Côtes DeBains, it is true, but that has nothing to do with this murder, I assure you." He tipped back his champagne flute for a long drink. "It was not business. Sally DeBains, she is not accepting, you know? She doesn't like it that *jéçois les femmes*. She doesn't like me."

I thanked him for the wine and the information and got up to go. "Those two bottles," I said, on my way out. "They were both 1945 Noir Côtes DeBains Pinot Noir."

"What bottles?"

"The ones in the general's compartment. One that you broke, I found the label, clinging to some broken glass. And the other one that wasn't broken—it was rolling around on the floor. Why did Thursby have two bottles of '45 DeBains Pinot out when you visited him?"

He gazed out the window. "I don't know. They were for the tasting, I suppose."

"All the other wines we had . . . he only had one bottle of each. Why were there two of those?"

Joe Damas gave me a cold stare. "Perhaps in case of an accident. General Thursby was a careful man."

17

At the Black Lizard Lounge

Y ou don't want to drink Champagne early in the day and then stop. That's a sure way to get a headache. On the other hand, if I kept drinking at the rate I'd been going, I wouldn't be upright for dinner. And dinner at *Chez Cici* would be late, so I needed something to tide me over until then. The best thing to do, I decided, was to get some solid food in my stomach.

I had planned to call on John McQuade, the wine critic, next. I consulted my list of suspects. Fenwick had provided a phone number for McQuade, next to the name and address, which was just south of Market. I stopped by a drug store to use the pay phone.

McQuade answered after two rings. "This is Frank Swiver. I'd like to talk to you about the murder the other night. Are you available now?"

He was. He sounded bored by my little problem, but willing. He hadn't had lunch yet and offered to meet me at a joint called the Black Lizard Lounge, which was right around the corner from his apartment.

I thanked him, and told him I'd be there in fifteen to twenty minutes. I returned to my Pontiac, drove over to Van Ness, and set a course south.

Traffic was light Sunday, and it was only about a ten-minute drive. I found the Black Lizard on the corner of Howard and Second streets. It was a storefront gin mill. There were bricks up to about my chest, and above that a couple of feet of glass window stretched the length of the building on the Howard side. A neon sign for Lucky Lager blazed in the window. There was also a neon black lizard, but it's hard to tell if black neon's lit or not in the daylight. The main entrance was set back on a diagonal in the corner of the building. Around the corner on Second, there was a small window and a back door. I parked on the side street and walked to the front.

It was dark inside the Black Lizard, but my eyes grew accustomed to the light in a few seconds. My ears were working immediately though, and I heard someone singing about a stormy Monday and playing stinging notes on an electric guitar.

Eventually, my eyes came around, and I saw a long bar running down the solid wall to my left. A long mirror stretched behind the bar, with shelves of liquor bottles in easy reach in front of it. In the center of the wall, between two sections of the mirror, was a splendid painting of a reclining, naked woman in a brazen pose. I'll never lose my enthusiasm for naked women in brazen poses.

Behind the bar was the bartender, a guy wrapped up to his sternum in a white apron, who looked like an ex-pug. His hair was cut short and a cauliflower ear decorated the right side of his head. He was wiping glasses with a dirty rag.

Business was slow. No doubt the regular clientele of such an establishment was still in church. I spotted the critic, John McQuade, in a booth in the back. He was wearing the same heavy tweed jacket he'd had on Friday night. With a friendly nod to the bartender, I made my way past the stools along the bar, some tables, and a beautiful new, post-war Wurlitzer jukebox, the source of the music, back to the booths.

"Hope I didn't keep you waiting, McQuade," I said.

"Not at all. I live right around the corner on Hawthorne. I just came over a couple of minutes ago."

I slid in opposite him and opened a black leatherette folder that contained a two-page menu card. "What do you recommend?"

"Everything's good here." He gave me an odd wink. "Of course, it's not like eating at *Chez Cici*, but then neither are the prices. Try the veal."

"I was thinking of a cheeseburger."

"You won't go wrong with that. Beef!" He had me puzzled with that comment, until the bartender strolled up with an order pad in his hand. "Beef's the owner," McQuade told me. "Beef Ballou, meet Frank Swiver, private investigator."

"Oh, yeah? We get a lot of dicks here at the Black Lizard. How d'ya do?" said Beef. Under the apron, he was wearing a rayon shirt in a light French blue. "Beef," embroidered in red script on the breast pocket, just peeked out over the top of the apron.

"Pleased to meet you. Cheeseburger for me. Slice of onion, side of fries."

Beef wrote it down. "Anything to drink?"

"Coca-cola," I said.

He turned to McQuade arching an eyebrow. "Bring me the meatloaf special."

Beef nodded.

McQuade touched a hand to Beef's forearm. "Beef, we'll have a bottle of the Échézeaux. The Meo Échézeaux, 1928."

"'28 Esh-shay-zo, cat's meow. Got you," he said. "Very good choice. You want it now or with the lunch?"

"Oh, bring it now by all means." I could see it would be difficult to have a therapeutic lunch. Beef toddled off to the kitchen. The word "Anchor" slanted across his back in embroidered red script. I wished I had a shirt like that.

McQuade said, "So, Mr. Swiver. What can I do for you?"

"What's your take on this murder case, McQuade?"

"You're asking the wrong man, Swiver. All I can say is the murder spoiled a perfectly good evening of wine-tasting."

"You must have an opinion."

"I told you my opinion. The veal's good here." Then he beamed and laughed at his joke. "Of course I have an opinion, Swiver. Opinions are my business. Give me two wines, wine A and wine B, and I'll give you an opinion as to which one is better."

"I can do that too."

"I can give you an informed opinion about wine," he said, "but not about murder. My opinion about your murder case would be as worthless as if you set a couple bottles of grand cru Burgundy in front of some wino in the park and asked him which was better. He might have a preference, but it would be of no value."

Another song was pumping out of the Wurlitzer now. A fellow was singing about what he wanted to do with a little schoolgirl, alternating with short bursts of torturing a harmonica. It was a different singer than the one who had been having a bad Monday, but the style of music was the same — raw and passionate.

"Suppose you cut the wine metaphor crap," I said. "You were on the train Friday night, right? Tell me what you think."

Beef returned to the table just then. "Fresh out of the esh-shay-zo, Mr. McQuade. I must of sold the last one last night. It was pretty busy."

"Oh, I know," said McQuade. "How about that bottle that I brought in last week — the one I wanted you to keep for me."

"The Clos de Vougeot?" said Beef. It sounded something akin to "claws duh voo-Joe," but I make it a point never to dispute anybody's French.

"Yes, that's the one," said the critic. "That's a Meo wine, though a bit younger." Making cat noises, Beef padded away again and down the stairs. McQuade turned back to me.

McQuade sighed. "Well, I really haven't thought about it much. I assumed if the police nabbed your secretary, they must have had a reason."

"The other night." I shifted gears. "You mentioned something about receiving threats. Tell me about that."

"It's true. Here's another one I found in the mail yesterday when I got back to town." He reached into his jacket pocket and produced a piece of wrinkled paper, which he laid on the table between us and smoothed so that I could read it.

It was brief and composed of letters or words cut from a newspaper and pasted on to a half-sheet of paper.

McQuade

If you publish anymore of your lying reviews about

Blackbird Noir I'll cut off your nose and stick it up your butt. Then you'll know what corked really smells like.

"And here," he removed a paper from a side pocket. "Here's another one. This came last week."

It was the same sort of paper as the first, and the note was composed the same way. The cutout letters and words had been glued to the paper with white paste.

McQuade

You're a fraud I'm going to expose you. And then I'm going to do much worse I'll get vengeance for what you've done.

"Has anyone handled these besides you?" I asked.

"No."

"Do you have the envelopes?"

"Yes, I think so." He fiddled in his jacket pocket and withdrew two envelopes. They were plain white, stationery size envelopes. McQuade's address was typed; there was a city postmark and no return address.

Just then Beef came out of the kitchen with thick cream-colored platters up one arm and a bottle and two big, balloon glasses in his other hand. He set the meatloaf down in front of McQuade on top of the one note and the cheeseburger in front of me. Then he set to work on the wine with his corkscrew. The meatloaf was steaming, and my fries glistened with hot grease.

"Your Coke'll be right out, Ace." The music was now a low, rolling tune about a crawling king snake.

"Are there any other notes like this?" I asked.

McQuade hesitated and then seemed to cover for the hesitation by watching Beef pull the cork on the Clos de Vougeot. "Ummm, no." Beef poured the critic a short taste that seemed lost in the large goblet. McQuade swirled the wine, then stuck his nose in the bowl and made sniffing noises. He looked pleased and drank the taste, holding it in his mouth and gargling it around rather than swallowing. Finally he gulped it down, but he still wasn't through—he closed his eyes and evaluated the finish.

"Superb," he said finally. He nodded for Beef to pour, but I placed my hand over my glass. "Later, maybe," I said. "Right now I need that Coke."

"Comin' right up," said Beef.

McQuade was tucking his napkin into his collar and began sawing away at a slice of meatloaf. "Suit yourself." He shrugged. "More for me."

I asked him, "Who do you think sent you these notes?"

"Mmmmph," he said, chewing. "I don't know. But I tell you, these notes are the reason I brought my Luger on the train Friday."

"Why? Did you think it was one of the guests?" I bit into my cheeseburger. It was hot. The bun was sourdough, the cheese was Sonoma Jack, the onion was crisp and purple, and it bit back. The hot juice of the meat slid down my chin. It was a great cheeseburger.

McQuade washed his meatloaf down with a drink of his Burgundy. "Not exactly a guest. I thought it might have been General Thursby."

"Why Thursby? You seemed surprised the other night that he owned the Blackbird vineyard."

"I couldn't have been more shocked. I had no idea who owned it, but I never really cared. I judge a wine based on what's in the bottle, not who put it there."

"So then what's the idea? Why suspect Thursby?"

"Well, my invitation." From his inside jacket pocket, he withdrew a khaki card and a cream-colored piece of stationery like the ones I'd received from Thursby. The tweed must have been the only jacket the man wore, and it acted as his filing cabinet. "You see, he sent me this note."

Beef dropped off my Coke and I took a long drink. *The pause that refreshes.* I read:

McQuade,

Come to cabin nine when the train leaves Oakland. We have some business to discuss before the tasting.

Thursby

The handwriting appeared to match that on the note Thursby had sent me. "What business was he referring to?"

McQuade shrugged and shoveled more meatloaf. He chewed, wiped his mouth with the napkin, and picked up his glass. "Mmmm. Really, you should try some of this. It's delicious. More finesse than power, but I think you'd like it." He drank. The music had more power than finesse now. A deep, whisky-ravaged voice was shouting about a gypsy woman, and the band played savage bursts behind the voice and between the phrases. "Here, have a whiff of the bouquet at least." He swirled the glass and slid it my way. I wiped the burger grease off my hands and taking the glass by the stem, I held it under my nose. The aroma was fresh, with strawberry notes and a little nutmeg. There were some earthy, dusty scents, along with the perfume of an old rose. Tempting. I passed it back and told him my impressions.

"Hmm. Very good." He evaluated me and my sniffer. "Did you notice the almonds? Unusual, but adds to the complexity."

"I had some Blackbird this morning. I think the bouquet on that was more profound."

"I'll ignore that crack, as I'm sure you can't be serious. What business did Thursby and I have? Good question. We never had *any* business. That's why I was suspicious of his note. General Thursby was a wealthy man who invited me to his tastings. This was a benefit to me because I make my living, such as it is, writing about the wine I taste. Marcus Wolff was usually there, and your friend Cicilia O'Callaghan . . ."

"Why do you say, *my* 'friend Cicilia?'"

He repeated that odd wink with his right eye. I didn't much like it and thought if he did it again, I might close that eye for him. "I know the young widow. I could tell she had some affection for you."

"All right, so what happened between you and the general?"

"Well, I was only in there a few minutes. He was in a rage. He had an advance copy of my May–June edition of *From the Spitbucket*. It's the one they found in my cabin. By rights, I'm the one who should have been angry. That's copyrighted material."

Some other patrons had drifted in while we were eating. A couple of brunos had swaggered up to the bar and occupied stools. A dame who may have been on the make perched at the other end. The tables were starting to fill up too, and a waitress came out of the back to take orders. She looked as hard as the dame at the bar.

"So Thursby had your next issue of the *Spitbucket*?"

"He did," said McQuade.

"What happened?"

"Well, the man was beside himself. He was complaining about what I'd written. His face was red. 'How dare you?'

he said. Well, I had expected the issue to set the California wine world on its purple-stained ass, but why was he screaming at me?" McQuade paused for another swallow of Clos de Vougeot. "And that's when he told me. 'You ignorant scribbler,' he yelled, 'I own Ravensridge Wines!' I was shocked. You could have knocked me over with a Frascati! But the general was livid. The veins in his neck were bulging. I had my Luger in my pocket; I could have drawn it, but I decided it would be more discreet to just leave. I grabbed the galley sheets out of his hand, turned, and bolted out the door."

"Did the general have his gun out?" I asked.

"I didn't see any gun."

"How would Thursby have laid his hands on these pages?"

"Don't you think I asked him that?" said McQuade. "He wouldn't say. He just raged on. Monday, when my publisher opens, I'm going to call and find out what's going on, believe me."

"Did you notice anything else?"

"No, not really. The room was larger than the others, about twice the size, fitted out a bit more sumptuously than ours, but nothing unusual."

"Did you see any wine bottles?" I said.

"Oh, yes, come to think of it. There were two bottles on the table next to Thursby. Both DeBains pinot noir."

We ate for a few minutes without speaking. Then

McQuade said, "You really should try this Vougeot. It was a gift from your friend, you know."

I don't have many friends or acquaintances who buy grand cru Burgundies. "Which friend?" I asked.

"Cicilia O'Callaghan." He winked again. "She sent it over to my apartment a couple of weeks ago. From her cellar at *Chez Cici*. Say, excuse me a moment, will you? I have to go use the toilet."

He didn't realize how good his timing was. I was getting steamed about his winks and innuendos about "my friend, Cicilia."

I took a slant at the bottle while he was gone, then at the cork, which I fingered idly. French corks always seem so much dirtier than American ones, or they're covered with crud or mold under the capsule. This one had white crystalline powder on one end, the wine-stained end.

Next I inspected the envelope from Thursby. To my surprise I found another sheet of paper underneath it. I turned it over and peeked.

McQuade,

I know how you won that bet You'll pay for your tricks
I've had wines with finishes that last longer than you.

There had been at least three threatening letters, and McQuade had lied when I asked him if there were any more. But why? ". . . wines with finishes that last longer than you." I couldn't figure it.

When McQuade came back, the record in the jukebox had changed again. A deep voice was complaining that he couldn't be satisfied. Despite that problem, the singer sounded upbeat and confident. I liked it well enough to ask McQuade who was singing.

"Oh, Beef, he collects this Negro blues music. He bought that jukebox last year, and stocks it with his blues records. What they used to call 'race' music. His pride and joy that Wurlitzer. Beef!" He shot up a hand and waved at the bartender. When Beef strolled over to our table, McQuade asked him, "Who is this singing? Sonny Boy Williamson?"

Beef grinned. "You know, Spitbucket, what gets me is that you can tell a '29 Cheval Blanc from '29 Haut-Brion blind, but you can't tell Sonny Boy Williamson from Muddy Waters." He cleared my plate, which I'd cleaned off down to the garnish.

"Ah, yes," said the critic. "Muddy Waters."

"From Rolling Fork, Mississippi," said Beef.

"Yeah, McQuade," I said, "that was pretty impressive the other night on the train, when you were identifying those wines we had. 'A Chambertin, pre-war, a '45 Noir Côtes DeBains Pinot.' How do you do it?"

McQuade's expression was smug.

"A good wine memory. An educated palate. I wish

I could say 'a million-dollar palate,' but so far it's not brought me much money, barely a living."

"But there are some benefits on the side, aren't there, John?" Beef nudged McQuade with an elbow, but the critic shook like it had been a solid jab. "It got him a piece of ass once. Did he ever tell you that story?" he asked me.

"No, John hasn't told me much," I said.

"Well, what the hell then, tell him, John." Beef set my empty plate back down and swung a chair around from an empty table and straddled it. I would have liked a piece of apple pie and a cup of joe, but I decided to listen first.

"Well," said McQuade, "it doesn't do to tell tales out of school, but, since you know Cicilia so well . . ." There was that wink again. I felt a slow burn starting. "I don't know if you knew her husband, Rusty O'Callaghan, the bootlegger from LA."

"Not to speak to," I said. "I'd seen him, years ago."

"Well, he was in the restaurant business here in San Francisco, but his first love was gambling. He'd bet on anything."

Beef said, "Right. I mean, you could sit out on the steps with this guy and a couple rolls of nickels, and he'd say, 'The next car comes by here, the license plate'll be an odd number.' And you'd say 'Even.' You could drink good whiskey, and do that all afternoon until one of youse had all the nickels. And most of the time it would be him."

McQuade fidgeted. He seemed a bit restless or

uncomfortable, but he resumed the tale. "Anyhow, one night I was at a party over at the O'Callaghan place. Rusty may have drunk whiskey, but he had a bunch of wine lovers over that night. He had choice French bottles over from the restaurant, as well as what he kept in his cellar at home. *Chez Cici* has a lot of excellent wine, even though they feature California wines. O'Callaghan was getting pretty loaded—"

"Everyone was," said Beef.

"Eh, right," said McQuade. "Beef was there too."

"I used to work for Rusty in LA," said Beef.

McQuade continued, "Well, O'Callaghan's pretty loaded, and he says to me, he says, 'I have a bottle of wine, and I'll bet you can't identify it without seeing the label. You tell me where it's from and the name of the wine.' I said, 'Fine. Bring it out. What shall we bet?'"

McQuade arched his back and neck, and rubbed his jaw. "Beef, I don't know if Mr. Swiver needs to hear all this."

"It's almost done," said Beef. "Besides, it's a swell story."

"Sure," I said, "I like a swell story. Tell it. You okay, McQuade?" He seemed paler than when I'd come in, and he was perspiring.

"Yes, I guess so. My jaw's a little tight. Well, the bet couldn't be money, because if you know me, you know I'm always on the nut. So finally, we bet wine, a couple of cases of the good stuff, right? Then Rusty O'Callaghan says to me, 'Remember, McQuade, you have to tell me the name of the wine and the origin. Otherwise, I win.' I agreed. I've done that many a time, and it was a good chance to win some expensive French wine from *Chez Cici*. And then I added, 'Suppose I can tell you the vintage too? What will I win then?'

"O'Callaghan says, 'If you guess the vintage too, I'll throw in a little something extra.'

"'I'll tell you what I want,' I says. 'I want your wife, for a night.' Well, you know yourself, Swiver, she's an exotic creature, probably not more than ninety-five pounds, and must be half of that is tits." He curled his lip, in a leer, and I wanted to wipe it off his mug. "Big boobs on a slender woman like that, you've got to figure she'll be dynamite in bed, am I right?" McQuade winked. Beef laughed and slapped his thigh.

"Now remember, Rusty was pretty well loaded by this time," McQuade resumed, "and besides, he didn't believe I could do it. So 'okay,' he says, 'if you tell me the name of the wine, where it's from, and the vintage too, you get a case of wine from my cellar, and you can sleep with my wife,' he says, 'for a night.'"

"Did Cicilia hear all this?" I said.

"Hell, yes," said McQuade. "She didn't like it. She started to scream and raise hell. You know, I think she even said, 'If you lose, I'll kill you, you dumb mick.' Don't mention that." He winked at me. "It would look bad, what with O'Callaghan dying in that accident. Anyhow, O'Callaghan had guests there, and he has his reputation to think about. So he says, 'Don't worry, McQuade, if you win, I'll deliver her to you, even if I have to tie her up.'

"Then O'Callaghan goes down to his cellar," said Spitbucket McQuade, "and comes back with a bottle of wine in a paper sack. He cuts the foil, pulls the cork, and throws them away so I can't see them. Then he pours me a glass."

I figured I knew where this story was headed. I felt myself getting tense. My left hand was squeezing the cork that had been lying on the table. It was bad enough to have lost Cici to O'Callaghan fourteen years ago. I can't tell you how many nights I tossed and turned awake in bed picturing the big gangster climbing on her. I didn't want to picture her with McQuade.

"It didn't take me long," McQuade continued. "Frankly, it was as easy for me as it would be for Beef to tell you the name of a blues song and the singer from the first four bars. It was a 1934 LaNerthe Chateauneuf-du-Pape. I got it *all* right, year and everything."

My eyes burned into the critic through a red haze that was forming. "And did O'Callaghan make good on his bet?"

"Oh, yes. Cicilia put up a fuss, but I guess I showed her a good time, because she sent me this bottle of Vougeot last week as a gift. I'd say she liked it all right, wouldn't you, Beef?"

I couldn't help myself. I rose up in the booth and grabbed McQuade by the front of his shirt with my left hand, yanking him toward me across the table. I gave him two hard slaps with my open right hand that sent his head jerking, and then I slammed him back down into his seat.

"Hey," said Beef. "None of that stuff in my place. This is the Black Lizard Lounge, not some goon box." He extended a thick paw to grab at my shoulder, but I shook him off.

"Don't get in a stew, Beef. I was about to drift anyhow." I pulled out my billfold, extracted a fin, and flipped it down on the table. Brushing past the big man, I strode out.

18

The Cask of Marcus Wolff

I tried to insert the ignition key into the Pontiac, but my hands were trembling too much. So I leaned back in the seat for a minute to calm down.

When I'd come back from Spain, in 1938, I'd seen enough violence to last me a lifetime. I was in rough shape, especially when I tried to sleep. More often than not, I'd wake up from nightmares. I staggered through the streets of San Francisco at night, afraid to get in bed and turn out the lights. After Pearl was bombed, I was called up for the draft. When the draft board invited me down for my pre-induction physical, I knew what I had to do. I told them I was a pacifist, a conscientious objector. That didn't go over well. If I was against war, what the hell had I been doing in Spain, they said.

Eventually, I got some help from a priest in Berkeley, and I learned a few things from the Catholic Worker movement, and I made my claim stick. The day I got my

CO status, the nightmares stopped. I spent most of the war cleaning out bedpans at St. Luke's hospital, but it was worth it.

Now, after all these years of non-violence, in a sudden rage I had slapped McQuade. A slap wasn't much. McQuade deserved slapping. It was the anger, not the slap that worried me. I'd been angry enough to kill McQuade. Why had I slipped into that animal rage today? Where had my rage been on the train when Vera was taken?

It didn't matter. I had to quit blaming myself for Vera and do something about getting her out. I found a pack of Camels on the passenger seat, fished one out, and lit up to steady my hands. Then I started up the straight eight, slammed the Pontiac into first gear, and roared off.

Marcus Aurelius Wolff resided, when he was in town, in a suite at the Hotel Biarritz, on Sacramento Street on Nob Hill. I made a right on Harrison, then another on Third, and headed up Kearny. Soon I found a parking space in the shade of Grace Cathedral and strolled over to the Biarritz. The brunette with glasses behind the front desk was cool and professional. I had the feeling that if I'd asked her for something in French, Spanish, or Russian, she would have answered as smoothly as she did when I asked in English for Mr. Wolff. I slipped her my card, and she called his room.

"Good afternoon, Mr. Wolff. This is Alice at the front desk. I have a Mr. Swiver here who would like to see you." Pause. "Very good, Mr. Wolff." She replaced the receiver. "Room 311, Mr. Swiver. Please go right up. The elevators are to your left." I thanked her and exited stage left.

I had pressed the call button and was waiting for an up car when I felt something poke me in the kidney. A gruff, "What's your business here, Mac?" came over my left shoulder.

I turned around. "Hello, Stosh. What's an honest cop like you doing in a classy joint like this?"

He removed his finger from my back and gave me a big grin. "Trying to keep mugs from bothering the paying customers, Frank. And it's 'honest *ex*-cop.'"

"Since when? The last time I saw you, you were an unhappy Polack walking a beat in Chinatown."

"Since I told the lieutenant where he could stick my badge," Stan Kosloski said. "Been over a year now I'm the house peeper here. How you doing, Frank? Still trying to save San Francisco from the bad guys?"

"Somebody's got to, Stosh. Say, pal, what do you know about the fat man in 311?"

He told me Wolff was loaded, "But that's true of most of the guests here. He lives alone, don't have many callers. But sometimes he has some young skirts up in the evening—some of the most expensive party girls on the Nob." Wolff took most of his meals out. Kosloski said the fat man entertained once or twice a month, but his parties were quiet, and aside from helping some of his guests who had drunk too much get into cabs and sending them on their ways, the parties were no burden to him. "During the months I been here," Kosloski said, "Wolff's been away twice for long periods. I think maybe overseas. You know, we got him in one of the best suites, with views. What's more, the management lets him store his wine bottles in a locker down in the bedrock under the basement. What a collection that guy has. It'd take months to drink all that, even for a wino like you. What's your business with him, Frank?"

"I'm on a case. We had a shooting Friday night up north. The Chico police pinched my secretary, and I want to get her out. Wolff was there. I'm hoping he can tell me something that would help."

"Wolff's in solid here. I can't let you run no grift on him," he said.

"No funny business, Stosh. But I've got to grill him a little, for Vera's sake."

"All right. If you need me, just tell Alice. She's the efficient little mouse at the desk. Good to see you again, Frank." He shook my hand and slapped my shoulder.

"Good seein' you, Stosh." I stepped into the elevator. "Thanks."

The third floor hallway had a high ceiling, tables with flowers, green wallpaper with a muted magenta flower pattern, mirrors on the walls, and it was brightly lit. I still had a grin on my face, thinking about Stosh, when I knocked on 311.

Wolff opened the door. He was wearing a three-piece suit in charcoal gray, with a watch-chain across his belly. He gave a little bow of his head and waved a pink hand to invite me in.

"Mr. Swiver, a pleasure to see you again so soon. Come in. Do come in."

After a short hike across the foyer and through a gallery, we pitched camp in the sitting room. I perused the polished walnut tables, fresh flowers, and the clean, soft rugs with their deep pile. The furnishings appeared dated to me, but my decorating skills are generally suspect. Nevertheless, everything seemed to be of the finest quality and maintained in tip-top shape.

Wolff motioned me to sit on the davenport and offered me a box of cigars. I helped myself to one and sat down. The fat man selected one for himself. "I like a glass of sherry in the afternoon. Would you join me?" I nodded, yes. He poured two drinks from a crystal decanter into thick lead-crystal stems, and brought those over to the cocktail table. "An amusing little *fino*." Then he waddled back to the sideboard, filled a matching crystal bowl with big, shelled almonds, glistening with oil, and deposited his bulk into a chair at my end of the sofa.

"Now, sir, to what do I owe the honor of this visit?"

He picked up a little gold pistol from the cocktail table in front of us and pulled the trigger, and a flame shot out of the barrel. He puffed several times on his cigar and then released the trigger and passed the toy lighter to me.

"The events on the train the other night," I said. "I was hoping you could tell me something about them. You see, my secretary's in the cooler in Chico, and I'd like to find out who really killed General Thursby so I can spring her."

Wolff blew out a big cloud of cigar smoke. I couldn't see his eyes while he talked to me. I just heard his voice going on and on in his purring style—a voice with a fat man's smile in it. "Oh, indeed, sir. I would be doing the same thing if I were in your place. I don't think for a moment that that lovely young thing is guilty. No, not for a moment. Trouble is, I don't know who is."

"I could see you for it," I said. I popped a few almonds in my mouth. They were salty; I hadn't had any that good since Barcelona. They made the *fino* go down easy.

"Oh, indeed, sir. You are a card. Me? No, it wasn't me."

"You had the opportunity—you were seen coming from the general's room. And you had the motive, which was the 1945 Blackbird."

"Ah." The smoke cleared away, and the warmth faded from his voice. "But I've already told you, the general gave me that bottle."

"Maybe you were lying," I said.

"'The lie is a condition of life.' Nietzsche."

"Sally DeBains visited the general's room after you left, and she found him dead."

"So Sally says. Hmmph. So she says. At any rate, he was dead when Sally *left* the room; we know that, don't we? But was he dead when I left? No, sir, he was not. I assure you General Thursby's death had nothing to do with me. If I'm to help you with this, you'll have to put me out of your mind. We must consider someone else as the likely killer."

I puffed on my cigar. "Who would you consider?"

"Oh, my, you place me in an odd position, sir," said Wolff. "Very odd, indeed. Those people on the train are my friends. How can I think of them as murderers?"

"Try."

"Well, let's see. Suppose we approach it logically, you and I. You say it was not the young lady . . ."

"Vera," I said.

"Yes, Vera. Miss Peregrino, I believe. And your presence here suggests it was not you either. Shall we accept that?"

"You can safely eliminate Vera and me."

"Then I trust, sir, that you will accept that it was not me either, that I had no part in this dastardly business."

I said nothing, but blew a puff of cigar smoke in his direction.

"Very well, then. Who do we have left? Let's see, Sally

DeBains, Joe Damas, John McQuade, and of course Cicilia O'Callaghan. That's four suspects."

"You're forgetting one —"

"What? Who else? I don't see who I could be omitting." He poked a big pink finger against one of his chins.

"Nick Fenwick," I said.

"Oh, yes, of course." He chuckled, shook from the belly, and leaned back in his chair.

"Did I say something funny, Wolff?"

"Oh, leave it to you, sir. The butler did it, eh? How droll." He blew some more smoke. "Very well then, we have five — DeBains, Damas, McQuade, O'Callaghan, and Nick Fenwick. How about Miss O'Callaghan, sir? How do you like her for it?"

"Why Mrs. O'Callaghan?"

"A dangerous woman, I think. You know what Nietzsche says, don't you? 'The true man wants two things: danger and play. For that reason, he wants woman, as the most dangerous plaything.' I noticed what passed between you two. You're a true man, sir, a true man. Anyone can see that."

"No, I don't think Mrs. O'Callaghan could have killed Thursby," I said. "She had no gun . . ."

"But the killer used the general's pistol."

"I think Thursby was more valuable to Cicilia alive. She needed money. Thursby could have provided some of that, but not if he's dead." I gestured at him with my cigar.

"Oh, dear me. Not Mrs. O'Callaghan, eh? What next then?" He pondered the problem.

"I'll tell you what, sir. Perhaps a glass of wine would help us. I know it helps me when I have some thinking to do. Sherlock Holmes had his pipe, and we shall have the grape. Why not?"

"All right," I said.

"Perhaps I could ask you to make the selection? My cellar will be at your disposal, eh?"

"Sounds like fun."

He rose from the chair and tugged his vest down. "Come," he said, "follow me. What sort of wine do you like?"

"Well, I spent some time in Spain. That's where I first developed my taste for wine."

"Ah, I have some lovely Riojas! Murietta . . . Riscal . . ."

"Actually, I was thinking of *garnacha*. That was always my style."

"*Garnacha*?" Wolff said. "Oh, dear. I'm afraid my selection in *garnachas* is not too deep." We had progressed as far as the front door, and he stopped sideways under the lintel. He filled the doorframe from side to side.

"Well, then, how about something from the Rhone," I said, "Reds from the Southern Rhone. Those are mostly grenache, aren't they?"

He positively beamed. "Ah, . . . *garnacha* . . . grenache. Of course. Splendid, sir, splendid. I have some lovely wines from the Chateauneuf region. Lovely wines." He waddled down the hallway to the elevator, and I kept pace at his side.

"So," he said, "what were you doing in Spain? Not the Civil War?"

"'Fraid so."

"Oh, dear. A beautiful country, Spain, wonderful people, but such a tragic history. The Inquisition and now that terrible civil war. Were you with the *generalissimo*?

"I fought on the Republican side," I said.

"Wonderful, sir. I'm a Republican myself. Were you with the Trotskyites? The Communists?"

"I was with some anarchists, out of Barcelona." We were in the elevator now, but the fat man continued to puff at his cigar. He pressed "B" for basement.

"Why, I should have known at once," he said. "An anarchist. Fits you to a tee, sir, yes, it does. Did you know Buenaventura Durruti?"

"Not personally."

"You two would have hit it off wonderfully. Many a cork I pulled with Señor Durruti, sir, and many a pleasant evening we two spent. God rest his soul."

This was so thick, I wondered if Wolff thought I believed any of it. I could not picture Durruti in his fatigues and rough peasant's cap sitting along *Las Ramblas* with this "Republican" in his custom-made suits, not unless one of them had a gun to the other's head.

Wolff led the way along a basement hallway of brick, painted in two shades of gray, light on top and dark on the bottom. Dim bulbs hung from the ceiling every twelve feet or so. We turned through a door into a large garage, crossed the garage and entered another door. We descended a flight of stairs into a sub-basement. In the stairwell was a large steel door. Wolff unlocked it and swung it open for me.

"You get your exercise when you need a bottle of wine," I said.

"Oh, I can call the desk and they fetch one up for me. They have a key. I don't make this trek every day, but I'm proud of my little cellar and love any opportunity to show it off. I wanted *you* to see it and pick something."

We moved down a short little hallway about as dark as where Stosh had told his chief he could stick his badge, and Wolff flicked on a light switch on the wall. I saw some chicken wire lockers, with wood frame doors, illuminated by a hanging naked bulb. Wolff stopped by the largest, produced a key, and undid a Yale padlock. We stepped inside the fenced area.

"Here we are, sir, the cellar of Marcus Aurelius Wolff, at your disposal." The hanging bulb in Wolff's locker swung, moving our faces from light to dark, light to dark. I thought of Vera's face behind the shadows of the jail cell bars.

"Is there a draft down here? It's chilly."

"We're in a sub-basement," he said. "If anything, it lacks ventilation, but it's naturally about 55 degrees." He coughed, and covered his mouth with his handkerchief.

"Are you all right?" I asked.

Wolff's face was red now and his eyes were watering. He answered into the hankie, "Oh, yes, umph! Umph! Uck! It's the cigar. And the stale, damp air, umph! Umph! Uck!"

The storage room was about ten by twelve feet, maybe bigger. Wolff's cigar smoke drifted along the ceiling. On the back wall away from the wire was redwood racking, about five feet high, from the floor up, all of it filled with bottles. And scattered about the floor between the wall and us were wooden wine crates, maybe two dozen of them. Most had been cracked open and the lids pried up. Many had the names of famous chateaux or *negociants* branded into the wood. Wolff started to cough again.

"Umph! Umph! Uck! Blast! I love these," he said, holding his cigar out before him, "but they don't love me. Umph! Umph! Uck!" He pressed the lit end of his cigar out against the top of a nearby crate.

"I'll put mine out too," I said.

"Nonsense, sir. I want you to enjoy it."

"But you're ill."

"No, no. I'll be fine now." He was bent over, leaning on a stack of wine crates. The bulb still rocked, and Wolff's face was in and out of the light.

"Now then." He straightened to his full height. "A grenache from the southern Rhone, eh? Here are my Chateauneuf-du-Pape; this section over here, sir. Pick out anything. Anything at all. The Domaine de Mont-Redon is always reliable . . . have you had Chateau de la Nerthe? Donjon?"

"I had a wine once that I really liked," I said, "but it's hard to find." I browsed through the bottles in the section Wolff had pointed out.

"Perhaps I have it. My selection in Chateauneuf-du-Pape is extensive."

"What was the name? Bouchet, I think. Have you heard of him?"

"Umph! Umph! Uck! Uck! Uck!" He had a coughing spell. "Excuse me. What did you say, 'Bouchard?' That's a Burgundy house."

"No, Bouchet," I said. "I distinctly remember it now." Had I surprised him? Or was it the cold and the smoke? It was hard to say, with the fixture still gently swaying, and Wolff's bulbous head peeking in and out of darkness.

"What was that name again?" he mumbled, and cleared his throat into his fist.

I found some. "Here it is, Bouchet. My, you have quite a vertical selection of Bouchet. Good pre-war years."

"Hmm. Yes."

"You know they're very hard to come by over here. I imagine one might have to go to France to find all these.

Did you ever visit the Bouchet winery?" I slid a bottle out of its rack, and saw it was a 1938. In that moment, I felt a wave of disgust for the fat man.

"Mmm, yes. Some time ago actually."

"Oh, then perhaps you met the owner. He's dead now, I believe."

"Is he?" He turned away to study his wines. "You know I have Chateau Rayas. That's almost 100 percent grenache. Maybe we should try that."

"Killed in the war. The Nazis got him."

Another coughing fit. "Nazis? Umph! Umph! Uck! Ucka-uck!"

I waited for him to recover. "Yes. At least that's what I heard. The Gestapo killed him."

"Oh. How tragic. War is hell, isn't it?"

"It sure is," I agreed. I set the bottle of Bouchet down on a wooden case. "I've changed my mind, Wolff. I don't care to have this with you. I'll find my own way out, thanks." I started to stride past him, but misjudged his bulk. Did I lose my balance negotiating my way around a crate? Or did the fat man give me an intentional bump with his big stomach? I was wondering about that as I shot out a hand to break my fall, but my knee bent over a stack of boxes and I toppled over fast. And then the lights went out.

19

In the Belly of the Beast

I was a bit worried about you, sir, indeed, I was." I heard Wolff's voice, but couldn't see him anywhere. I tried opening my eyes, but that didn't work; they were already open. I couldn't see anything. I could smell cigar smoke. It had the freshness of a filling station toilet.

"Wolff, where the hell are you?"

"Over here, sir." I heard a click, and a small flame flared above my head and about six feet off to my right. When my eyes adjusted to the light, I could see the fat man, perched on a stack of three wooden cases, holding his little toy gun lighter in one hand and a glass of red in the other. "You know, this was an excellent choice, Mr. Swiver. The '38 Bouchet seems to be at its peak. I'll pour you some." He let the lighter go out, and I heard him lay it down.

I was lying on my back, my knees draped over some crates, and my head using the edge of another as a pillow.

I curled forward a little and felt the back of my hair. It was sticky, and it wasn't that greasy kid stuff. "How long have I been out?"

"Don't know. Don't know exactly, but not long. Less than ten minutes I'd say. My first thought was of reaching the light switch, but I found we were locked in. Locked in my wine cellar in the dark. Plenty of good wine. Damn little fresh air down here though." He wasn't coughing, but panted for breath.

"Don't you have the key?" I was sitting up now but stayed on the floor.

"Alas, sir, no. I had left it in the open lock. It's gone. I did have time to open this bottle, while you were out, and pour a glass." Wolff flicked on his lighter and stepped toward me. He positioned a glass of red down on the crate by my arm.

"Douse that light, you fool," I said.

He let his lighter go out. "Yes, I suppose it might be in our best interest to conserve oxygen."

"Someone locked us in here and then turned out the lights. He means to come back and kill one of us."

"Oh. One of us?

"Yeah," I said. "It's someone we know. And if he meant to kill us both, he wouldn't need darkness. There'd be no survivor to identify him."

It was quiet for a few moments. "Oh, dear. I see what you mean. Which one, I wonder."

Holding onto my wineglass, I shifted a few feet to my left. "Wolff, why don't you get down on the floor? Behind a crate or something," I whispered. "Did you search for the key? Maybe it fell."

"Might have, sir, might have. But I hardly think the lock locked itself and the key fell. More likely whoever locked us in has taken the key."

I had a sip of wine. My mouth was dry and fuzzy, and the wine was refreshing, so I had some more. "Did you call for help?"

"Humph. Call for help?" he said. "No. We're in a sub-basement, under the garage. The door we came in through is shut, and the walls are thick. Very solid structure the Biarritz. Survived the earthquake in '06, you know. How are you feeling?"

"A little groggy still. Hell of a headache. What the heck happened?"

"You must have lost your balance trying to squeeze between me and a stack of wine, just when the lights when out."

I wasn't so sure about that, but I couldn't prove different. It all happened so fast, and my head felt split in the back. Wolff coughed again. "Umph! Uck! Ucka-uck!"

If things weren't bad enough, locked in this cage with the fat man, the image of Vera locked in her small cell haunted me in the dark.

I needed to get my bearings. Then perhaps we could

see about busting out of the chicken wire. I drank some 1938 Bouchet Chateauneuf-du-Pape.

Some ten minutes later, I'd finished my glass and was ready to try to stand. I couldn't tell if the room was spinning; there were no points of reference in the dark. But I managed to maintain my balance.

"Marcus, use your lighter about two seconds, and see what's between you and the door. Then kill the flame and move that way."

We did this twice, and I reached the chicken wire. Extracting my pocketknife, I set to work on the fencing near the door latch. It wasn't long before I had the latch hanging loose and we pushed our way through the door.

"Where's the switch?"

"On the far wall, umph! Uck! Umph! Uck! Down the hall by the door," said Wolff.

Groping along with my hand on the wall, I found the switch, but no lights came on when I flicked it. "Someone's tampered with the fuses or something. Doesn't matter." I yanked open the door to the garage. Someone shined a flashlight in my eyes.

"Frank. Mr. Wolff. What the hell are you doing down here in the dark?" It was Stan Kosloski, the Biarritz house dick.

I hiked up the ramp of the Biarritz garage. Dusk was

snuggling down on the hills of the City, but it seemed lit up like an operating room compared to the sub-basement. I donned my shades and drove home. It would give me a chance to feed the cat and freshen up before going to Cici's for dinner — my suit smelled of cigar smoke.

"Yeah, you gents are lucky," Stosh had said. "Alice was done with her shift and headed down to the garage for her buggy. She had just got in her car when the lights cut out.

"It was dark," said Alice. "I turned my headlights on."

"She must have spooked whoever was playing with the electrical panel, which is right down there, by the entrance to the sub-basement. Half the fuses were unscrewed. When Alice turned her lights on, the guy scrammed. She came back upstairs and got me."

"He drove off in a big black sedan, like a town car, maybe a Buick. I didn't get the license number," said Alice.

"That's okay," I told her. "You saved our lives. He locked us in, killed the lights, then was probably going to come back and kill us too." I thanked her with a kiss on the cheek, and she flushed a little.

Back at my apartment, I doffed my jacket, tie, and shirt. I opened a can of sardines for Chardonnay, and poured her a bowl of water. Then I put on a fresh pot of coffee and washed up in the bathroom while it brewed.

With a mug of the hot java and a clean pad of paper, I sat down at my desk to see if I could puzzle out the movements in the corridor of the train.

Wolff had visited Thursby, and McQuade saw Wolff leave with the magnum of wine. McQuade and Damas had each made a pilgrimage to cabin nine sometime after we left Oakland. McQuade left with his *Spitbucket* copy, and Damas left with his hand cut. McQuade must have gone first, because he saw two bottles of DeBains Pinot Noir, and Damas admitted he broke one. Fenwick had seen Damas leaving with the injured paw. All those comings and goings were before Wolff saw DeBains in the hallway with her heater drawn, because Thursby had been alive for all the visits before DeBains. Vera had come to my room before seven, opened the door and that's when she'd seen Cici and me together. Damas had seen Vera in the corridor. No one denied any of these comings and goings, so we'd take them as facts. I thought about these facts in light of the evidence I'd collected today through my questioning, to see if I could come up with a theory.

After an hour or so and a second cup of joe, I hadn't made any progress on a theory, but my head was hurting. Just then, a pounding at the door interrupted my thoughts. I slipped my notes under the blotter and answered the knock.

There were two guys in cheap overcoats and hats. One of them flashed a buzzer at me. "Snoots," he said.

Then the other one flashed his and said, "Overby. Lieutenant Overby. Can we come in?"

"Sure, fellas." I stepped back. They brushed past me into the living room.

"You Swiver?" asked Snoots.

"That's right."

"Been home long, Swiver?" asked Overby. I wondered if it was about the incident at the Biarritz. I didn't think Kosloski would wake the law for that.

"'Bout an hour and a half. What's this about, Lieutenant?"

"We'll ask the questions," said Snoots. Apparently, that was a standard line. "Tell us, where did you have lunch today?"

"I ate in a little saloon south of the slot. Why?"

"Would it have been the Black Lizard Lounge?" asked Lieutenant Overby.

"Yeah, that's right," I told him.

"And did you happen to see a gent name of McQuade there?" Overby continued.

"What if I did?"

"We're with homicide division. His landlady found him dead on the stairs this afternoon," said Overby. "Being a good citizen, she gave us a call."

"It seems he was coming back from lunch," said Snoots. "Never made it up to his room. He died on the steps. She found him a little later."

I hadn't expected that. Could it have been a coincidence? Or was there a killer at work, the same killer who'd been on the train Friday night. I didn't believe in coincidence. "Geez, that's tough," I said, "but . . ."

"We backtracked," said Overby. "He had lunch at the Black Lizard too. Quite a coincidence, ain't it, Snootsie?"

"The lieutenant don't like coincidences."

That makes two of us, Snootsie, I thought to myself.

Snoots consulted his spiral notebook. "The proprietor there at the Black Lizard, one Beef Ballou, and some other good citizens who happened to be on the premises, told us a fellow fitting your description took offense at something, struck Mr. McQuade, and then marched out."

"Mr. Ballou was nice enough to remember your name," said Overby. "He said it was a party named Frank Swiver that had lunch with McQuade."

"I slapped McQuade, but it was nothing. An open hand across the kisser and back."

"Like this, you mean?" asked Snoots. He slapped me quick with his right hand, left cheek, right cheek. He wore a high school ring, and it stung. "Or more like this?" He tried again and I was quicker. I leaned back. His fingertips just grazed my chin. I turned away, to the kitchen and chewed a couple of aspirin for my headache. The sting on my tongue distracted me from Snoots. Calm, I returned to the parlor.

"The slap wasn't important," said Overby. "But maybe

you waited outside his building and followed him in."

"Or maybe you were waiting on the stairs and finished him off. When there weren't so many witnesses around," said Snoots.

"That's ridiculous," I said. "What did he die of?"

Sergeant Snoots regarded Lieutenant Overby. Overby considered Snoots. "We don't know. We're waiting for the autopsy. It looks like somebody worked him over, though. We have to assume it was foul play."

"Or maybe he just fell down the stairs, got a black eye, and broke his neck," I said. "Don't you guys have anything better to do? You're homicide dicks for Christ's sake, and you don't even know if it's a homicide."

"The coroner's man at the scene called it a probable homicide, Swiver, so we've got to look into it," the lieutenant said. "What'd you two argue about?"

"We didn't argue . . ."

"Then why'd you slap him?" asked Snoots.

"Why'd you slap me?" I countered.

"Hey, maybe I should slap him again, Lieutenant."

We were in a little circle in the middle of my living room floor. I was tense, and I figured they were too. It wouldn't do to let this boil over and be taken downtown. If I were locked up, there'd be nobody to help Vera. I turned slightly and backed away from the circle. "Can I get you boys anything? Smoke? Coffee? Drink?"

Overby eased out of the circle too and crossed to my

desk. "Naw. We don't drink on duty." He reached for his own pack of cigarettes, Old Golds. He shook one out and grabbed it between his lips. "What are you working on, Swiver?" He could have been glimpsing a corner of my notepad that was peeking out from under the blotter.

"What am I working on?"

"Beef said he thought you were a private dick," said Overby. "Let's see your license."

I showed him the photostat from my wallet.

"Who are you working for?"

"You know that's confidential, Lieutenant," I said. "But I can tell you there was a murder up north Friday night. McQuade was there. I went to ask him some questions."

"What murder?"

"Don't worry. It was on a train, between Sacramento and Chico," I said. "It's out of your jurisdiction."

"Was McQuade a suspect?" said Overby.

"Could be."

"Don't play with us, Swiver. If McQuade was a suspect in a murder and then he gets bumped off in San Francisco, we need to know why."

"Lieutenant, you don't even know yet if McQuade was bumped off. And even if he was, it might not have had anything to do with my case."

"He had a couple notes in his pocket," said Overby, and he showed me two of the threatening letters McQuade had at lunch. Great, and I had their sister here in my apartment. Where was it, still in my coat? Or on the desk where I'd been working on the puzzle. "You know anything about these?"

"McQuade showed them to me this afternoon." There it was, the third note, on my desk next to the blotter. It was only about a foot away from Lieutenant Overby, but it was folded over. "He didn't know who they were from. That's all I know. Listen boys, this is fun talking to you, but I have a dinner date, and if I don't get going, I'm going to be late." I herded them together with my body, and guided them toward the door.

"Now hold on," said Snoots. "You can't give us the bum's rush."

"Look, you know where to find me if you want to talk some more. I'm not investigating McQuade's death, but if I find out anything in my investigation that might help you, I'll call, okay, Lieutenant?"

Somehow, I pulled it off and got them out. Then I leaned with my back to the door and willed my heartbeat back down to normal.

20

Chez Cici

hez Cici was in a converted townhouse on Union. A boy opened my car door when I drove up.

"Complementary valet parking for *Chez Cici*, sir." I climbed out, left the keys in it, and pocketed the ticket stub he traded me for the Pontiac.

A green canopy and a Chez Cici sign, done in cast iron lettering, like the Paris Metro, arched over it. A guy in a monkey suit held the door open for me, so I didn't stop to peruse the menu in a lighted shadow box on one side of the entrance.

"Good evening, sir." The hostess was a tall blonde in a black evening dress down off one shoulder. A hot pink diagonal slice slashed down from the other shoulder. I asked for a table and gave her my name. "Walk this way, Mr. Swiver." She picked up a menu, which had a red velvet tassel hanging from the binding, and a second, thicker red folder. Turning around and revealing a long bare back, she set off with long strides. She moved with such action that the tassel coming out of the menu started to twirl. I couldn't walk that way, but I could follow.

Downstairs was a dark, wood-paneled room, but the hostess led me up one flight. In the second floor parlor, I followed her to a table near a gas fireplace. "I'll tell Mrs. O'Callaghan you're here."

The room was lit by red or white candles in straw-covered Chianti bottles on tables covered by long red and white cloths. The only electric light spilled in from the hall where we'd come up the stairs. It was a busy night. Most of the tables were taken. Some of the swells were in dinner jackets, but there were enough casual dressers that I didn't feel out of place in my sport coat. Ice was sprinkled on the fingers, in the ears, and around the necks of the dames, and it sparkled wildly in the candles' flickering light.

The place buzzed with lively conversation, punctuated with women's laughs at the appropriate breaks. Waiters and waitresses in white shirts, black pants, and red bow ties flitted among the tables with loaded trays. The intoxicating aroma of warm garlic and the sizzle of recently cooked meat drifted through the air. These scenes must go on all around the world, Paris, Rome, New York, wherever beautiful people with money gathered to have a good time. But I'd never been anyplace like Cici's.

I cracked open my menu. On the left were "Sunday's Specials" typed on a crisp sheet of parchment and clipped in.

Lasagna Bolognese

Grilled Breast of Muscovy Duck

Rack of Lamb

Steelhead Trout a la Cici

Beef Wellington (for 2)

I looked up and saw Cici across the aisle at a table to my right. "I'm Cicilia O'Callaghan, the owner of *Chez Cici*. Is there anything I can do for you?"

She was talking to a bald gent with a soft face. He gestured at the black shells on the plate in front of him. "I can't eat these."

"What seems to be the trouble, sir?"

"These mussels are not fresh."

"That's impossible," said Cicilia. "I bought them myself this morning at the wharf."

He dabbed at his mouth with his napkin. "No, I beg to differ. I know mussels, and these mussels are not fresh."

"I assure you, sir, all our food, all the ingredients here at *Chez Cici* are the freshest possible."

"I can't eat these. I know mussels."

"Perhaps they're overcooked. I'll replace them for you."

"No, I don't want them anymore." His companion, a peroxide blonde, who must have been twenty years younger than him, seemed bored with him and his mussels. She appeared to be concentrating on chewing her gum.

"I'll take them off your bill. Can I get you something else, sir?" asked Cicilia. "Perhaps you'd like to try the oysters. Westcott Bay oysters. They came in from Washington State this afternoon. Very fresh."

"No, I'll just have my main course."

"Very well, sir. Giorgio."

The waiter, standing by quietly until now, said, "*Si, Signora?*"

"Giorgio, please remove these mussels and bring this party two glasses of the Moet. Compliments of Cici."

"*Si, Signora* 'Callaghan."

Cici looked my way, leered, and came over. She laid a hand on my shoulder, and in her deep smoky voice said, "See anything you like, sailor?"

"Hmm, I do now, Cici." She wore a light champagne-gold, double-breasted blazer, buttoned just under her left breast. She had a short skirt to match the jacket. She touched my ear and ran her fingers through the back of my hair as she did so.

"You don't need a menu, Frank. I'll take care of you. I hope you brought your appetite."

"My mouth's watering—for you, doll." Cici's Mediterranean skin had a warm glow in the flickering light from the fireplace, in dark contrast with her pale gold suit. I no longer smelled the garlic. Once again, I was under the spell of Night of the Honeysuckles. "So, where's the apron and the toque tonight?"

"Don't you like this outfit?" she vamped for me.

"It's great, what there is of it."

"I work most of the day, Frank. I buy the groceries, I draw up the menu, and I start some dishes that cook slow." She drew out the word "slow." "But at night, I take off the work clothes. I hand over the stove to my assistant chef. I like to dress up in something glamorous, and I come out to be with the guests. You see that asshole?" She flicked a thumb toward the guy whose mussels weren't fresh. I nodded. "Well, that's what the owner needs to deal with. Those fucking mussels were still alive twenty minutes ago. That son-of-a-bitch wouldn't know fresh mussels if they clamped themselves onto his crank." Her green eyes blazed.

Dinner was great. You'll have to trust me on that. I couldn't tell you what I ate. I do remember that Cici brought out each course, hot from the kitchen. She brought the wine too, a bottle of '45 Noir Côtes DeBains "Old Vine" Zinfandel. She lingered a bit with each dish and drank from a second glass of the wine that she'd poured for herself and left on my table. We smiled at each other and talked like old friends. We tantalized each other, like we had fourteen years ago. We used to go to North Beach when Cici wasn't waiting tables. In the afternoons, we listened to the café owners sing Italian love songs as they sautéed garlic. In the evenings we drank espresso and listened to jazz or poetry. We made a bubble bath in my tub with cheap shampoo and soaked in it face-to-face and laughed with our legs entangled. And tonight Cici treated me the same way as she had back then. She teased me, tempted me, and stoked my fire for her.

By the time I had my dessert, the place had emptied out. Cici was sitting on the arm of my chair. Her legs were crossed above the knees, and her skirt was up enough to expose the tops of her hose and black garters. She was feeding me forkfuls of her raspberry crème brulee and laughing as her dark hair fell down in front of her eyes. At about a quarter past ten, the last couple, from the other side of the fireplace, got up. The woman flung the end of her mink around her shoulder and stuck her nose in the air, but the man paused to sneak a glance up Cicilia's skirt as they toddled by.

"Now that we're alone," said Cici, getting out of my lap, "scoot up close to the table, and I'll show you why we have these long tablecloths." Before I could say anything, she'd disappeared under my table. I knew what was coming next. You can't get service like that in many joints.

21

On Lafayette Square

I had decided to spend the night at Cicilia's if she offered. I didn't want to go to my place and take a chance on Snoots and Overby coming back and taking me downtown. She offered.

"Kitchen's closed," she announced. "I'll just grab the night's take, and we can let the staff lock up." She scooped the bills out of the register without counting them, and stuffed them in a gray canvas bag. "Come on with me, Frank. I'll show you where I live."

Two valets brought our cars. Cici's was a dark '41 Caddy. She drove off at a good clip, and I had to goose the Pontiac on the hills to keep from losing her. The O'Callaghan house was on Lafayette Park, so we didn't have far to go.

The house was an old white stone building, and the walls glowed in the moonlight. It impressed me as being at least as large as General Thursby's residence.

Architecture's not my game, but I'd say the place was in the French country-chateau style, but on more of a city-sized scale. Cicilia whipped the Cadillac into the driveway and under an archway. I found a spot to park the Pontiac a couple of houses down on Octavia. I had brought a change of clothes in my duffel, and I brought it out of the back seat and slung it over my shoulder.

It was a crisp moonlit night, and I caught a whiff of *yerba buena* in the air. When I arrived, Cici was waiting for me under the arch in her driveway. She undid the button on her blazer as I approached and let her jacket slip open. She was naked underneath. Cici's areolas are as big as Morgan dollars, and I love them. They were a rich pomegranate color in the darkness, and her nipples were hard in the cool evening air. I massaged one of the breasts in my right hand until the nipple felt like a little cork. "Forget your underwear tonight?"

Cicilia fished a wad of cloth out of her purse and shook it out into a tan silk slip. "I removed it on the drive home. For you." Well, she is petite, and the Caddy's roomy. And she had one of those Hydra-Matic transmissions.

I pressed her to me and kissed her as good as I've ever kissed anyone. Cici kissed me back, and she kissed good too. We kept this up for about as long as we both could. Then she buttoned up and invited me in. "The girls will be in bed. Maybe you'll get to meet them in the morning."

Of course, I hadn't seen her in fourteen years, and

had never thought of Cicilia Ricci as a mother. But I had read the news story of Rusty O'Callaghan's death, and the mention of "survived by two daughters" came back to me. "Who puts them to bed?"

"I have a woman come in when I work late, which is usually six nights a week. She gets here in the afternoon, so that Brigid and Meaghan don't come home from school to an empty house. Fix us a couple drinks, Frank. I'll be right back." I draped my jacket over the back of a chair and made myself at home while Cici dismissed the nanny and went up the stairs to kiss her girls goodnight.

I found the fixings for a couple of martinis, shook them well, poured them out, and positioned them on a silver tray, which I brought into the living room. I set the tray on the cocktail table, and set myself on the davenport.

When Cici came back down, she was in a silver satin men's pajama top, long enough to come down to mid-thigh. Only the top button of the three it had was buttoned. "Oh, it's good to get out of all those clothes after a long day."

"All those clothes? You barely had on enough to ante up in a game of strip poker."

"Sure I did, Frank. I had enough on because when I play cards, I win. Runs in the family." Cici plopped down on the davenport next to me. She lifted her martini with her right hand, crossed one bare leg under her, and draped the other on my lap. She propped her left elbow on the back cushion and rested her head against her hand, smiling at me.

"I don't know, doll. I saw Fenwick today. He doesn't think the general lost all that money to Rusty."

She sipped her drink and eyed me hard over the rim of the glass. "Fenwick don't know nothing about it, Frank. I've got the paper. As a matter of fact, I want you to take those IOUs down to the probate court for me and file a claim. Now that Thursby's dead, that's the only way I can collect."

"Well, that might have to wait a day or two."

"Why wait, Frank?"

"I have to go up to Sonoma tomorrow. I'm going to go talk to Sally DeBains. I think I'd like to see the Blackbird vineyard too. I'll have to take care of your claim on Thursby's estate later in the week."

She shrugged. "There's time, I guess."

"There'll be plenty of time. I didn't find any wine. There's an abundance of good gin around, so I made martinis. How's your drink?"

"It's just what I needed. Thanks. There's some wine in the cellar, but most of it's at the restaurant. Rusty didn't drink much wine. He liked his gin though."

"Did he drink much when he gambled?"

She hesitated, and then nodded. "Sometimes."

"Fenwick thinks he had plenty to drink when he was over there. You know, maybe his judgment wasn't so good when he drank. Maybe he didn't win all that money from Thursby."

"Yeah? Well, maybe he did. What difference does it make what Fenwick thinks?" She sipped her martini. "Jesus, Frank, who says Fenwick thinks at all? He seems like . . . like such an animal."

"He was okay when we dipped our bills today—just the two of us—in Thursby's kitchen. Anyhow, I talked to some of the other suspects today too," I said.

"Suspects?"

"People from the train. Suspects in the Thursby killing."

She had another swallow of her martini and then set the glass down on the table. She leaned forward and wrapped her arms around my neck. The cool satin sleeves slid around me, just above the collar. "Frank, are the police hunting for any suspects in the Thursby killing?"

"No, they've got Vera."

"Maybe you should just leave it that way." She planted a kiss on my yap and gave me some icy cold tongue. Then she crammed a salty surprise, an olive, into my mouth.

"She didn't do it." I chewed the olive.

Cici picked up her drink again and leaned back. Was she pouting? "We found the gun in her drawer."

"Somebody planted it."

She had a drink and sighed. "Oh, I suppose you're right. It's just that . . . well, damn it, Frank. These days seeing you again, after so many years . . . It's been a long time since I've felt this way. I feel like a woman again. If Vera were around, she'd just complicate things."

No more than you've complicated things for Vera and me, I thought, but didn't say it. "Listen, if I'd had my way, you and I would have been together the last fourteen years. But Vera's my pal. I'm not going to let her take the fall for this."

"Your 'pal?' Isn't she a bit more than that?"

We both drank. "Okay, she's my colleague, my confidante . . ."

"Your lover," said Cici.

"You left me, Cici. Did you expect me to be celibate all these years?" I took another sip, and placed my glass down. "I saw Joe Damas today."

"So?"

"I was thinking about how he smashed the bottle in Thursby's cabin and cut his hand. It seemed odd. There were two bottles of the '45 DeBains Pinot Noir in there. There was only one bottle of everything that Fenwick opened for the tasting."

"You know," Cici said, "Joe came along from nowhere. He built up a good trade. Then he lost his best customer, Noir Côtes DeBains. Did he tell you why?"

I shrugged. "He told me Mrs. DeBains doesn't like

gay cats."

"Sally? That's true, she don't. But if Joe was making money for her, she wouldn't have cared if he was buggering altar boys."

"They must have been making money. I see the wine everywhere, and Sally says she wanted to buy the Blackbird Vineyard."

"Well, you know, 1945 was a good year for California pinot noir. Sally's a good winemaker. She knows how to make wine as well as I know how to run a restaurant. I tasted her pinot up at the winery." She paused and sipped her martini. "It was first-rate juice. I bought a fairly large quantity for the restaurant. I was going to make the Noir Côtes DeBains the house red wine at *Chez Cici*. I placed the order through Joe Damas, like any other customer. Well, the stuff I took delivery on, it's inconsistent. I opened up bottles at random. I'd say 60 percent of it is bad. But why? How could Sally have had such variance from barrel to barrel?"

"So where did the bad wine get into the process? Why does it have Sally's name on it?"

"I don't know," Cici said, "but I can't sell it to my customers. I know what Sally thinks. She thinks it has something to do with her distributor. That's why she canned Joe."

"Well, I'll ask her about it then." We drank. "I also saw Spitbucket McQuade today."

Again she said, "So?" as if she didn't care, but it wasn't as smooth as last time.

"Funny thing. I was the last one to see him."

"What's that supposed to mean?"

"I mean he's dead."

Now she was surprised. "Dead? McQuade?"

"Yes. I'm sorry to have to tell you."

"Don't be. I couldn't stand the bastard."

"Really? I thought maybe you were friends. After all, you sent him a bottle of good Burgundy."

Cicilia was quiet for a few moments and stared hard at me with her green eyes. "You're quite a detective, Frank. Who says I sent him a bottle of wine?"

"He did. We had lunch. He opened your bottle. A Clos de Vougeot, from Meo. Good bottle of wine."

"Did you drink it?" She touched my forearm with a tentative hand, just a feather's touch.

"No. I only sniffed it. McQuade loved it though."

"If he said it was from me, maybe it was something he bought at the restaurant."

"There was a gent there at lunch, name of Beef."

"Beef Ballou? You must have been at the Black Lizard."

"You know him? He doesn't seem like the sort you'd meet in Lafayette Square."

Cicilia gave a little snort. "Beef worked for Rusty in LA. He tagged along when Rusty came up to San Francisco after Prohibition. Rusty was very loyal, Frank. He gave

Beef a job. He was the first bartender at *Chez Cici*, back in '35. Two, three years ago, Beef had saved up a stake and bought that saloon south of Market. Then, even though he was no longer an employee, Rusty would still have him over to the house." Cici extended a hand to the cocktail table for her glass, and the men's pajama top slipped down off one shoulder. "We could be having a party with people like Thursby, Wolff, and the Nob Hill crowd, and Beef would be there, circulating with the guests. Rusty never understood that my friends, my customers at the restaurant, they don't want to socialize with those people." She squirmed a little on the davenport and snuggled closer to me. If she was any closer, she'd have been behind me. "Sure, it was fine when Beef was behind the bar. They could order a drink from him and say 'How ya doin', Beef? How d'ya like the Seals this year?' But Rusty, oh, well . . . he never knew where to draw the line, you know? He was even friendly with Fenwick, I think."

"McQuade told me an interesting story today."

"You don't say?" She sipped her drink and made a face as if no story McQuade told could interest her.

"Yeah. It was about you and him. Here, let me have your glass. I'll fix us a couple more of these and tell you about it."

So I fixed a couple more martinis. I found a bottle of vodka, and this time I used that instead of the gin. I made them strong and dry, and I raised the olive count to three in each glass. I brought the drinks in to the living room, and I told Cicilia the story I'd heard. As I did, she lowered her green eyes and seemed to stare at her olives. She shivered, and she wrapped one arm across her chest and over a shoulder and made herself small on the couch. When I finished, she said to the olives, "You believe that story?"

The olives said nothing. I replied, "Yeah. I believed it so much I slapped McQuade down when I heard it."

Cicilia snapped her head around to face me. "Did you, Frank? You slapped him? For me?" The corners of her mouth turned up.

"Yeah. And now two homicide dicks are watching me. They think I might have waited for McQuade to come out of the Black Lizard so I could finish him off."

The glow was back in Cicilia's eyes. "It was terrible, Frank. It was the most humiliating thing that ever happened to me."

I sipped my drink and thought about this. "Cicilia, it got me sore when I heard about it. It's a dirty story and it made me sore. But besides that, I couldn't picture you going quietly into something like that, not against your will."

"Yeah? Well I did, Frank. Because it wasn't exactly the way McQuade told it." She set her glass down and hugged herself with both hands. She was shivering. I got up and lit the gas fireplace on the opposite wall.

"Tell me."

"There was a bet all right. But you didn't hear the true stakes. McQuade didn't ask for me. He asked for a share of the restaurant." She took a long drink. "He wanted to be part owner if he won, Frank. He told Rusty, 'I want to run the wine program.' Rusty was smoked. But he probably would have agreed even if he'd been sober. Rusty thought it was a safe bet."

"McQuade wanted in on *Chez Cici*?"

She shrugged again. "He thinks *Chez Cici* brings in plenty of jack. McQuade was perpetually broke. He knew I wanted to expand. What is he—what was he, forty-five, forty-six years old? He didn't want to grow old and die alone and poor in that shabby flat with nothing but his wine. He didn't know anything about running a business, so he tried to win his way into a successful business on a bet." Cicilia drank. "Of course Rusty can't welsh on a bet. The big dope. His reputation was more important to him than the restaurant. *My* restaurant."

"You think he actually would have made McQuade a partner?"

"I know he would have. McQuade was like Rumpelstiltskin. Rusty would have forgotten about it the next day, wouldn't have thought about it until Rumpelstiltskin came around to collect. And then Rusty would have had no choice. He gave his word, and because of the guests who'd overheard, he would have had to keep it. I had to do something. I didn't work in a hot kitchen six nights a week for thirteen years to lose 49 percent of what I'd built.

"So, I made McQuade another offer—one night with myself, now, instead of the rest of his life with my business. It made me sick, Frank, physically sick. But I'm the owner, the cook, the manager. It's my restaurant. I had to do it, not for Rusty's sake, but for myself. For myself and the girls. And now the bastard's dead."

Cicilia leaned back on the couch with her hand on her forehead and her face down. She rubbed her temples behind her eyebrows. Her petite frame sank back into the overstuffed couch. The pajama top slid down, and I could see her left breast in the gaping opening. An hour ago it had been an object of desire, hot in my hand. Now it was just a tired tit.

I was tired too. Our drinks were about gone, and it had been a long day. I wanted nothing else now but to go upstairs and get in bed. But first I had to ask her.

"So did you kill him?"

"Kill McQuade? You're the suspect, remember? Not me."

"Did you kill Rusty?"

"You already asked me that, Frank." She considered her olives again.

"I don't remember you giving me an answer."

She brought her head up and stared straight at me.

"Look at me, Frank. Look me right in the eye." I did. We were sitting close, and she gave me an intense stare. Her words came out of the burning green irises. "Now I'll tell you what you want to know."

"Did you murder Rusty O'Callaghan?"

"No." She never blinked. "No, I didn't kill him. Now I don't want you to ask me that ever again."

We climbed the stairs to the master bedroom. There were dark wooden Doric columns built into the walls and some paintings, mostly still-lifes. In the master bedroom, a naked, sleeping Endymion on a grand scale covered most of the wall opposite the bed. Behind the bed, a double swag of heavy dark-green curtains framed a mirror.

"Do you still want me, Frank?"

"What three things does drink especially provoke?" I mused out loud. "Nose-painting, sleep, and urine. Lechery, madam, it provokes and unprovokes; it provokes the desire, but it takes away the performance."

"What are you talking about, Frank?"

"Shakespeare, Cicilia. Never mind." I was dead-tired, but I knew what answer a woman needed. "Of course I still want you."

We made love. Afterwards, Cici quickly drifted off to sleep, while I lay awake on my back, staring up at the ceiling, across at Endymion, or back at the mirror hanging behind us. Fourteen years ago, Cicilia Ricci, my first girl, had been a good lay. Now she was spectacular.

She was also quite a cool liar.

22

A Bad Dream, a Bad Finish

I finally drifted off but into a bad dream, one of my first bad ones since those Spanish Civil War nightmares had stopped.

I dreamed I was disheveled and groggy, lurching down the stairs of Cici's house, wearing a shabby yellow robe, unbelted. I paused at the threshold of the kitchen and beamed peacefully under bloodshot eyes. Cici was in the kitchen. "*Introibo ad altare Ciciliae,*" I said.

Crossing the threshold, I pulled out a chair from the kitchen table, bowed to Cici before sitting, and rubbed my hands on my unshaven cheeks. Cici turned to the stove to make my breakfast.

"You're sore at me, ain't you, Cici?" In the dream I could see what she was cooking, and I watched her arrange a line of little golden brown fungi down the center of a pan of flat yellow egg and fold one side over the other.

"Ain't you?" I said. "You're still sore at me about the

other night."

"I'm not sore, Rusty." I didn't know why she would call me Rusty. That was her dead husband. I was Frank. "Why should I be sore at you?" She was talking to the tiled splash guard on the wall behind the stove, so maybe she didn't know it was me, not Rusty O'Callaghan.

Cicilia flipped the omelet and placed some flabby strips of bacon on my plate. The white fat at the curled ends reminded me of pale flesh, and I closed the top half of my robe and crossed myself in the air before gurgling through grace in my phlegmy morning throat. Yes, I should pray for this omelet. Cici dashed it with pepper. Plate in her left hand, skillet handle in her right, she turned, as I finished praying and crossed myself again.

"Cici, we've been married fourteen years. I know when you're sore at me."

"Well, I'm not sore, damn it." She slung the omelet onto the plate, and slammed the pan down on the stove as if the burner were my head.

"Is there coffee?" Cici brought over a thick white cup, rattling on the saucer as she poured from the percolator. The coffee splashed over the rim when she set the cup on the table in front of me. I grinned and dashed Tabasco on the eggs, then salted them.

"Hmmm. Delicious, Cici. As always. These mushrooms are rich and meaty. What are they?"

"Toadstools."

"Ha, ha," I said. "I'll wager they're chanterelles."

"That's the trouble, Rusty. You'll wager about anything." I wished she'd quit calling me Rusty. She turned to the sink to start the dishes.

"How are the girls?" I asked.

"Brigid and Meaghan have already gone to school." I heard my fork scraping on the plate as I shoveled egg, herbs, and mushrooms into my yap. The herbs were bitter. It seemed I could even hear the sound of my teeth gnawing at the soft bacon, but that was unlikely with the water running in the sink. I looked at the plate. Only a few more bites to go. I must finish it all for Cici.

She kept rinsing out the skillet. "Oh, Cici," I called. "I must have eaten too quickly."

"What is it, Rusty?" She didn't sound cloying, just concerned. She came over to me. My hands were on my belly now, and I moaned as the chair toppled over backward. Did I hit my head? Maybe I had the wind knocked out of me. "What's wrong?" said Cici.

"Can't breathe."

"Maybe it's your heart, dear." She knelt down beside me.

"I knew you were sore." My eyes stared up at the ceiling, unblinking. I gazed across at Endymion; I looked back at the big mirror on the wall behind us. I was waking up in Cici's bed.

A dark-haired girl of about ten was peering at me. I

sat up, bare-chested. The girl raised a hand to her face and called, "Mommy, Mommy."

"Good morning. Eh . . . you must be Meaghan," I said. "Mommy's still sleeping." I gave her a grin. The girl circled around to Cicilia's side of the bed. Cici was lying on her front, her head turned away from me, face covered by her hair. The girl got close enough to see that it was Mommy and watched her for a second or two. Then she turned and fled the room as quickly as she'd come in, running out on tiptoes. That was fine with me. I was naked under the covers; I had to pee, and my morning wood was as hard as a railroad spike.

My Timex said it was about six thirty. I had places to go today and people to see, so I climbed out of the sack and set off to find a toilet and a shower.

The shower was excellent, with two showerheads and great water pressure. Ah, the comforts money can buy. In about ten minutes, I was dried off and back in the bedroom, slipping into something from my duffel bag suitable for a drive into the country. Cici was on her back now and raised one eyelid, as if to say, this is all the energy I'm going to use and you're lucky to get this. But she did have a languid smile on her face, and she stretched her lips a little at the corners for me.

"Good morning," I said. Cici said nothing, I told her Meaghan had been in, and she gave a little nod. "I'll have to get up in a few minutes and get the girls off to school."

She stretched her arms up over and behind her head. A tit rose up and the nipple peeked over the top of the sheet, like a pomegranate sunrise.

"I'd better go then."

"After I pack their lunches and feed them, I'm getting back in bed for a couple more hours. Stay and join me?"

I stepped over and brushed my lips across her eyes and then her mouth. "No, I have a lot of ground to cover today, doll. I'm on a case."

"You and your case. I'll make you breakfast."

I love breakfast. I almost said yes. "No, I gotta run."

"All right, then. I'll see you tonight, Frank." We followed that quick kiss with a slower one that left me with Cicilia's taste on my tongue, at least until I had my morning coffee.

A man in a Chrysler was easing out of the first driveway I came to. I said, "Good morning," and he nodded from behind the closed window. Then he pushed down the lock button on his door.

It was a cool, dry morning. I thought about what it would be like to live on Lafayette Park. A grand house instead of that run-down apartment in the Haight. I would wake up here and leave from here for work each morning. Good food, excellent wine, great sex last night with Cici. Why not every night? Was this what the next chapter of my life could be?

You could hear birds singing in the park. You could pick up the paper off your doorstep and mosey across the street and sit on a bench in the sunshine and read about the world. I thought it would be swell. All I had to do was forget about McQuade's death, O'Callaghan's death. All I had to do was forget about Thursby's murder and Vera in the Chico jail.

I found my car faster than you could say Sam Spade. I wanted to get an early start to Sonoma County today, but I needed to stay in town until Wells Fargo opened to cash that check from Friday evening so I could eat today, or buy gas.

Snoots and Overby might have been waiting to pinch me. Or, they might at least have had someone planted outside my apartment, ready for a tail job. I decided against going to my apartment, but I thought I could risk the office.

I drove downtown to Post Street and parked the Pontiac in my monthly garage space. It was just seven thirty. The traffic was flowing into the City like a transfusion into the veins of a patient on an operating table. I gave a newsie a nickel for a morning paper, walked to a hash house that was opening up, and spent my last ninety cents on a stack of wheats and my fill of strong mocha java. I chose a table where I could gaze out the window and see the front entrance to the Rose Building.

The hotcakes were dismal, and so was the news. Beneath the fold on page one, I read:

Writer Dies on Building Steps
Police Say Wine Critic Has Bad Finish

John "Spitbucket" McQuade, a well-known figure in the world of wine, was found dead Sunday on the steps of his apartment building in the 100 block of Hawthorne St. Although officers on the scene refused to comment on the cause of death, the Chronicle has learned that the Police Department's Bureau of Inspectors is interested in the case and has ordered an autopsy from the Coroner's office.

Mr. McQuade's landlady, Mrs. Flannery, found the body at approximately 2:30 in the afternoon. "I had just spoken to him when he was going out to lunch," Mrs. Flannery said. "He seemed perfectly fine then." Neither Mrs. Flannery nor any of the neighbors knew of any recent or chronic health problems from which Mr. McQuade may have suffered.

Mr. McQuade had taken his lunch at a nearby tavern on Howard St., the Black Lizard Lounge, where he had been a regular patron. The owner of the Black Lizard, Mr. Beef Ballou, related that the critic's luncheon companion had lost his temper and struck McQuade.

"The Black Lizard's a classy joint," said Mr. Ballou. "We don't tolerate any rough stuff in here, so I ran the other fellow off." Patrons of the Black Lizard Lounge corroborated Mr. Ballou's account of the episode. Police are seeking the other man for questioning. Readers with information should contact Sgt. Snoots of the Bureau of Inspectors.

Mr. McQuade was forty-seven years old. He lived alone, and had no close relatives in the area.

The wheat cakes had the consistency of shoulder pads from a cheap dress. A fleeting image of breakfast at Cici's crossed my mind, and I poured more syrup on the hotcakes. They tasted like shoulder pads from a sweet dress.

I would have liked another cup of coffee, but I was uncomfortable. The counterman seemed to have nothing better to do than to watch me. I hadn't seen any law on the street staking out my office, so I paid up, tugged the brim of my hat down a little farther, and headed over to the Rose Building.

23

A Road Trip for Vera

My office was empty and quiet. I opened the filing cabinet to "W" and found out a bottle of white, Italian Swiss Colony Gold Medal Label. I rinsed out a tumbler and poured myself about eight ounces. It wasn't chilled, but the heat hadn't been on in my office since midday Friday, and the drawer temperature was cool.

It was quarter past eight. I called Lorenzo Peregrino's number in LA. A dame answered.

"My husband left last night on business. This is Mrs. Peregrino. Who's calling?"

I identified myself to Vera's sister-in-law and found out Lorenzo had taken the Sunday night train north. He could be in Chico by now for the arraignment. Well, the little mouthpiece might turn out to be all right.

"You know, he's got all the business he can handle right here in LA," Mrs. Peregrino said. "There's a big case right now at Paramount he should be working on. I don't know why those dago farmers think he should drop everything . . . Oh, excuse me. You're not Italian, are you?"

"No, *signora.*"

"Hunh? Oh, a wise guy. Well, listen, Mr. Wisenheimer. Lorenzo better get paid for his time, see? He could be billing the studio twenty-five dollars an hour down here, but now he's off on some wild goose chase."

"I'll pay him, Mrs. Peregrino." Twenty-five dollars an hour. I billed twenty-five dollars a day. I might be cutting Lorenzo's lawn all summer. "Listen, I told him to call me today when he has some news. But I'm going to be out of the office, so tell him to call his mom, okay? I'll be up in Sonoma County, and I'll check with her this evening."

"Yeah, sure. And if I don't hear from him, you check with his office. He'll call in there."

She gave me the office number, and we broke the connection.

I dumped last night's rags out of the duffel bag and stuffed in a couple of things I might need for the day's work. At the last minute, I grabbed the office roscoe out of the bottom drawer and packed it, along with a full box of cartridges. Then I finished the glass of Italian Swiss Colony, slung the duffel bag over my shoulder, and locked up. I walked down seven flights of stairs and out into the alley. Next I made my way over to Union Square, where I could sit outside with the other winos to wait for my bank to open. I started to get my mind off Cici and the damn dream, and focused onVera and getting her out of jail.

By ten a.m., I was crossing the Golden Gate Bridge headed north on Route 101. I had money in my pocket, the sky was blue, and there were no traffic lights ahead of me for miles. The Improved Eight was running smooth with steady oil pressure.

I had the window down and my left arm on the sill. By the time I came to Mill Valley, I was running smooth too, just like the Improved Eight. I thought about singing a song.

I'd been born in Mill Valley thirty-five-and-a-half-years ago, in 1912. I loved the big city. Make no mistake about that. San Francisco and I were made for each other. But I'd learned my values in Mill Valley — good, American pre-war values. People watched out for each other in my hometown. Mill Valley values kept me focused on my mission to save Vera.

I turned off the highway and found a café where I ordered a small java. I asked them to pour it into a large cardboard take-out cup. I held the coffee in my left hand and tried to keep it from sloshing on my pants while I got back on 101 and shifted up through the gears, using my knees on the wheel to keep the Pontiac on the road.

I passed through San Rafael quickly, and then it was open country and farmland up to Novato. I stopped to take a leak at a roadside rest between Novato and Petaluma.

As I pulled off the road, I saw in the mirror a large black car slow and ease onto the shoulder eighty yards or so behind me. And when I left the roadside rest, the large black car got back onto the road too. A tail? It was possible they'd picked me up outside the Rose building, whoever *they* were.

In Petaluma, I knew some side streets that would let me get off the highway on the south side, just after I hit the rail crossing, and then re-connect with 101 on the north end of town. Just before the tracks, I stuck my arm out the window to signal for a stop, and I used enough brakes to light up my taillight. Then I downshifted to second and accelerated around a corner to the left just after I crossed the tracks.

Halfway along the block, I pulled over to the curb beside a Mexican grocery and, sliding down in the seat, checked the mirror. The black car squealed its tires coming around the corner and rushed on by.

It could have been a sedan. It could have been Thursby's convertible with the top up. I let a grin cross my face, eased back out into the road, and followed the scenic route through the east side of Petaluma.

At a little after eleven, I arrived at the Sonoma County Courthouse in Santa Rosa. I spent some time going over the recorder's plat books and deeds in the county clerk's office. I found what I was looking for and was back out to my car before noon.

Between Santa Rosa and Healdsburg, I turned left onto River Road, which followed the Russian River through some of the best wine growing land in the valley. I passed some old established vineyards, some post-war plantings, and even some vacant land that hadn't been cleared for farming. There were also orchards of Gravenstein apples and even some rangeland for grazing sheep. River Road was the main road into town for the farmers who worked in Windsor, Guerneville, and all the way out to Monte Rio, and the farm traffic made for slow going.

I hooked a right on Wohler Road and crossed to the north side of the river on a small iron bridge. The bridge fed me onto Westside Road, which runs along the other side of the Russian River down from Healdsburg. By twelve thirty, I had come to a wooden sign for Noir Côtes DeBains Vineyards and Winery. The swinging gate was open, and I turned through a eucalyptus grove onto a wide dirt track.

This track crossed some rolling vineyard land. There were rows of vines on either side of me, semi bare in early April but with impressions of new green leaves and buds. I could see the thin, young plants, tied and supported, and rows of taller vines with trellis systems built around them. The vines poked up through fields of unharvested mustard plants. At the road end of each vineyard row was a solitary rose bush with the green or red shoots of spring just budding.

The dirt road wound up and down along these little hills, but overall we were climbing, and soon I saw a large Victorian farmhouse ahead, at the end of the vineyards along the right. Opposite the house, the last vineyard on the left sloped about a half mile down to the flat, brown Russian River below. This vineyard was the most unusual of them all. The vines looked like tree stumps in a petrified forest. They were as thick as my leg, black and gnarled, and they were pruned short. Most were only a couple of feet high. The sun was directly overhead and the short black vines threw even stubbier shadows, which intensified their stunted aspect.

I drew up to the house and climbed out. It was a peaceful morning out in the country, and all I heard were the robins singing and the crows calling—until the two gunshots rang out.

24

Sally DeBains

I dove back into the car. One more shot echoed down to the river valley. I stretched a hand up and gave my horn a couple of toots. If I wasn't the target, I wanted to let the shooter know someone was here.

There were no more shots. A voice yelled, "Halloo!" and I poked my head up a little. Sally DeBains was coming toward me out of the vineyard on the north side of my car. She carried a pistol in her right hand, but it was hanging down at her side.

"Hello!" I called, and climbed back out of the car.

"Oh, it's you, Mr. Sleuth. I didn't expect to see you again. Welcome to Noir Côtes DeBains."

"Thank you, Mrs. DeBains."

"Sally." She came up to me, and changing hands with the gun, offered me her right hand to shake. "You can call me Sally, especially after that frisking you gave me on the train. I feel like we're old friends. Ha, ha, ha!" What a laugh this old dame had. It was a wild hoot, like the call of a loon on tea, but it was infectious. I had to laugh with her.

"Sorry about that, Sally. I had to check you for a concealed weapon."

"Sure you did. Maybe you need to check me again, hunh, shamus?" She hooted again with that laugh. She seemed relaxed, in a blue denim work shirt and loose khaki pants tucked into rubber boots.

I pointed at her heater, which was a mid-weight automatic, bigger than the .32 caliber Smith & Wesson I'd taken from her on the train. "Taking target practice?" I asked.

"No." She looked at the gun. Her smile faded. "As a matter of fact, I was hiking through the chardonnay and I saw a snake. A rattler."

"I didn't know wine making was so dangerous."

"Well, it was for the snake." She laughed again, then said, "Hey, come on up to the house. I haven't had lunch, and you look like you could use a glass of wine."

People are always telling me that. I guess I have a thirsty expression. "I could use some lunch," I said. "I hope it's no trouble."

"Hell, no. C'mon. You like rabbit?"

I allowed as to how a rabbit would be an interesting change of pace for me. She seemed to find that funny too. We strolled on up to her house.

Sally DeBains kicked off her high rubber boots and

slipped into some espadrilles that were waiting by the door. "Follow me."

I followed her along a center hall, into the kitchen in the rear of the house, and straight out the back to a large patio. The house was at the top of the hill I'd driven up and featured a great view. On the west side, the patio overlooked that old vines vineyard I'd driven through coming in.

A couple of rabbits waited on a steel spit over a low wood fire. Sally poked the fire with a set of cast iron tongs, and then she gave the spit a turn. "These are done," she proclaimed. "Think you can set that table while I get us a bottle of wine? You'll find what you need in the kitchen."

I told her I'd manage, and while I selected the place settings, she padded through to the far wall, opened a door, and disappeared downstairs.

By the time Sally DeBains came back out to the patio, I had a redwood table ready for a meal for two. Sally was holding a bottle by the neck in each hand and a corkscrew. "Here." She placed them on the table and handed me the opener. "Do your duty while I slide these rascals off the spit. We'll have the '42 first."

I proceeded to work on the '42, which was a Noir Côtes DeBains Pinot Noir "Sally's Reserve." The much cheaper DeBains Vin Rouge that was the house red at *Chez Cici* was a decent wine in my price range. I was looking forward to trying this. The bottle was cool in my hand, cellar cool. I had the cork out in a jiffy and poured a taste in each of the big goblets I'd found. In the same time, Sally had served the rabbits on a big orange Fiestaware platter and carved them into individual pieces. She made one more trip inside and emerged with a salad in an aqua Fiestaware bowl. Sally sat down facing west, and I sat at her left with the sun on my back.

"What the hell's this?" she asked, peering in the goblet in front of her. She picked up the bottle, poured another eight ounces or so into her glass, and passed the wine to me. "I sprinkle more Chanel behind one ear than you poured in my glass. A-ha-ha-ha!" When I'd topped up my glass, she held hers out in a toast. I raised my goblet, and she said, "If you drink no noir, you'll pinot noir." She cackled, we clinked glasses, and I gulped a large mouthful. It was delicious wine, serious pinot noir, and it captured in a bottle the joy of her crazy laugh.

The rabbit wasn't bad either. Good meat, well seasoned with paprika and sage, and nicely cooked on a wood fire. Good wine, bright ruby in the spring sunlight. This was California.

"So what brings you out to my place, shamus?"

"Please, if I'm going to call you Sally, you can call me Frank."

"What's on your mind, Frank?"

I told her I'd been investigating the Thursby killing hoping to spring Vera. "Tell me again what you saw on the train."

"Well," she began, "after the train left Oakland, I stayed in my room for a while. The first time I opened my door, I saw Fenwick standing outside the kitchen having a smoke. I thought if I tried to visit the general then he might interfere. So I closed my door and waited a spell."

"When was this?"

"I don't wear a watch, so I can't say for sure. It must have been after six, but we hadn't come to Davis yet."

"How long did you wait?" I asked.

"I'm not sure. At least ten minutes though. Maybe twenty."

"So it was after Wolff had been in the corridor with the magnum. Did you believe Wolff's story about Thursby giving him the wine?"

Creases in her forehead came together in a little v over her nose, and she drank wine while she thought about it. Then she said, "It's more than a little hinky, knowing the history of those two."

"Anyhow, after fifteen minutes, give or take, you tried again. What did you see?"

"Nothing in the corridor. I slipped down to Thursby's room. I knocked. I didn't hear anything. I tried the door handle. The door wasn't quite latched, I remember now, so I opened it a little. I saw enough to know something was wrong — a mess on the floor — so I opened the door all the way, and slipped in. Right away, I saw the table was overturned and Thursby was down on his back. That must be when I drew my piece.

"Well, I looked at Thursby and saw the hole in his chest. I knew right away he was dead. The first thing I thought of was to get the hell out. I did. I didn't see anyone in the corridor. I stepped out into the hallway, and I returned to my room."

"Didn't you think to tell someone that Thursby was dead?"

She shifted her gaze down into her wine and didn't meet my eye. "No. What I thought was here was a dead man, shot through the heart, and I was coming out of his room with a roscoe in my hand. See, that's when I realized I'd better put it away, and I stopped and hoisted my skirt." She looked up at me. "I guess I should have yanked on the emergency cord or something."

"Or just called out for help. Why not? You didn't shoot him. Your piece hadn't been fired."

"The thing is, Frank, and I think most of the people on the train know this, I could have shot him. I was there to buy the Blackbird Vineyard. I'm a businesswoman, and I was ready to do business. But if Thursby'd said no to my offer, well, I might have held my gun to his head and asked him again."

I was impressed. "What about the others? Could they have killed Thursby?"

"Hell, yes! I don't know about you or your blonde

friend, but the rest of them, I've known them for years. I don't think there's a one of them who wouldn't have killed the old man if he was crossed, or if he saw some gain in bumping Thursby off."

"He?"

"Or she. Don't think that petite little Cici wouldn't kill." She wagged a finger in my face. "There's ice runs through her veins." Fenwick, Wolff, and now Sally cast aspersions Cici's way. It worried me. Was I denying her true nature?

"Most people didn't know of any connection between Thursby and the Blackbird," I said. "How come you knew?"

"I visited the courthouse a few weeks ago. I did some research."

"I stopped at the courthouse this morning," I told her. "The deeds say the Blackbird Vineyard is owned by Wine Partners' Trust, Ltd. That's what the public knew. The story was that Wine Partners' Trust was a couple of orthodontists in San Francisco."

Sally dismissed that with a wave of her fork in her left hand. "Bullshit. I don't even know what an orthodontist is. But I doubt if an orthodontist could make wine like comes out of those Blackbird bottles. It's the best wine I've ever had."

I raised my glass to her. "I'm glad *you* said that, because this Sally's Reserve must be a close second. *Salud*."

"Ha-ha-ha-ha! I'll bet you say that to all the girls. *Salud.*" We drank. "What did you do when you saw Wine Partners' Trust on the deed?"

"Well," I said, "I checked the maps in the plat books. They said the same thing, Wine Partners' Trust, Limited."

"Right. Did you stop there?"

"No."

"Neither did I." She twisted off a piece of rabbit at the joint. "I looked up the limited partnerships in the county clerk's office. It was right there for anyone to see, all these years, but I guess 'Wine Partners' Trust' was good enough for most people who checked. Hell, what's in the bottle says all anybody ever needed to know, right? Drink it and enjoy it, and who cares who owns it?"

"But you wanted to know more."

"I had to know because I wanted to buy the vineyard. You could have knocked me over with a feather though when I saw Wine Partners' Trust is 'General Lloyd Thursby.'"

"'General Lloyd Thursby and V. Thursby,' actually," I said.

"That was another surprise. I never knew of the old bastard being married. I thought he was a nance."

"Thursby? Queer?"

"Well, I'd never seen him with any dames. Maybe he had a brother or something. Vince? Victor? You know, Frank." She paused and looked me in the eye. "I used to skate around plenty myself. You wouldn't think it, I know, 'cause I'm forty-seven now and respectable, but I used to be quite a skirt. Thursby never even made a pass at me. God knows there were nights when we'd both had a smell from the barrel, and I gave him every chance."

Sally was young at heart, anyone could see that, and she might be respectable. But if she ever saw fifty again, I'd eat my fedora. With a glass of her zinfandel.

"He was always with his man-servant, that creep, Fenwick," she continued. "And of course, Damas."

"You used Damas as a distributor yourself, Sally."

Sally held a leg of rabbit by the bone. She tore off a bite with her teeth and shook the rest of it at me. "That little daisy. He could have ruined me. You know, I've worked years to build up this business. My husband, Mort, he died in 1935. I had this house and a barn and forty acres of hops and barley. Mort made beer, you know, during Prohibition. Well, I decided to go into the wine business. How hard could it be, right? I started planting grapevines. Where's that bottle of the '39, shamus? My glass is empty."

I got busy with the corkscrew and the second bottle while Sally talked on. I gave her a hearty pour this time. "While I was waiting for my vines to come in, I bought grapes. Mort had a little dough socked away, enough to get me started. Times were still tough back then. The Depression wasn't over. A lot of farms were foreclosed on, and land was going cheap. I bought everything around here that I could, any piece of ground you could stick a vine in or finagle a mortgage on. Noir Côtes DeBains grew. Did you know, I'm the second biggest vineyard owner in Sonoma now?"

"Who's first?" I asked.

"The Gallo brothers. But I'm respected here. My wine is in the finest restaurants. My wine is so good one year that the next year, I can ask an extra two bits a bottle. And you know what? I can get it." She swigged her '39. "You'll like this. I sold it for fifteen dollars a case back in '41. I should have charged more."

I swirled, sniffed, and downed a mouthful of the '39. She was right about me liking it. It was a big, full-bodied pinot noir with a texture that dragged across my palate like the lick of a cat's tongue.

"Well, it wasn't easy getting to where I am now," she continued. "During the '30s and even during the war, I had to load up the truck, one of the old flatbeds Mort used to carry the beer barrels on, and drive the goods into town. Cases of good wine for the restaurants and the posh trade, jugs of Noir Côtes DeBains Blanc and Rouge. I even sold boxes of grapes, fifty-pound crates of zinfandel, Alicante bouschet, and petite sirah.

"At the end of the war, Joe Damas came along. I met him at Cici's, at a tasting. Let's walk."

Sally rose and topped off both our glasses. I followed her around the patio. "Noir Côtes DeBains was growing, see, and I couldn't do it all myself. So I needed a distributor, and Joe and I made a deal.

"He grew the demand for the reserve wines, especially the pinot noir and the old vines zinfandel. Everything was great, I thought, but then last year, I started to get complaints. The '45 pinot noir wasn't as good as usual, they said. In fact, it was awful, thin, under ripe, over cropped, too bitter, no acidity, no fruit. It was piss. It couldn't be, Frank. I knew."

I was gazing at clouds on the western horizon as Sally talked, but there was a shift in my perspective, and now I realized I'd been looking at the Pacific Ocean.

"It was one of our best pinot vintages here. But I kept hearing grumblings from restaurants and customers. Cicilia O'Callaghan called me. General Thursby told me. Even Spitbucket McQuade had the balls to tell me, and usually McQuade's just kissing my ass.

"Well, I bought a couple bottles of my wine at random in San Francisco, and I bought some at the market in Healdsburg. Cicilia gave me back a couple from her cellar. It was my wine, see, it said right on the label, 'Noir Côtes DeBains.' But it wasn't my wine in the bottles. It didn't taste like anything I had in my cellar. So it had to be Damas's doing. Somehow, he was selling cheap wine with my name on it. I couldn't prove anything, but it had to be him.'"

"Did Joe ever tell you what he did in the war?" I asked her.

"No. I think he was still in Europe then."

"Yeah. He forged documents for the French resistance."

"He was a scratcher?"

"Yeah," I said. "I imagine he was good at it. He had to be. It was life or death for them."

"My God! That's it then. Forged labels. He could buy other wine for a quarter of what he paid me. He could bottle it and slap a phony DeBains label on it. Damn him. I ought to shoot his balls off."

We drank our wine and looked out over the valley down to the river and out toward the sea. Sally was quiet, but I wouldn't have liked to be in Joe's shoes. Or shorts.

"Can we prove it, Frank? Can we prove Joe Damas is selling rotgut wine under my name?" she finally asked.

"We could prove that the '45 Noir Côtes DeBains is not all the same wine from bottle to bottle. I don't know the business, but I imagine there are wineries where not all the wine of a certain type is the same from barrel to barrel. There are probably some barrels better than others. So that might not mean a lot."

"I ferment the wine in large tanks, then fill the barrels. My barrels are pretty consistent."

"Okay, then. Maybe a chemist could prove it's not all from the same batch, that there's counterfeit 1945 DeBains Pinot Noir in some bottles. How many cases did you make?"

"Three thousand of the regular, and another 450 cases

of Sally's Reserve."

"That's probably the number Joe's books show. But maybe there's 10,000 cases on the market. And Joe probably moved the ringers as fast as he could. I don't think we'll find any of the bad stuff still in his warehouse. If it's all in the stores or in the hands of consumers, we'd have nothing on him except circumstantial evidence."

"Shit," she said.

"You fired him as your distributor. Who knows about this?"

"My friends. Not many people, I guess."

"Well, all you've done is you've stopped Joe Damas from selling genuine Noir Côtes DeBains," I said. "But if he could counterfeit the '45, who's to say he can't do the same thing with the '46? Or he could lay low a couple years and then do it again with the '49."

"How could he do that? I fired him. In fact, the '46 is sitting in the winery. It ought to be on its way to market by now."

"If he's a good scratcher, why would he need to buy *any* of your goods to sell counterfeit Noir Côtes DeBains?"

"Damn! I *will* shoot his balls off."

"Don't be a boob, Sally. Use your head. If you shoot Damas, what happens to Noir Côtes DeBains? What happens to your dream?"

"Ah, hell. I sure would enjoy it though. Just like I enjoyed blasting that rattler."

"Who do you like for the Thursby killing?" I asked.

"I never thought much about it. I suppose you don't think it's your blonde friend. What was her name?"

"Vera. Vera Peregrino."

"Peregrino. Oh, yeah. Some of my neighbors. Here, I'll show you something." She led me to the Southwest edge of the patio. Pointing at the vineyard of stunted vines that sloped down to the river, she said, "See there? This is my best holding. I bought these four acres back in '36. It's old vine zinfandel, planted in 1888. It's the second best vineyard in Sonoma County. The old vines don't produce as much fruit as younger ones. But old vine fruit has depth and complexity you can't get in young zin.

"We're on Black Mountain, 1400 feet. Now look right across the river there. See that hill? That's Blackbird Hill. And on top of that hill, on the eastern slope, is the Blackbird vineyard. That's the best there is."

Blackbird Hill had a steep rise up from the south side of the river, whereas Sally's vineyard lay on a more gradual slope. The sun was above and behind Blackbird Hill, which appeared to be a little higher than we were up on Black Mountain. It was hard to believe anyone could farm such a steep hillside, though I could see even in the shade that the hillside was planted in vines. Old man Fenucchi must have been a mountain goat. There was a tall tree near the top, and I don't know if it was the light, but I imagined I saw a brooding raven or black hawk perched in the top branches. Here I was drinking an old pinot noir, one of the best I'd ever had from California, and as good as some of those Burgundies we'd had on the train Friday night. And my mouth was watering—for another taste of the Blackbird.

"Now from the river up toward that hill," she pointed, "well, that's the old Fenucchi ranch, what's left of it, that is. You can see their house at the base of the hill. Mrs. Fenucchi, she still lives there. Alls she's got is a couple acres of yard in front of the house. Her husband sold the rest. Went crazy during Prohibition. Too bad for the old widow he couldn't have held on to the land a couple more years until Repeal. The Blackbird is the last piece he sold. Now just over there to the east of the Fenucchi ranch and the Blackbird, that's all Peregrino land. Angelo Peregrino, he bought a lot of the Fenucchi ranch. Everyone who was buying during Prohibition wanted a piece of the Fenucchi spread. Of course, what kind of fool buys vineyards during Prohibition?"

"General Thursby," I said.

"Damned old fox."

Then I heard a growl from down in the river valley that sounded like an unmuffled truck exhaust at first, but it wound out through the gears much faster than a truck might. A big motorcycle, I thought. Sally suddenly took off at a fast trot for her kitchen. Then along the Westside road, I saw a little blue open roadster. Sally came running back with a rifle in her hand.

"Speak of the devil. That's Joe Damas down there." She brought the rifle up to her shoulder, but I jostled her to ruin her aim before she could fire.

"Sally, I thought you were going to forget about plugging him."

"I could shoot a tire," she said. "He might go into the river. It would look like an accident."

"Are you that good a shot?"

She relaxed and lowered the gun. "Damn him, he's around the bend. Must be headed to one of his other wineries, in Healdsburg, maybe." Then she smiled at me. "And by the way, yes. I could probably knock off his hood ornament from here with this gun. This is a 30-caliber Springfield, model 1903. It was Mort's in the war. The first war."

"How did you come to shoot so well?" I asked.

"Well, I'm only seven miles from the coast, you know, as the crow flies. After Pearl Harbor, I thought, what if I was out there in the vineyard alone and a Jap popped up out of the morning fog? I learned to shoot. I even formed the Sonoma Gunner Girls."

"Listen, Mrs. DeBains . . . Sally, forget about shooting Joe or taking out his tires, okay. That won't solve anything."

"Maybe not." She rested the rifle against the low parapet on that side of the patio and picked up her wine. "Listen, Frank, how'd you like to work for me?"

"What do you have in mind?"

"Seems to me, the way things stand now, Damas can go right on counterfeiting my wine. I want to end that, and you need a fall guy to take the rap for the Thursby job so's you can get Vera out. Maybe you could squeeze Joe. Do you like him for the rub-out?"

"I don't know," I said. "I talked to Wolff. He mentioned that when he was in Thursby's room, he saw two bottles of your '45 Pinot Noir on the General's table. When we found Thursby dead, one of those was rolling around on the floor and the other was broken. Damas told me that he had smashed one of those bottles. That's how he cut his hand. Well, unless they're both lying about the same detail, that means in the fifteen minutes or so after you saw Wolff, Damas paid a call on Thursby."

"See, Joe probably drilled him."

I shook my head. "If Joe drilled him, he didn't use his peashooter. Thursby was killed with his Army Colt. But Joe had his little automatic in his hand when he smashed the bottle, remember? McQuade said the gun smelled like your wine. Anyhow, Damas came out into the corridor, and the general's .45 ended up in Vera's drawer."

"So what difference does it make?" she said. "Maybe Joe didn't kill Lloyd, but I say he's still our patsy. Tell him to lay off my wine, or he'll step off for chilling Thursby. Tell him Sally DeBains is ready to testify against him."

"Would you?"

"Let him think so. Let him know I know about the counterfeit '45 pinot, and he won't take any chances with me."

"It's good, but a threat won't spring Vera. We'd have to give Joe to the law."

"On the other hand," Sally said, "squeezing Joe might just stir things up a little."

Maybe that's what this case needs. "All right, Sally. I can help you on that."

"I'll make it worth your while."

"I get twenty-five dollars a day," I told her. "Plus expenses. In this case, one visit should do it."

"Done, and I'll throw in a case of my '46 Zin. It's just ready for release this month. Oh, and Frank." She winked, "I don't mind if you have to rough him up a little to make sure he gets the message." Then she cut loose with that crazy laugh again.

I winked at her, and we held our glasses out and clinked them. I had another client, and I was enjoying both the '39 Pinot Noir Reserve and the view across the river at Blackbird Hill. The Fenucchi house had been shaded by the hill all this time, but now as the sun poked around to the west, some light spilled across the front yard, and a sudden bright flash blinded me for a moment.

When my eyes recovered, I asked, "Sally, what kind of a car does the widow Fenucchi drive?"

"Car? I don't know that she has a car. I don't even

think she drives."

The sunlight reflected off the chrome bumpers of a large black sedan parked out front. I wondered if it was the same car I'd seen behind me that morning on 101.

25

Soaring with the Peregrines

At the bottom of Black Mountain, I turned into the sun on Westside Road. I made an acute left and crossed the Russian River, heading east with the sun at my back now and the shadows stretching out for their afternoon nap. The river was on my left and a large ranch planted with grapevines was spread out to my right. According to what Sally had said, this was Peregrino land, and when I came to the mailbox, I saw that was right. The Peregrino gate was closed, but not locked, so I climbed out of the car, let myself in, and then closed the gate again.

I recalled I had been here before one time with Vera, a couple of years ago. A few months after she'd started to work for me, she invited me home to meet the folks and spend a Saturday in the country. We hadn't a care in the world that day.

It had been a warm day in late summer. Vera had walked me out into the vineyard, where the clusters of grapes hung plump, round, and purple on the vines. She carried a picnic basket and I carried an old army blanket. Angelo Peregrino had cleared most any land he could plant a vine on, but a little stand of eucalyptus trees remained on rugged ground way east of the house. I'd spread out the blanket, and we had our picnic under those trees. We drank too much wine, hiked down to the Russian River, lost our inhibitions, shed our clothes, and waded out to the middle on the smooth stones along the bottom as the cool water washed over us.

The Peregrino house and barn were well back from the river. The house was a functional family farmhouse, not a fanciful Victorian like Sally DeBains's, and the barn hadn't known a right angle since Taft had been president. Behind the house and tucked flush up against the hill was a hulking building with a sign, "Peregrine Winery." It needed a coat of paint. The sign wasn't much to look at either.

I pulled up by the house, and a couple of run-down mongrels came out to sniff me. Either they lacked the usual dog enthusiasm or my smell didn't excite them. They soon lost interest in me and began to smell each other's butts. Then the screen door slammed and Louisa Peregrino came out on the porch, wiping her hands in her apron. Her hair was dark brown, and her skin glistened in the sun as if it had been rubbed with walnut oil

"Hello, Mrs. Peregrino." I touched the brim of my hat

and nodded at her.

"*Buon pomeriggio, Signor Swiver,*" she said. "Come up to the house. Come in." I'd been hoping for good news, but Louisa wasn't smiling.

Inside it was warm, and the smell of garlic in hot olive oil made my mouth water. "Come in the kitchen," she said. "I'm going to fix dinner." I followed Louisa out to the kitchen, where the garlic odor was strong enough to ward off vampires. Louisa worked an indoor pump over the sink, and as she did, I could see the still-firm muscles moving and the outline of her flank beneath the thin cotton of her dress. Like mother like daughter, I thought. That was where Vera got her physique.

Louisa gave me a glass of cool water, and then found a clean tumbler and a jug of red wine and poured me a measure. She poured some for herself, replaced the cork, and set the jug on the floor. The wine had a hard acidic edge, but was not bad. The Peregrinos grew a lot of barbera, and I pegged this as some. It probably would have been damn good for washing down a plate of spaghetti and meatballs.

"We'll talk while I work," she said. "Okay?"

"Sure, Mrs. Peregrino."

In the kitchen by the table, Louisa Peregrino was feeding dough into the rear of a machine like the top part of a wringer washer, and turning the crank. Fettuccine oozed out the front and hung limply, and she cut it to lengths about twelve to fifteen inches as she turned it out. Louisa's apron protected a navy dress with white polka dots. It had short sleeves and a V-neck that disappeared behind the top of the apron. Her sun-tanned bosom shimmered with drops of perspiration as she bent to the crank. She was a sturdy woman, shorter than her daughter in the legs, and though a little heavy, she was harder all around than Sally and about the same age. All around that is, except for a soft pillowy bosom that rocked from side to side like the ferry from Naples to Ischia as she turned the crank on the pasta maker. The wine may have been a little thin, but Mrs. Peregrino was ripe and full-bodied.

"Lorenzo called about an hour ago," Louisa said. "They had the arraignment right after lunch. The judge says it's a murder case, and he don't turn no murder suspects loose with no bail. He set it at $25,000. *Madre di Dio.* Where I'm a gonna get $25,000? My poor Vera."

"Well, now that's not so terrible. All we need is $2500 and we can post a bond." I explained to her about bail bondsmen.

"Only $2500? Oh, good. I feel — a so much better. How much you got?"

I had to tell her I couldn't help with the bond.

"Oh, that's okay." She quit turning the crank and stepped across to the counter where she opened the lid of a big ceramic jar that said *Farina.* She extracted a small handful of lettuce with a rubber band around it and flour falling off. "Look, this is the money I get selling chickens and eggs. Maybe I got $2500 here." She snapped off the rubber band and counted out the bills. She had twenty-six dollars and tears were starting to roll across Louisa's cheeks.

"Mrs. Peregrino, I didn't expect you to have the cash. Is your husband here? Did you tell him?"

"Angelo is here. He's out in the winery. He's bottling the harvest from last fall this week. I went out there and told him. He just kept the bottling line running. He didn't look at me. He said, 'We'll talk at dinner.' You want to stay for dinner, Mr. Swiver? Because if you want to talk to Angelo, you have to wait until dinner."

I told her I'd stay.

"Good," said Louisa. "Don't worry. Angelo likes an early dinner. Maybe he'll be in at five." She returned to work at the pasta maker, and I sat with her and sipped my wine.

We didn't sit in complete silence. On a whim, I asked Louisa if she knew Joe Damas. She stopped chopping peppers and turned to me.

"Who?"

"Joe Damas. He's in the wine business. He buys from a lot of the families around here."

"No. I don't know him." She attacked the pepper with renewed vigor.

Having fried up a load of garlic in oil, Louisa browned

some coarsely chopped beef. She sliced and diced onions, tomatoes, and mushrooms, and added them all to a large skillet. She lifted the jug of wine and poured a generous dollop in her glass, then another in the skillet. The pan sizzled and splattered, and the smell of a good meat sauce began to come together in the kitchen. When she sprinkled in oregano and basil, the aroma nearly knocked me off my chair.

Five o'clock came and went, and I was on my second tumbler of barbera, but only because there's something sad about a woman drinking alone and grinding fettuccine in her own kitchen. I hate to see that, so I drank with her, and I thought about Vera in the Chico cooler.

Vera had been home Easter weekend and gone out in the vineyard with her dad. She told me she'd been having a tough time communicating with him.

"Peregrine Vineyards holds 200 acres of the best land along the Russian River," she'd said when she came back to work. "Old vines from before Prohibition. Pinot noir from 1914. Zinfandel from the 1890s. We were out there in the zin. Those old vines are some of the best in the county. Thick, twisted, healthy, and strong, and Pop's turning out truckloads of cheap plonk. He sells his wine for fifty cents a jug, and he thinks that's great.

"I said to him, 'Poppa, let me make a wine here this

year. Give me a few acres here on the west end of the ranch to work with. I'll cut the yields and make a wine that will make Peregrine Vineyards soar.' He says, 'No,' and just keeps working."

"No?" I'd asked her. "Is that all?"

"That was all."

"Angelo Peregrino is an immigrant, Vera," I'd said. "He came over here with nothing. He worked and saved 'til he could buy that property, and then he planted vines. Then Prohibition comes along. The government tells Angelo he can't sell wine. By the time Prohibition ends, the market has crashed and the Depression's here. How old is your dad, sixty? He works hard and he's never had enough. He's probably afraid. When times are good, when he's got a good crop, he wants to make and sell all the wine he can."

She'd dismissed it with a wave. "No, there's something wrong. My brothers and sisters, they don't give a damn about the family farm. But I've always been interested. I cared. I worked with my dad, side by side in the vineyard and in the winery. But he cuts me out of the business. I could be a better winemaker than Pop, I know it."

"Maybe that's why he cut you out. Jealousy?"

"Oh, hell, Frank, I don't know."

At a quarter past five, I heard boots on the back porch and the kitchen door opened. Angelo Peregrino's silhouette loomed in the doorframe. He saw me sitting at the kitchen table but ignored me and crossed to the sink, where he operated the pump handle. After removing his fedora, he stuck his head under the gush of water that came out. Then he grabbed a kitchen towel, rubbed his curly black hair, and spit some Italian at his wife.

"You speak English, Angelino," she spit back. "We have a guest for dinner. This is Mr. Swiver. You remember him, don't you?" He considered me, and I rose and offered my hand. He didn't want it, but he looked at Louisa and she stood there with her hands on her hips and stared him down, so he dried his hand and shook mine. His grip was nothing special. I stuck my hand in a grape press once that did less damage and didn't hurt nearly so much.

"*Benvenuto,*" he said. "I was only asking Louisa if dinner was ready yet. You want some wine? Come on. We're going to eat in the dining room." Bringing the jug of red, he led the way.

Angelo was about five eleven, big-boned but lean, and he stooped slightly. He wore denim overalls over a blue-plaid flannel shirt. He moved to the far end of a dark wooden table, and I parked myself on his left. Angelo filled our glasses, and Louisa began wearing a path from the kitchen to the table and back, bringing in big cloth napkins, forks, bowls, a loaf of crusty bread, a small plate with a slab of farm butter on it, a wedge of stinky hard cheese and a grater, and finally a platter of steaming fettuccine and a tureen of meat sauce. Although Angelo helped himself to a full bowl of the pasta, he surprised me by going light on the sauce. He drizzled it around the top of the noodles with the serving spoon and then blended it in with his fork. "Just enough to color it," he told me, and grinned.

"Mr. Peregrino, I'm trying to get your daughter, Vera, out of jail."

"*Buono*. You get her out."

"It's a murder rap, Mr. Peregrino. We need to post bond."

He chewed for a while without saying anything, so I dug into the fettuccine myself. It was still hot, but it was delicious, more meaty than tomatoey, with a smooth, rich consistency. Then I tried to explain bail and bond to Angelo, but he broke in.

"Murder? Who'd Vera kill?"

"She didn't kill anybody, Mr. Peregrino."

"Then she's gonna be okay, hunh? American justice is good, no?"

"Sure, but these things can take time. Jail's a bad place to be. I want to get her out now."

He ate and thought again. "You're the detective fellow she works for, right?" I nodded. "You been banging Vera, coupla years, and now she's in a jail. You ain't get none, so you're in a big hurry to get her out, hunh?" He winked at me. "Sure, we're men of the world, you and me. I know why you want to get Vera out of jail."

I was sore at that insult right away. He was wrong to attribute motivation to me, but he was the father, and yes, we'd been lovers. It was awkward. I didn't want to quibble with him; I wanted to get his help with the bond. Before I could say anything, Louisa lashed out in rapid Italian. Louisa's words were too fast for me to catch, but it wouldn't have mattered if she'd been speaking Ruthenian. I got the gist. So did Angelo.

He patted his mouth with his napkin. "*Mi scusi*, Mr. Swiver. I meant no disrespect. Vera, she can do as she pleases. She's twenty-eight. It's okay. I know she's no nun, hunh? Who do they *say* Vera killed?"

"A man named Lloyd Thursby." Louisa knocked over her wine, and started to wipe up the spill with her napkin. Angelo's eyes grew wide, but then he decided to scrutinize the noodles he was twirling. Louisa poured herself another glass of wine.

"You knew him?" I asked.

"No," said Louisa.

"I don't know him." Angelo looked up at me again. "But I heard the name. There was an Army man between the wars used to drive up sometimes from the Presidio. A big-shot officer. I think he's name of Thursby. He was looking to buy vineyard property, I think."

"Lloyd Thursby *was* a retired US Army general ," I

said. "Anyhow, I thought you might know him because he owned land near here. You might say he was a neighbor of yours. He owned the Blackbird Vineyard." I was in the middle of the table, with Angelo at the head to my right and Louisa at the other end near the kitchen door. It would have been tough to keep an eye on them both if they'd been playing with me, but now they both seemed as surprised as a chicken who'd just laid a meatball. They didn't hide it.

"*Potrebbe questo essere vero?*" said Angelo to Louisa.

"*Non lo so,*" said Louisa. "*Perchè me lo chiedi?*"

Angelo Peregrino set down his fork and regarded me. He held up an index finger. "I *have* seen that man. He hires people to do most of the vineyard work, but sometimes he comes out here, in a big black car. He never come and speak with me. I didn't know he was name of Thursby. Vera kill *him*? How she do it?"

"Thursby was shot through the heart," I said. Angelo was studying his bowl, engrossed again in twirling fettuccine. Was he smiling?

I told him how I'd called Lorenzo and sent him up to Chico. "Lorenzo's a bright boy," he said. "He get Vera out." I told him Lorenzo couldn't get her out because the judge set bail. I told him we needed twenty-five grand to bail her out. I suggested that if we used the farm to make bond, we could spring Vera. She wouldn't have to wait in jail, and there'd be no risk. All Vera had to do was show up for the trial, and Angelo's land would be safe.

At first, he didn't say anything either way, but his expression darkened. We ate, and we drank more Peregrine wine. It had a bad reputation, but it was quite passable washing down the food. As an accompaniment to the meal, the Peregrine "burgundy" had developed a dry, earthy tone and a medium-body. And you would have had to be a very bad winemaker indeed to fail with that ripe Russian River fruit. It was a bad imitation of a good pre-war Chianti. Or maybe a good imitation of a bad post-war Chianti.

It was clear he wasn't going to speak about the bail again until he'd sucked up his last noodle, so I tossed out the Joe Damas question.

"Do you know a man named Damas?"

"Who's he?"

"Joe Damas, foreign gent," I said. "He's in the wine business. Buys at wholesale and distributes to stores, restaurants, you know."

"No." Angelo finished chewing, patted his mouth with his napkin, and looked me in the eye. "I don't know the man." He returned his concentration to his dinner.

I had seconds on the fettuccine and meat sauce. After a late rabbit lunch, I was surprised I had much of an appetite for dinner, but Louisa's cooking was good. I'm not a fast eater, but I finished before Angelo. I complimented Louisa on her cooking and lost myself gazing at her big dark-brown eyes and thinking about Vera. Could she have known Thursby before we boarded that train? Well, they *were* neighbors. That might be enough for a vindictive Delgado and a hotshot DA to string a jury along and railroad her. I had to solve the case and give Chief Bidwell and Delgado the real killer. But deep down, I started to wonder. What if Vera was as dangerous as Cici? Did she have a dark side I didn't know about?

When Angelo finished he wiped his mouth and placed his napkin down next to his bowl. He tried to straighten his back and relax but couldn't seem to do both. He looked directly at me. "Come. We talk." Angelo slid his chair back, stood, and turned to the china cabinet. Bending down and opening doors, he produced a bottle of clear liquid and two small glasses. I followed him into the living room.

Angelo filled the two glasses with a shot each and holding one out to me said, "Grappa."

I returned the toast. "Grappa." I clinked my glass against his and threw it down. The liquid slid down my gullet as easily as Sherman marched through Georgia, and it left a burnt-out swath in its wake too.

"I make it myself." Angelo beamed as my eyes watered.

"With what?" I coughed out as I struggled for breath. Gasoline?

"Oh, skins, seeds. The pulp that's left in the crusher when I make wine."

"I've never had anything like it," I said through teary eyes. Maybe I would turn him in to the treasury boys for moonshining to get even — if I survived.

Louisa had been clearing the table and now she came into the living room, wiping her hands in her apron folds. She crossed to the davenport and sat down. I selected an armchair opposite Angelo. The upholstery was worn and tattered but was in better condition than my guts right now.

"Louisa, your place is in the kitchen," said Angelo.

"No, we talk about my Vera. I stay." She produced a little cordial glass from an apron pocket and helped herself to the grappa.

Angelo reddened and turned away from Louisa. He poured himself a second grappa. When he addressed me, he deepened his tone. "Mr. Swiver, the land is very important to me. It's all I got. I cannot risk it. My answer to you is no."

"Mr. Peregrino, I understand how you must feel about the farm. I know you've faced some tough times with Prohibition and then the Depression. But surely you would do this for your daughter. You know what they say, 'Blood is thicker than water.'"

Angelo winced. "Don't tell me about blood, Mr. Swiver. I know about family." He reared up, as tall as he could, with his thumbs hooked in his overall bib. "You don't got to lecture me about family. You don't understand how I feel. The answer is no, Mr. Swiver. That's all I got to say." He swigged down the rest of his grappa. I stood up too. My head was hurting. Angelo brushed past me and stepped out of the room in a couple of long strides.

Louisa was still sitting at my left side, her chestnut eyes moist. I plopped back down. Louisa didn't speak but didn't attempt to leave, either.

"I don't get it," I told her after a while. "It's his daughter in jail. How can he do that?" She was quiet. I pressed on. "You know, Vera thinks the world of that man. The other kids, I'm not saying anything against them, Mrs. Peregrino, but what do they do for Angelo? What do they do for the farm? Vera comes up here every fall to work the harvest, to help with the crush. She's like him. She loves the land. How can he be so cold to her?"

"She's not his daughter, Mr. Swiver."

26

The Old Fenucchi Place

Louisa tipped another little glass of the grappa down her throat and made her exit to the kitchen. I waited in the living room a few more seconds, trying to puzzle out how it was that Vera Peregrino was not the daughter of Angelo Peregrino. Adopted maybe? Vera'd never told me she was an orphan. Then I weaved my way into the kitchen after Louisa.

She had boiled water for the dishes and was pouring it into the sink. "She's not his daughter?" I said. "What do you mean by that?"

She kept her back to me and scrubbed the large skillet. "What do you think?"

I thought as best I could. A glass of white wine for breakfast in the office, the two good bottles of pinot with Sally DeBains, the several glasses of Peregrine Burgundy—I'd developed a nice edge, and I'd kept it all day. The grappa had shoved me over the edge. "I don't understand," I said.

Louisa turned around and faced me. "I spell it out for you, Mr. Swiver. Vera is not Angelo's child. I had a lover."

I said nothing.

"Angelo's a proud man, Mr. Swiver. There's nothing else I can do. The property is in his name, not mine. Now, I appreciate it if you go. I have dishes to do, and I'm not in the mood for company."

The sky was a carpet of tiny stars, undimmed by the lights of any town. A cup of java would have hit the spot just then, but odds were against me finding one this far west of Healdsburg. Besides, my esophagus was on fire with heartburn from the tomato sauce, garlic, and grappa. Coffee wouldn't help that. I turned the key in the Pontiac and eased my way down the rutted driveway. I opened and closed the gate, but when I headed west on River Road, I hadn't gone much more than a hundred feet when the Pontiac stalled out, just as we moved around a left-hand bend. The evening was colder than I'd realized, and I had forgotten to set the choke. I rolled along and pressed the starter a couple of times, but I must have flooded the damned thing. It wouldn't catch. I steered her off onto the right shoulder and waited.

I heard a dull roar. At first, it was just the river washing along on its way to the ocean. Then I heard more of an ongoing blasting noise over the sound of the river. The blasting noise was behind me, coming closer, and changed pitch. It could have been the exhaust of a powerful car engine. Then I heard a definite downshift and a sound of ripping canvas. It could have been Joe Damas in his sports car.

No car came by, and the intensity of the roar diminished. It burbled to an idle, then it ran a little in first gear, then it idled again. Then the car started up again and moved away from me. Finally, there were a couple of short blips of the throttle in the distance, then nothing.

I climbed out of my heap and traipsed back along River Road the way I'd just come. Just the soothing rush of the water now, and a bullfrog calling, "Ribbit."

"Pinot," I answered.

"Ribbit."

"Merlot."

"Ribbit," said the frog. This was fun.

In a minute or so, I was back at the Peregrinos' gate, and for the second time that evening, I let myself in. It was a couple of hundred yards up to the house. I didn't mind the hike, but I worried the dogs would tip my hand.

There was a little blue foreign job sitting in front of the house with the porch light shining on one side of it. I slipped into a low crouch and trotted up to the dark side of the car. It was a Bugatti; it said so on a red oval just under the radiator cap. Big old-style headlamps, capable of lighting the road for fast motoring after dark, were like wide-open eyes on either side of the radiator, and two fog lights were mounted on the bumper. The top was down, even though the air was turning quite chilly now after sunset. I bent in and looked for the registration. I found it and turned it to the porch. I had just enough light to make out the name "Joe Damas" and the address of Joe's Magnolia Street apartment.

I saw no point in making any kind of play now. I could always catch up with Joe back in town. I thought about leaving him a flat tire. But the Bugatti had two spares mounted on the trunk, and anyhow, it wasn't my style. Besides, I was cooking up an idea about how Joe, being a good scratcher, could be helpful in springing Vera, and this gave me a little more ammunition for the squeeze I was planning to put on him.

For now, I filed the information away—Joe Damas knew the Peregrinos. Angelo Peregrino said he didn't know Joe Damas. Joe Damas called on the Peregrinos after dark. Angelo Peregrino was lying. I headed back down toward the river. "Don't wake the dogs on my account," I said.

My little excursion had given the Pontiac time to unflood itself, and now the Improved Eight fired right up. I eased back onto the road heading west. I hadn't even pushed the choke in before I came to my next stop.

There was no gate and no name and no lights, either,

at the next driveway; it was country dark. Still, I was confident from spotting the ranches in daylight from across the river with Sally that I had found the Fenucchi property. I turned into a rutted drive and bounced across a yard to a little farmhouse. There was no porch light. I stopped and parked with my headlights angled across the front of the house. It was a small one-story, wood-frame farmhouse with a front porch. The house was painted a deep weathered red; the porch had white trim.

The Peregrino place had been shabby, but this house was as old and gnarled as Sally's old zinfandel vines. Even so, a window box hung over the porch rail, with shoots of fresh spring flowers budding up to give the place a little cheer. The Peregrinos may have had only a pump for water, but they'd had electricity. I didn't see any electric wires running in from the road to the Fenucchi house.

I gave the horn a couple of friendly toots. No dog responded, which out here in the country meant either there was no dog or there was a particularly mean one eyeing me right now, keeping silent, and just waiting for me to open the car door and stick a leg out. I opened the car door and stuck a leg out.

Still no dog. So far, so good, so I turned off the engine and slid out. The boards on the porch steps creaked, but they were very clean. There were no cobwebs around the porch frame, and the front windows of the house were spotless. I could see the backs of neatly pressed curtains inside. The window closest to the door displayed a small white flag with a single gold star sewn to it. It was the sign that a family member had given his life for his country in war. I knocked on the door three times.

There was no response, but it was a dark night to be out on foot, and the Widow Fenucchi didn't drive. It seemed likely she'd be home, unless she'd departed earlier that afternoon in the large black car. I knocked three more times. The curtain on my left may have fluttered.

"Mrs. Fenucchi?" I called out. "It's all right. I'd like to talk to you. Mrs. Fenucchi?"

A soft glow moved in the room behind the white curtains, and a board creaked. The door opened a few inches, and a short white-haired woman looked up and out at me. Her face was gently lit from below by a kerosene lamp.

"Mrs. Fenucchi?" I said.

"*Si*. Maria Fenucchi. Who you?"

"I'm Frank Swiver. I'm sorry to call on you so late, but it's very important. I'm up from San Francisco, and I wanted to ask you some questions before I go back."

"What questions?"

I didn't really figure she could tell me anything about the murder, but I wanted to talk to her and see how her piece of the puzzle fit in with everyone else's.

"It's about the Blackbird. Can I come in?"

"The Blackbird?"

"Yes."

"You have my wine?"

"Your wine?"

"*Si*. The Blackbird."

"No, I don't have it. But I can get it. Can we talk?"

She opened the door and stepped back. "*Si*, we talk. Come in."

I had pictured the Fenucchis and the Peregrinos as being from the same generation. Louisa, who was probably fifty to fifty-five, had looked a voluptuous forty-five. Mrs. Fenucchi, on the other hand, was showing a hard-earned sixty. The widow Fenucchi was starting to shrivel and shrink with old age. Louisa Peregrino had a healthy tanned color; Maria Fenucchi was pale. She wore a gray woolen cardigan with a hole in the left sleeve and a plain black dress, probably from before the war.

"Sit down," she offered, and she placed the lamp on a tidy end table, gestured toward a dark blue davenport, and headed for her rocker.

"Mrs. Fenucchi," I began, "before we sit down, could I trouble you for something?"

"*Si?*"

"Baking soda. Do you have any baking soda? Or a bi-carbonate?"

She made a face as sour as my stomach acid. "You knock on my door to ask me for baking soda?"

"No, ma'am. But something I ate disagreed with me,

and I think a little bi-carbonate would help." She shrugged, and picking up the lamp, padded toward the door at the back of the sitting room.

That left me in a dark room. I could see pressed doilies, yellowing on the back of the davenport and on the end table. A basket with a checkered cloth rested on the table, and I peeked in—wild mushrooms, freshly picked. I saw an old gramophone, but no radio. On top of a cabinet were some framed photos, but it was too dark for me to see who was in them.

Mrs. Fenucchi soon returned with an orange box of baking soda, a teaspoon, and a small glass of water. I mixed myself a strong one and drank it down. Almost immediately, the flames quit backing up into my throat.

I told Mrs. Fenucchi that I was a private dick and that I was a friend of Vera Peregrino. She remembered Vera and broke into a warm smile.

"Oh, Vera. She was a sweet girl. She used to bring me fresh eggs. How she doin'?"

I told her that Vera had been arrested for murder.

"Oh, no. Who she kill?" There seemed to be a readiness in this neighborhood to equate murder charges with guilt.

"A General Lloyd Thursby, from San Francisco."

"Thursby? *Bene.* Thursby's a bad man. He kill my Vito. How can I help?"

"Vito? Is that your husband?"

"*Si, si,*" Maria Fenucchi said, "my Vito. Thursby kill

him."

"Are you saying that Lloyd Thursby murdered your husband?"

"No, no. But he kill him, as sure as we are sitting here. He cheat him. Thursby take the Blackbird from him. Vito, he no can read. He make his mark on the papers. Thursby cheat him. That kill my Vito, same as if Thursby cut his throat."

I asked her to tell me how it happened. Her English was a little rough. I got the impression that she didn't use it much. She may not have had anyone to speak to, in any language. What she had to say fit in with the story I'd heard from Fenwick and from Vera about the Blackbird Vineyard, and with the transfers I'd found recorded in the Santa Rosa courthouse.

Putting all of that together, I concluded that young Lloyd Thursby was no stranger to the Russian River Valley in the years after the First World War. He was a junior officer on his way up through the ranks, and he had some money to spend. In 1931, the Volstead Act had been in force for more than eleven years, and the Depression was deep. Vito Fenucchi had sold off more than eighty acres of good vineyard land with mature vines to neighbors like the Peregrinos just to make his mortgage payments on the remaining property. All he had left was the homestead—the land I'd driven across between the little farmhouse and the river—and the Blackbird Vineyard, the acreage planted in mixed black grapes behind the house on the steep slope of Blackbird Hill.

By 1931, Thursby must have been a familiar face in the valley. He was serious about good wine, and he wanted to take advantage of the depressed prices and buy himself a piece of land. He probably could have afforded a fair price, helped the Fenucchis, and still swung a good deal for himself on the Blackbird. With Prohibition, what value did the property have anyhow? You couldn't make and sell wine, and the steep slope made it useless for most any other agricultural activity. Thursby could have used it as pasture for sheep or goats, maybe, but it was poor pastureland, and besides, the area was notorious for coyotes.

"The coyotes carry off my dog, Brando," said Maria Fenucchi. Too bad for Brando, I thought, but just as well for me tonight. On the other hand, maybe Brando would have been preferable to coyotes.

But instead of paying a fair price, Thursby decided to take advantage of Vito Fenucchi's illiteracy and immigrant background and cheat him. Apparently, Fenucchi had thought he was signing a lease or rental agreement and that he would still own the land, but Thursby had tricked him into exchanging title for the land for one dollar and a case of wine each year.

"That's why I ask, 'You bring my wine?'" she said. "I no have the 1945 yet. Now Thursby is dead . . ."

After the loss of the Blackbird, Vito Fenucchi went downhill fast. First he had a nervous breakdown, and then in '33, a stroke. He was dead within a year. Maria had lived there modestly ever since. The couple had one son, who helped his widowed mother, but now he was gone too, killed in the war.

"I'm glad Thursby is dead," said Mrs. Fenucchi. "The vendetta is fulfilled. Now Vito find peace."

There wasn't much more for me here. I rose to go and ambled over toward the cabinet with the photos on top. Maria Fenucchi saw me and brought the lamp over.

I saw a photo of a young man and a woman on their wedding day. It was a formal pose in a studio, with a classical backdrop. There was a hand-tinted photo of the same man, a few years older, in overalls this time, dots of blue for his eyes, squinting into the sun and smiling, holding the hand of a little boy, maybe three or four years old. The little boy had lots of dark hair on the top of his head and was beaming, happy to be with his dad.

I pointed to the wedding picture. "This is you and Vito?"

"Si, si. And here is Vito and our little boy, Niccolò."

"Niccolò, that's a nice name. Lots of American boys named Nick."

"No, not Nick. Only Niccolò. And here is Niccolò in his uniform. When Vito had his stroke, Niccolò take care of him. Then Niccolò join the Army, in 1934, after his father died." She showed me the third framed photo on the top of the cabinet, this one of a handsome young man in a khaki uniform. Niccolò wore his army dress cap cocked across his forehead, had dark hair like Vito, and the dark five o'clock shadow of a man with a heavy beard.

"He looks like his father." I had another slant at the second photo, the one of the father in overalls. Vito seemed vaguely familiar, but I couldn't place the face.

I said goodnight, thanked her again for the bicarbonate, put on my hat, and stepped out onto the porch. "There's a man looking after Thursby's affairs. I'll ask him about your wine when I get back to town, Mrs. Fenucchi. I'll see that you get it." But she had the door closed behind me before I even finished speaking, and I heard her turn a deadbolt lock. Poor old lady, I thought.

The temperature was dropping. Well, it was only early spring, even in California. A fog bank covered the river and would soon be spreading across the road toward my car. I had covered a lot of ground and done a good day's work. It was time to head back to San Francisco. I wondered how the police investigation into McQuade's death was going, and if Snoots and Overby would be laying for me back in town.

It was nice out in the country, I thought as I circumambulated my car. With a hand on the door, I paused to take one last gaze up at the stars from the darkness of Mrs. Fenucchi's yard. I was standing there peeping up at the Milky Way, like a turkey with its head tilted up at the rain, when my outside mirror exploded.

27

The Highway Is Fraught with Marauders

I hit the dust by the running board on the driver's side. Pieces of glass, shattered by a bullet, sparkled in the dirt inches from my face. Somebody was going to have seven years of bad luck. I heard a couple more gunshots and the metallic thud of a lead slug slamming into my car door. I rolled under my heap and crawled fast to the passenger side. The Improved Eight Coupe has plenty of ground clearance. Reaching up, I opened the door, hoping my car was between the shooter and me.

The '35 Pontiac Business Coupe is a 2-door, and the door handles are at the front. The term "suicide doors" never seemed so apt as I sat up and stuck my hand into the glove box. I plucked out my revolver and slid back down and under the car.

I tried to get a fix on the source of the shots, but then I heard a car engine start up. It sounded like a big powerful motor, not Joe's high-strung mill. I couldn't be sure with the gunshots and the clanging of the bullets on sheet metal still echoing in my ears.

Spinning back out from under the car, I climbed in on the passenger side, shut the door, slid across to the driver's seat, and started up my machine. I hung a U-turn across the dirt driveway and through the yard. By the time I reached the road, I had it pretty well wound out in second gear. The rear end bounced around on the rutted ground. I stabbed at the brake pedal and spun the wheel to the left. The Pontiac drifted beautifully out onto the River Road pavement, and when I had her pointing west, I straightened the wheel and gave her full-throttle.

There in front of me but drawing away around a curve were the taillights of another car. I was willing to bet that was the shooter, and he was headed west. I decided to give chase. Nothing like a good high-speed chase to focus the concentration when you've been drinking, I always say.

River Road winds alongside the Russian River. With its twists and turns and narrow surface lined by trees and bushes on the left side and a riverbank to the right, it wasn't a good road for speed at any time, least of all with the fog rolling in. On the other hand, at around nine thirty at night, I didn't expect much traffic, and as long as I could see the other fellow's taillights, I kept my foot on the gas. I just hoped I wouldn't follow his lights if he drove down into the river. I had to admit it was fun trying to ride him down. I started to think about what to do if I caught him.

We roared along, and I couldn't see much of the fellow in front of me, but I had the impression it could have been the big black car I'd been seeing all day. He may have had more horsepower than me, but he was hauling a heavy load. My Pontiac was lighter and shorter, maybe nimbler. Besides, the Improved Eight had the power of a twelve, because my heart was pure.

When the bad guy disappeared around a particularly sharp corner, I dropped down to second gear, but mostly, I just used a heavy foot on the gas and the brakes, gas, brakes, and steered like hell.

I was gaining ground as we hit Guerneville at fifty miles per hour and roared on through. Never a cop around when you want one.

River Road came to a stop sign at California 116. The bad guy didn't stop. No respect for the traffic laws. I didn't stop either. One-sixteen was a little bit broader and a little bit straighter and it seemed to be taking us out of the fog. Past Monte Rio, the big car picked up speed and started to increase the gap. I decided to squirt a little metal his way.

I don't much care for gunplay, but unless you're in the same room as the party you're shooting at, gunplay is just that—play. At this distance, probably fifty yards now, I could drill the back of his crate if I was shooting right-handed, and standing still. But at sixty miles per hour, shooting out the window with my left hand, I was about as likely to knock an owl out of a tree. Still, it might test his nerve if he knew I was throwing lead. And I could always get lucky and hit the gas tank, or a tire.

Holding the wheel with my right hand, I squeezed off two rounds with my left. The big bucket weaved suddenly left, then right, and the driver lifted off the gas and steered to regain control. Meanwhile, I kept on the gas and closed to seventy feet. Then I noticed bright headlights in my rearview mirror, closing fast on me.

Up in front, the black sedan dove into a right-hander. I was in darkness, except for the lights in my mirror, and I backed off the throttle. I tilted the rear view mirror up to kill the glare from behind me.

The three of us were coming to the coast—I could taste the Pacific in the air. The big black sedan was in the lead, I was in the middle in the Pontiac Improved Eight, and the heap with the blinding lights brought up the rear, crowding closer on my tail. We climbed over the headlands, another spot where the fog could hang dense. The air was cold at altitude, and I turned my car heater on. As the road ascended, it became twisty again, and I gained back most of the distance I'd lost when I'd been dazzled by the lights.

It was amazing how much the temperature had dropped, and the damp air flowed in like cool rain. But I was close, so I stuck my arm out the window to shoot another bean. Just then the big boiler disappeared into a thick fogbank. I had to slow down, so that I didn't outrun my headlights, and I found myself bathed in a weird glow. The dashboard reflected yellow. I tipped the mirror and saw a low car right on my tail. In addition to the blinding headlamps, he was burning a pair of big yellow fog lights. I stole a glance over my shoulder, willing to bet it was Joe Damas in his little Bugatti.

I had to slow down some more to follow the road, and I kept it in second. When I could see taillights again ahead of me through the miasma, I gave it the gas until I was as close on his tail as I could be. Behind me, the driver laid on his air horn. In a hurry? I grinned and waved him around with my left hand, but he didn't have the *cojones* to try a pass.

Then suddenly we had crested the headlands and the road began to wind down to the coast. We descended out of the fog, and I could see the black heap ahead again, speeding downhill toward California Route 1. His brake lights came on, and I heard him crunch his gears. He slid through the stop sign and turned left down Route 1. I double clutched and did the same. An old flivver was running north at about twenty miles per hour, and the tail car had to stop for him at the intersection in a squeal of brakes and tires.

Route 1 is treacherous but visibility was good — the fog had climbed in over the road — and I was gaining again on the bus in front of me. When I was as close as I'd been all night, I fired another shot. The lead probably sank into the Pacific, but the car in front of me reacted by swerving so violently that he went into a left-right-left pattern of steering and correcting. Had I hit him with a lucky shot? Had I just washed eleven years of non-violence down the drain? Gunplay. Yeah, it's play, all right, until somebody loses an eye. Somehow, wounded or not, he pulled out of it and recovered control before coming to a sharp, downhill right-hand bend.

But now the car behind me was coming up fast again, this time flashing his high beams at me. I couldn't go any faster, so I had to let him go by, but I'd be damned if I was going to make it easy for him. Coming out of the right-hander, I kept the throttle to the floor and shifted up to high. We were racing downhill, and a pair of lights was coming up toward us. I heard the wheezing wind of a climbing truck engine, but the driver behind me whipped out to pass.

He moved out into the left lane as if we were playing crack the whip on the playground at recess. I wondered if they played that in Marseilles. By the time he started to draw even with my rear fender, he must have been doing seventy to seventy-five. Downhill. Straight at a truck.

Well, it was probably only three seconds but it felt like everything was slowed down. The Bugatti came up alongside me, and I saw that it was Joe Damas all right. He was wearing a white scarf around his neck, and goggles, but through the goggles I saw surprise in Joe's eyes. He hadn't known it was me. He was just driving his sports car fast and having fun. And then I saw the surprise in his eyes turn to something else, recognition. In that second of recognition, Joe decided to kill me.

The truck kept coming uphill. When Joe had a fender on me, he cut across my bow. It was about 200 feet straight down to the Pacific, and I was in no mood for a moonlight swim. I stood on the binders and cut the wheel a little to the right myself. Joe whizzed by at speed and the teamster laid on his horn. My front tire hit the gravel, and I only had two or three feet between me and a low stonewall, and then a long drop.

I fought the wheel for control and somehow straightened the tires as my running board and fenders started to scrape along the stones. The truck rumbled uphill past us; the driver shook his fist at me out the window. He yelled something about my mom, but it wasn't true. Besides, she'd been dead for a number of years now. The Pontiac ground to a stop and somehow stayed up on route one.

I leaned on the wheel and hung my head over it. I felt like I'd been at sea for a week, and I wanted to plant my feet on solid ground. Thank God we weren't moving anymore. I saw Joe's taillights growing smaller, hurrying toward the horizon. It wouldn't be long before he passed the big black car, and I wondered if he'd recognize that driver too.

28

A Small Death in the Kitchen

When I climbed out to check the damage, I found that the right front fender was crumpled and the tire on that corner was flat. The chase was over; the night's adventure was ended. I rolled the Pontiac just enough so I'd have room to squeeze in between the car and the cliff to jack it up and replace it with my spare.

Oscar Wilde said, "All of us are lying in the gutter, but some of us are looking up at the stars." I liked that one, and I thought about it lying on my back along the cliff edge, as the stars twinkled down at me from a black sky.

The lug wrench and the jack worked well; the spare had enough air in it to drive on. Soon I was on my way, at an easy pace. I stopped in Bodega Bay, a little town on the coast, where I pumped some more air into the spare. I found a cafe open across from the gas station, and despite my earlier heartburn, I grabbed a cup of java.

Traffic along the coast was light, and I was back in town by 10:00 p.m. I cruised past my block on Haight from both ends. I didn't see Snoots or Overby anywhere, but there were a number of parked cars with a good view of the front door of my building. The streetlight just opposite the entrance to my place was out, and I couldn't see if anyone was inside the black Ford sedan parked under it. Coincidence?

I don't trust coincidences, and the bulls drove Fords that year, so I dropped my heap at an all-night garage a few blocks east on Haight and left it to have the flat repaired. I walked to my block via Waller and arrived at the back entrance.

I climbed the stairs and entered my apartment quietly, leaving the lights out. Right away I knew she'd been there — Night of the Honeysuckles, Cicilia's scent, lingered in the air. However, it wasn't Cici, but Chardonnay who came to greet me, and she bent herself around my ankle. The way I felt then, I'd take a hug wherever I could get one.

"Hello, girl." I crossed to the window, lowered the shade, and drew the curtains. I lit a candle I kept in the kitchen for power failures. Then I bent down to pet Chardonnay. She was a light golden color, more of an old Montrachet, really, and she had long hair. Soon her purr-motor was running smooth. In the light, I found a half a fried chicken, cut up, on a plate covered with wax paper.

There was a note under it, in Cicilia's hand:

Frank, dearest,

I brought our dinner over. I waited all evening, hoping to see you, but I finally had to get home to the girls. You know, there's always a place for you — in my heart, and in my bed. Join me.

Cici

P.S. Did you know, in the early years, I built the restaurant business on my fried chicken? It was my signature dish, and it's still our biggest seller. Eat well, my darling.

"Meow." I couldn't remember when I had last been home to feed Chardonnay, and I realized maybe she had a motive behind her affection. She wanted some food. I couldn't fail Vera on this. Springing her from the Chico jail was still a tall order, but I promised her I'd take care of the cat. So I sliced some strips off the chicken breast, and then cut them into cat-sized bites. I gave Chardonnay fresh water, then I lit the oven, turned it to low, and put the rest of the chicken in there in a covered pan to warm it. Chardonnay dug in to hers.

"You were hungry, weren't you, girl?"

It had been a tough day. I'd covered a lot of ground, drunk a lot of wine, and more grappa than I ever hoped to drink again. I had been shot at, been in a car chase, and changed a tire. I also had eaten well at Sally DeBains's and at the Peregrinos', so I wasn't in any hurry for Cici's chicken. I decided to take a quick shower while it was in the oven. I slipped out of my suit and headed for the bathroom, where I could turn the light on without it being seen from the street.

Under the warm spray of water, I eased the tension out of my neck, back, and shoulders, and rinsed away some of the dullness from my mind. I remembered back to Saturday night when Cicilia had come in the shower with me and worked the tightness out of me. That led me to thinking it wouldn't be so bad to spend the night with her. Why sit here in the dark, trying to dodge the cops? Of course I knew Cici was dangerous, but as Marcus Wolff said, (or was it Nietzsche?) "The true man wants two things: danger and play." Well it wouldn't be so bad to play with Cici. It would be wonderful. And, if it were dangerous, well, does that dissuade the male black widow spider from mating? Of course not. You just have to be careful afterwards.

The steam heat was on in my bathroom, and it gave me a feeling of well-being. Fresh steam and your problems don't amount to a hill of beans. I rubbed circles in the mirror and lathered up for a quick shave, so that my whiskers wouldn't scratch the soft skin of Cici's inner thighs.

Then I slipped into clean underwear, but before getting dressed, I decided to gnaw on a chicken leg. In the candle-lit kitchen, I saw Chardonnay stretched out on the floor, asleep already. Cats sleep sixteen hours a day, I've heard. What a life! She didn't have to catch bad guys, just the occasional mouse.

I removed the pan from the oven, and selected a plump thigh for myself. I know, you probably thought I was a breast man. Some Paul Masson Burgundy was open in the icebox, and I poured a short glass to wash down the chicken. I rubbed my foot along Chardonnay's back, but she didn't respond. "You fall asleep, you lazy girl? Dreaming about mice?" I rubbed her some more with my foot. "Meow," I said. Nothing. I bent over to tickle her under the chin. Her head and neck were limp. Cats can be very slinky. They can make you think they're boneless. It's funny. I played with her, rolled her over, but she just stayed limp.

Maybe I'm slow sometimes. I set my chicken and my wine down on the table, and I lifted Chardonnay with both hands under her front shoulders. Her chin drooped down between her front paws. Her eyes stayed shut. No question about it. Chardonnay was a dead cat. Vera was going to be pissed.

29

My Pound of Flesh

"Hi, ya, doll."

"Frank . . ."

"You seem surprised to see me." I was at Cicilia's big house on Lafayette Park, and I brushed past her and stepped inside.

"Well, yeah, I was in bed." She wore a black silky robe, with pink satin lapels, cinched loosely at the waist with a pink belt, and golden slippers with heels.

"You invited me over, didn't you?"

"Uh . . . yeah, sure. But I'd given up hope that you were coming. It must be after midnight." She was right about that. It was after midnight. I'd gone back to the garage where I'd left the Pontiac and redeemed it. They hadn't finished patching the blown tire, but I told them to keep the wheel and tire until morning. I was out in the City, operating without a spare.

"Chardonnay's dead."

Cici blinked at me. "You could be right. But I think it's our best-selling white wine at the restaurant."

"The cat, doll. Vera's cat. Don't play dumb with me." I felt like grabbing her and shaking her, or slapping her good.

"What are you talking about, Frank?" She was trying to catch up, but she couldn't.

"Vera's cat, Chardonnay, ate the chicken you left me."

"So?"

"So?" I opened up the pillowcase I was carrying and held up a dead cat by the scruff of its neck. It was a tacky thing to do, but I elicited a reaction. Cicilia screamed and her hands flew up to her mouth. "You expected *me* to eat that chicken, didn't you, Cici? Me. You're trying to kill me now, like you killed Rusty."

"No!"

"No? You didn't wait to eat with me, did you? You left it there for me to eat alone."

"You're crazy, Frank. It was getting late, and I had to come home to the girls. Weren't you up in Sonoma? Hell, I didn't even know *if* you *were* coming back tonight. I just left you a little something to enjoy if you came in late. You know, a snack before bed. Anyhow, I didn't kill Rusty. I told you that. I'm getting tired of telling you that." Her green eyes were blazing now. "And get that damn cat out of here. I didn't kill it either. If *you* gave her the chicken to eat, did you think to de-bone it, for God's sake?"

"Listen, Cici, you can fool the cops. But Thursby was on to you. You poisoned Rusty, and now Chardonnay eats your chicken, the chicken you left for me." I was waving the cat now. "Ten minutes later, she's napping the big catnap. How dumb do you think I am?"

"Frank, you're scaring the girls." I noticed Brigid and Meaghan on the steps in their little flannel nighties, eyes wide, hugging each other around the shoulders. I put Chardonnay back in the pillowcase and looped the top to close it.

"Oh, hi, girls. I'm just showing your mom a stuffed animal I won at the fair."

"Is it really dead?" the taller girl asked.

"Naw, you girls know a fake cat when you see one, don't you?"

"It's okay girls, go back to sleep. Mommy's fine." She was so confident with me. "I'll see you in the morning." Brigid and Meaghan watched us, and I grinned at them and tossed the pillowcase on the davenport. It bounced on the cushion, tumbled to the floor, and the cat head plopped out. I imagined crosses on the eyes, like in the comics. I don't think that from where the girls were they saw it. At any rate, they turned and ran upstairs.

I drank Cicilia in with my eyes. She may have been petite, but she was still a strong drink. Her arms were on her hips now, one knee cocked. Her head was back, her chin and, of course, her breasts thrust up and toward me.

"What the hell are you thinking, Frank?"

I wanted to beat her. I wanted to slap her tits for my dead rival, Rusty; I wanted to blacken her eye for the dead general, and make her cry for the dead cat. I wanted to leave her moaning in a heap because she tried to kill me. But I'm a peaceful man. I couldn't do it, and I'll bet she knew it. I plopped down on the couch. I could smell Night of the Honeysuckles.

"I wish I could believe you, Cici."

"Listen, Frank, maybe you're too worked up about your case. You want a drink?"

"Are you having anything?"

"Sure, I'll have one with you. How about a nice glass of Beringer?"

"Fine," I said.

Cici brought the wine and sat down beside me. We drank in silence for a while. Then she opened her robe and lowered a strap on her black lace nightdress down off one shoulder. Her black-cherry nipples poked into the sheer lace. "Bring here your lips and place them on my lips; and bring here your hand and put it on my breast, and be not unbelieving but believing," she said. Or did she? Cicilia was a religious experience for me.

I scooped her up off the couch and tossed her head first over my shoulder. Holding her by the legs, I carried her to the stairs. She was light, as light as a dead cat.

"What are you doing?"

"You know what you need, Cici?"

"Bring the wine, Frank."

"You're not going to be able to sit for a week." As I carried her over my right shoulder, I brought my left hand around and slapped her butt with a resounding crack.

Even a pacifist can deliver a good spanking.

And so I extracted my pound of flesh. Tuesday morning, I woke up early but I felt rested and at peace. At least Cici had a story, answers for everything. No, she said, she didn't kill Rusty O'Callaghan—that was accidental toadstools in the omelet. No, she hadn't poisoned the chicken. If Chardonnay died after eating it, maybe a chicken bone caught in her throat. I didn't necessarily believe Cici's answers. I believed her ass in the sack.

Cicilia was lying face down in a deep sleep. Her olive colored butt-cheeks had a reddish blush that morning, and they were pointed gloriously up toward the heavens, as if I'd draped her over a log. The hem of the lacy nightdress had slid up to the small of her back, where she had a little patch of dark downy hairs. Did she know she had a little hair there? Had she ever seen the beautiful small of her beautiful back? Probably. Cici knew every inch of her body and how to use it.

The girls weren't up yet. Downstairs in the kitchen, I put on some coffee. Dressed in my trench coat, with my fedora down low on my forehead, I picked up the pillowcase containing Chardonnay and headed out. First I dropped the dead cat in my car trunk, and then I strolled to a newsstand where I bought the morning *Chronicle*. I held it up to my face on my way back for anonymity.

I left the paper on the kitchen table and looked in Cici's fridge for eggs. If I ate anything there, I was going to cook it myself.

I spooned a little bacon grease from a can by the stove into a pan, and heated it up. I found a half a loaf of sourdough, still fresh, in the breadbox on the counter, so I sawed off two thick slices and popped them in a chromium toaster. Then I broke a couple of eggs into the pan, slit the yolks with a knife, and basted the eggs with the hot grease. The edges curled and bubbled, and I cooked them over hard. A grind of black pepper, a dash of salt and *voilá*! All the basic food groups—protein, cholesterol, grease, sodium, nitrates, caffeine—and it tasted great too.

It was a cool morning, but dry, so I carried my eggs, toast, and coffee out to a cast iron table for two on a little patio off the kitchen. Cici had a neat back yard with an attractive garden. I recognized Lilies-of-the-Valley, in front of a border of rhododendrons, already in bloom. Blue hydrangeas, some odd-shaped daffodils, tall spires of green with purple and pink bell-shaped flowers hanging down, curvy, greenish-purple blooms with eye-catching, shiny berries, and an ornamental shrub with fragrant white blooms growing in the shade of the house. Nearest the kitchen was a little green parsley type herb, with small, white flowers growing in umbrella-like clusters, probably for gourmet cooking, very convenient for the chef of *Chez Cici*. Or maybe they were just weeds that needed to be yanked up.

I opened my *Chronicle* while I ate, and found what I was looking for, the latest on McQuade, inside on page five.

Poison Killed Writer, Cops Say

John "Spitbucket" McQuade, a writer who had been found dead Sunday on the steps of his apartment building, died of poisoning, a San Francisco police spokesman announced. "We have no choice, now, but to treat this as a possible homicide," said Lieutenant Overby of the Bureau of Inspectors.

Mr. McQuade had eaten lunch at the Black Lizard Lounge, on Howard St., where he had been a regular patron. The Black Lizard has a clean record with the Department of Health, and their inspection certificate was posted and up-to-date. "We adhere to the highest standards of food safety and cleanliness here at the Black Lizard," said Mr. Beef Ballou, the owner, who had served Mr.

McQuade his last meal. "There's never been any poison in the joint because we serve food. I use traps for the rats."

Police said preliminary indications are that the poison was a "powerful neurotoxin," not a common household poison. They are seeking Mr. McQuade's luncheon companion, Frank Swiver, of the City, who has since vanished. "We'd like to talk to him," Lt. Overby said. "It's possible if he shared a meal with McQuade, he could be at risk too. He might be lying sick or dead someplace." The lieutenant confirmed that he had interviewed Mr. Swiver briefly Sunday, but that the latter had subsequently disappeared.

An obituary for Mr. McQuade appears on today's obituary page.

So McQuade was still dead and Overby was still looking for me, eh? It was a good thing I had spent the night at Cicilia's. Now I needed to keep clear of the cops just a little while longer to pull together a few loose threads on this case.

Upstairs, I turned Cici over onto her back, and woke her up. "I am the Little Red Rooster," I sang, a line I had heard at the Black Lizard Lounge.

30

A Longer Rope

Bureau of Inspectors? Let me speak with Lieutenant Overby, please." It was still early Tuesday morning, and I was in a phone booth in a drug store on Van Ness. I had helped send Meaghan and Brigid off to the school bus. It wasn't so hard. Cicilia hadn't said much, but she'd seemed fine.

A voice came on the other end of the blower. "Overby, here."

"This is Frank Swiver, Lieutenant. I hear you've been worrying about my health."

"Where are you, Swiver?"

"Macao or maybe Hong Kong. I don't know. I had too much to drink last night. All I know is I woke up and everybody's speaking Chinese."

"Funny man," said Overby.

"Listen, Lieutenant, I might be able to give you something on the McQuade poisoning, but it's tied into a case I'm working on. If you haul me in, I can't deliver for my client. Can you give me a little room on this? I promise I'll bring you the whole package, as soon as I can."

"What have you got?"

"Nix, Overby," I said. "I can't have you and Snoots crashing in and queering the deal for me. Listen, man, you know I didn't hurt McQuade. And even if I had wanted to, I wouldn't have bumped him off in a public restaurant with poison. That's not my style."

"You might have, if you'd wanted to finger somebody else for the job," he said.

"If I'd wanted to finger somebody else for the job, I would've left a clue pointing to somebody else, not to myself. I wouldn't have had lunch with the victim just before he died. I certainly wouldn't have slapped his map in front of witnesses."

"I can't let you run around loose, Swiver. How do I know I'll ever hear from you again?"

"You'll hear from me," I told him. "I'm running around loose now, Lieutenant, and still I spent my nickel to call you. I'm not going to run out on you because I have to get Vera Peregrino out of the cooler up in Chico. She's your security deposit. I'm working on the murder of General Lloyd Thursby from Friday night, and the bulls up north pinched my secretary, Vera, for it. The Chico police aren't going to do any more work on the case. The only way I can spring her is by finding the real killer."

"I don't know."

"Lieutenant, what if it was Snoots? He's your partner right? If your partner were under glass, wouldn't you try to do something about it? Well, Vera, she's only my secretary, but she's like my partner, see? You wouldn't just stand by and do nothing and let your partner take the fall, would you?"

"You're breaking my heart, Swiver."

"I didn't know you had one, Overby. Listen, I'm a detective, just like you're a detective. Well, it wouldn't be good for the detective business if you or I let the real killer get away with this."

He sighed. "How much rope do you need?"

"It's Tuesday, right? How about if you come to my place Thursday night, around ten? I'll have McQuade's killer there for you, but that's just my little gift. I'll have General Thursby's killer too."

"You're giving me two birds?"

"That's right," I said.

Nothing for a couple of heartbeats, and then Overby said, "Okay, Swiver. Thursday at ten at your place. And if you don't have your suspect on the McQuade poisoning all wrapped up for me with a neat little bow, I'm taking *you* in. Somebody's having his elbows checked Thursday night, and I sure don't mind if it's you. The chief's lighting a fire under me."

"Thanks, Overby. I knew you were a white dick."

It sounded like he spit. Then he said, "And listen, Swiver. Me and Snoots won't be looking for you, but be careful. I can't cancel the order to pick you up. Don't run any stop signs. Don't stick up any crippled match girls."

"Don't worry, Lieutenant. I'll behave like a regular altar boy. Thanks again. Thursday at ten, my apartment, okay?"

"We'll be there, shamus." He hung up.

Now that I'd bought some time, I had to use it well to set everything up for Thursday, so I headed over to the Rose Building. In case any sharp-eyed young button had his eye on the front, I parked at the Clift Hotel on Geary instead of in my garage space at the building. I walked over, slipped up the alley, and entered via the loading dock. Tommy's shift was over but he was still back there, half-conscious in a haze of Anchor Steam. His eyes widened when he saw me. "Holy cow! Mr. Swiver. They been asking for you. Holy cow!"

"What'd you tell 'em, Tommy?"

"Nothing, Mr. S. They couldn't get nothing from Tommy." I wasn't surprised to hear that, but I thanked him and gave him four bits.

"I'm still not here, Tommy, got it?"

"You bet, Mr. S. They can't get old Tommy to sing."

Up on seven, I let myself into the office and proceeded straight to work. My office stationery wasn't fancy like General Thursby's, but it would have to do.

Old Vine Detective Agency
Suite 711, Rose Building
650 Post St.
San Francisco 9, California
You are cordially invited to a Noir Evening of wine tasting,
7 p.m., Thursday, April 8, at the home of Frank Swiver, 1421
Haight St. Apt. 3-B
RSVP. UNion-1-8503 or AShbury-2-7112

Then I crossed out the last line. It was less than even money anyone would find me home or in the office, so why RSVP? I used to have a service for the office, but I had to drop them in the winter for lack of funds. Forty-five minutes later, I had five invitations typed up and signed. It's hell not having a girl in the office when you type like me. I addressed them to Sally DeBains, Joe Damas, Nick Fenwick at the general's house, Marcus Wolff, and Cici.

At nine thirty, I placed a call to Thursby's lawyer at the firm Fenwick had named for me, and I booked a half hour with Attorney Wolfowitz for two thirty that afternoon. While it was still early, I dropped my invitations in the mail and drove over to Thursby's place on Maple Street. It seemed quiet when I cruised past. I parked on a nearby block on Clay Street and ambled back to the big corner house.

I stayed in the shadows as best I could on the west side of the corner and made my way to the garage. I could see through the garage door windows that the big Buick was inside. I wanted a closer look, so I tried the overhead door, and it was unlocked. It was a creaky, noisy affair, so rather than shoving it all the way up, I raised it two feet off the ground, dropped, and rolled in.

The Buick turned out to be a pre-war Phaeton 4-door convertible, probably a '39. From the top of a hill a mile away, I supposed it might appear to be a regular black sedan. On the other hand, it had been a sunny spring day up in Sonoma yesterday, and if it were my car, I would have lowered the top. I needed to see something more.

A thin layer of mud lined the wheel wells. If it were wine, I might have been able to identify the origin as the Russian River Valley, but my dirt tasting skills were a little rusty. I circled all the way around to the front and found the something more I needed — a spider web in the glass with a neat hole drilled in the middle, high up on the passenger side windshield. Completing my circuit to the back, I found it lined up with a small hole through the back of the black canvas top. If somebody had drilled the top a year ago, Thursby would have had it fixed. On the other hand, if it had happened last night . . .

The door from the garage into the kitchen was unlocked, so I decided to let myself in to the house.

Inside, it was cool and quiet; a couple of windows were open and a nice breeze blew through. Exiting the kitchen, I crept up the hall and chose a door in the front of the house on the right, which turned out to be Thursby's study. But before I could start to search the place, I moved the curtain and peered out the front window. Guess who I saw coming up Maple Street with a large brown paper grocery bag in his arms? Nick Fenwick in a leather bomber jacket over a white tee shirt.

If what I suspected about last night was true, Nick wouldn't be eager for a visit from the law. But neither was I. It was best to dust. I headed back up the hall fast. On the way through the kitchen and out, though, I paused long enough to pop into the pantry, where I found a half dozen magnums of Blackbird Noir. I helped myself to an old one. There were also some bottles of Sally's '45 Pinot Noir and I lifted one of them too. I slipped through the garage and out the drive. Staying in the shadows, I turned the corner and watched Fenwick come up the porch steps whistling the caisson song and pulling keys on a chain out of his right pants pocket.

It was ten thirty now. Next stop was the Presidio of San Francisco. I spent a couple of hours there, including a break for lunch on base, and I found some history about General Thursby's postings. He had indeed been stationed at the Presidio between the wars. Everything I found in his records checked out with what I'd heard. There was no record of him ever being married or having dependents in his household.

Niccolò Fenucchi checked out too. Missing in action in

February 1944, in the Marshall Islands — some place called Kwajalein. In June of that year, he'd been "presumed dead." Kwajalein. It seemed like a raw deal, some unknown rock in the Pacific, but no worse than what a quarter million other GIs were dealt. When your time comes, what does it matter if it's Normandy or Anzio or Kwajalein?

I didn't find any records for Nick Fenwick. The corporal in the records room said that didn't mean anything. The Presidio didn't have records for everybody, just the ones who served in the Pacific theater.

31

Who Is V. Thursby?

By 2:25 p.m., I was sitting in the reception room of Agnello, Lamm, and Wolfowitz, attorneys-at-law, on the nineteenth floor of a modern, post-war office building on Sansome. They had a girl behind the front desk, a platinum blonde with straight hair cut short and brown eyes that didn't give-a-damn. She was working on a new coat of red nail polish that looked like Chinese lacquer. She had good posture, generous round breasts, and a tight blouse. But she seemed more interested in her nails than in me and my snappy repartee, so I parked myself in a green-leather wingback chair and flipped through the new *Esquire*. I consoled myself that she wasn't a real blonde, anyhow.

At about 2:36 p.m., the nail polish was dry enough for her to risk doing some work, and she circled around the desk with a leatherette appointment book clutched up against her bosom. "Mr. Wolfowitz will see you now,

Mr. Swiver. Follow me, please." She swung hips sheathed in a snug tweed skirt and marched on gams like Gwen Verdon's. I followed. Her seams were straight, but the rest of her was all curves, and she wore red shoes that matched her nail polish.

I remembered coming to San Francisco one day with my mom to go shopping. She saw a woman leaning over the counter at the old Emporium, grabbed my hand, tugged me in the other direction, and said, "When I was young, nice girls didn't wear red shoes to town, Francis."

Nice girl or not, I'd follow this one anywhere, but it was only a short hike, through an interior door and down a hallway along a soft thick carpet. She rapped twice on the last door on the left and opened it without waiting for an answer. "Mr. Swiver to see you, Mr. Wolfowitz."

She stood in the open doorway and invited me in with her expression, so I turned slightly and stepped past her breasts with a nod and a thank you. Meanwhile, Meyer Wolfowitz, slender and short, was up out of his seat and coming around to greet me. He had a firm grip for an aging gray-haired gent and an alert smile. Wolfowitz ushered me into a comfortable chair, the sister of the one I'd used in the lobby, and returned to the high-backed leather swivel chair behind his desk. His office sported an expensive view to the east out over the financial district to the top of the Ferry Building. "Thanks for seeing me, Mr. Wolfowitz." He didn't say anything but gave a slight graceful gesture to indicate there was no way he'd rather spend a Tuesday afternoon than swapping lies with a down-and-out private dick. I got right to it, in case he was billing me for this time, and told him I was working on the Thursby murder, and that I understood he was the General's attorney.

"That's right, Mr. Swiver. I've handled General Thursby's legal affairs since 1925. In fact, he was one of my first clients when I joined this firm, before I made partner. May I see some identification, please?" I showed him the copy of my license.

"The police would like to talk to you, Mr. Swiver."

"Yes, sir."

"Did you think I wouldn't know that?"

"No, I figure a man in your position reads the papers. I don't flatter myself that I'd come to your attention, but even if you missed it, perhaps your clerk would have told you your two thirty appointment is hot."

"But you came to see me anyhow?"

"This is important to me, Mr. Wolfowitz. It's not just about the general. I have to help a friend."

"You have nothing to fear from me, Mr. Swiver. What can I do for you?"

I told him that I was there about General Thursby's will.

"It's on the calendar for next week," he says. "We'll be opening and reading it here in my office. You're welcome to attend."

"I was hoping you might be able to help me sooner than that. There's a young woman in jail for a crime she didn't commit, and I hate to leave her there another week."

"Your friend?"

"Yes."

"You're a private investigator, Mr. Swiver. Your profession must have certain ethics regarding privileged information about your clients."

I told him I did have certain ethics. "Even if I didn't care about legal or ethical requirements, I know that if someone comes to me in confidence, it would be bad for business to divulge his secrets." Business had been bad, but I don't think it was my ethics.

"Then I'm sure you understand I'm bound by professional ethics as to what I can divulge about General Thursby's will. Besides, I don't see how any information I give you can get your friend out of jail. Information won't post bond."

I acknowledged that with my eyes. "You keep well-informed, Mr. Wolfowitz. There's a killer on the loose. General Thursby's killer. My secretary — my partner — is charged with the shooting. The cops aren't looking for the real killer. They're content to sit on my partner and pick their teeth. If I can nab the real murderer and turn him in, I can spring her. I'm wondering if there's something in the will, like a motive for killing Thursby. He was a wealthy man, right? Someone must stand to gain from his death."

Wolfowitz held his fingertips together and eyed me over the top of them. "Over the last twenty years, General Thursby became more than a client to me. He was my friend, Mr. Swiver. I understand about friends. I am glad you are searching for my friend's killer. Why don't you ask me some questions, and I'll see what answers I can give you without breaching professional ethics."

"Thank you, Mr. Wolfowitz. The will you have, is it a recent one? Have there been any changes?"

"This will dates back to 1942. Before General Thursby went into combat, he made an appointment with me and updated it then. It was duly witnessed by me, and aside from the stress of the war, General Thursby was under no duress when he signed it."

"And are you familiar with the provisions?"

"I am," he said.

"So who stands to profit from General Thursby's death?"

"His heirs. He was a wealthy man."

"And who are his heirs?"

"That's privileged information, Mr. Swiver."

"I see. How wealthy was he?" I asked.

"Sorry, I can't answer that either."

"I thought you said you wanted to help."

"I do. Perhaps you'd like to ask me a different question." He smiled, like a man with low blood pressure, money in the bank, and a deaf and dumb wife whose father owned a liquor store.

"Is General Thursby's estate worth, say, more than a quarter of a million?"

"Yes."

"Higher?"

"Considerably."

"More than a million?"

"Yes." Now we were getting somewhere.

I tried again on the heirs. "Are there many beneficiaries named?"

"Fewer than a million."

"Are you having fun with me, Mr. Wolfowitz?"

"Why not, Mr. Swiver? I am helping you, I trust, but I'm enjoying myself too. You don't begrudge an old man that, do you?"

"Are there fewer than ten heirs to the estate?"

"I think I can tell you that there is one principal heir, who stands to inherit the bulk of it. And there are some smaller bequests." He held up four stubby fingers, and wiggled them.

"So one person gets the bulk of it; I could say that somebody is going to be at least half-a-million berries richer this time next week."

"You could say that, Mr. Swiver."

"Does General Thursby have any living relatives?" I asked.

"I can't say."

"Thursby owned Ravensridge Wines," I said.

"Yes."

"And is that property, the Blackbird Vineyard, and the assets of Ravensridge Wines, included in the estate?"

"Thursby's share, yes. You are probably aware that he owned it in partnership."

"Yes." It was my turn now to say that. "The partner is listed as 'V. Thursby.'"

"Yes."

"Who is V. Thursby?"

"I can't say," he answered.

"You can't say, or you won't say?" Silence followed for a time, and I rubbed my chin.

He sighed. "Mr. Swiver, the general once told me of his desire to leave his estate to his only child, a daughter."

"So V. Thursby is his daughter."

He shrugged. "I can't say. Perhaps I've already said all I can. I do have more information, of course, but I believe that what I have not told you falls into one of two categories — that which would not help you with your investigation, or that which I cannot ethically tell you now. It has been delightful talking with you. Dee-lightful." He pressed a button on an intercom box on his desk. "Miss Wonderleigh, would you be kind enough to show Mr. Swiver out, please."

Wolfowitz came around the desk again and laid one

mitt on my shoulder while he shook my right paw with the other. "I do hope you'll come next week, Mr. Swiver. It may be that the firm could use your services."

"How's that, Mr. Wolfowitz?"

"Well, sometimes we open a will and read it but not all the beneficiaries are present. In some cases, that's a trivial matter. They may be represented by an attorney or they may have chosen not to come. We just mail them a check for their portion of the proceeds. But other times the executor of the estate is unable to locate one or more of the principals. In such a case, we hire a private investigator, Mr. Swiver. A man like yourself."

"I see," I said, as Miss Wonderleigh stepped into the doorway, chest out, heels together, butt cheeks and shoulder blades against the open door.

"Good." He shook my hand. "We haven't found General Thursby's daughter, a Miss Vera Thursby. Good afternoon, Mr. Swiver."

32

In Which I Throw a Little Soiree

By Thursday, I had a good idea of who the murderer was. Or perhaps I should say who the murderers were, since we had more than one body: General Thursby (U.S. Army, ret., dec'd) and John McQuade (Spitbucket, dec'd.) Not to mention Rusty O'Callaghan, but Cici wouldn't want me to mention him. Trouble was, I didn't have any solid proof, nothing that would convict Thursby's killer. But I did think if I brought everyone together and stirred things up a bit, I might get something, maybe even a confession.

I had tidied up my apartment on Haight Street as best I could. It wasn't as spacious as the digs of some of my suspects, but it was as big as the lounge of *Vieux Désirs*, Thursby's private car, so I figured our dwindling little group could fit.

I wore my Harris Tweed sport jacket, a green,

burgundy, and beige pattern, with moss-green khaki slacks, but no tie. At 7:05 p.m. my bell rang, and I opened the door to Joe Damas.

"Am I the first one?" He glanced around.

"Hello, Joe. You are. Glad you could make it." We seemed to have an understanding, now, and shook hands. He wore a dark charcoal suit with a puff of lavender silk in the breast pocket, a lavender tie, and a fly yellow shirt. He carried a walking stick, which he handed to me along with his bowler hat, as he slipped off his lavender gloves. I caught a whiff of his cologne as I stashed his accessories in the hall closet. He smelled marvelous. Joe slid a blue box of Gauloises out of his side pocket and lit one up. So much for the marvelous smell.

After I had left attorney Wolfowitz's office the other day, I'd paid a call on Joe. We had talked about our *tete-a-tete* on the coast highway, but Joe just said that was how they drive in France.

When I had leaned on him about the DeBains counterfeiting, he'd admitted nothing, but agreed to ride with me up to Chico. Using the deed I'd pilfered from the Santa Rosa courthouse, and Joe's forgery skills, we signed over the Peregrino Ranch to post bond and got Vera Peregrino out of the Chico cooler. I'd dropped Joe at the train, thanked him, and bought his ticket back to Oakland. But I warned him that if any more bottles of counterfeit Noir Côtes DeBains turned up in future vintages, I wouldn't stop Sally from coming after him with her guns.

Now I poured him some sparkling wine, some Korbel, which he frowned at, and asked, "By the way, did you overtake that black sedan I'd been following on the coast highway Monday night?"

"*Mais oui!*"

"Did you recognize the driver?"

He hesitated. "I'm not really sure. I didn't take a good look." Then the buzzer rang again. It was Vera, in the trench coat I'd bought her once with a bonus from a happy customer. It was a Burberry, like mine, but a woman's cut, with the buttons reversed. She was sporting a jailhouse pallor, not her usual healthy glow, but was still lovely in an off-the shoulder robin's egg-blue dress. It had a sash tie at the shaped waist, V-neck and tight around the bust, and full in the skirt. She wore sunglasses to cover what remained of the shiner Delgado had given her.

"Vera, you look swell, sweetheart. I'm glad you could make it." I tried to give her a hug and a kiss on the cheek, but she drew back.

"Keep your distance, Frank. I'm only here because you said we could crack the case."

Vera had seemed so happy when I sprung her. I thought she was going to forgive me for Cici, but I'll be dammed if she didn't ask about her cat right off as we drove south. I had to tell her Chardonnay was dead.

"Dead, Frank, how? I thought you were taking care of

her for me?"

"Bad luck, chicken bone in the throat. I'm sorry." I took the blame. That wasn't such a great move. I got another scratch to the face and almost lost control of the Pontiac. Then she wanted to get out and walk. It was all I could do to get her to ride with me as far as the Russian River Valley where I dropped her at the Peregrino home.

Louisa welcomed Vera right inside, but I hung around on the porch to speak to Angelo.

"Somebody shot at me after I left here the other night."

"Wasn't me," said Angelo. He was amused. His eyes twinkled with mischief.

"I think it was Niccolò Fennuchi."

"Niccolò? No, he never came back from the war."

"Would you know him if you saw him?"

"Sure. But Niccolò *è morto*." I didn't think he knew what was going on, so I thanked him and said good night. I drove the rest of the way back to town alone.

The fat man arrived next. "Marcus Aurelius, how are you? Glad you could come." I grabbed his hand and started to pump, while I guided him in by the elbow. "I haven't seen you since someone tried to kill us in your wine cellar."

"Yes, that's right," said Wolff. "I probably shouldn't be here now. I had plans to go to the theater . . ."

"I'm sure we'll have a good show for you Marcus. A-ha, ha, ha," I laughed.

"You did say something about the Blackbird, did you not, sir?"

"Yes, indeed, Marcus," I said, "yes, indeed. You will love this."

Fenwick arrived next. He wore a sport coat over an open neck shirt and appeared a little uncomfortable. His sleeves always seemed too short. Then Sally DeBains arrived.

"Hey, is my car going to be okay out there, shamus?" she said.

"Should be, Sally."

"I brought a couple bottles, like you said," Sally added, and deposited a bag on the table.

"Oh, I say," said Wolff, "were we supposed to bring something?"

"Oh, no. No need, Marcus," I said. "The drinks are on me tonight. There was some Noir Côtes DeBains I couldn't get, and I took the liberty of asking Sally."

At seven thirty, Cicilia arrived with a small entourage from *Chez Cici*. I'd asked her if *Chez Cici* could supply some food to go with the tasting, and told her what sorts of wines I planned to serve. "Mrs. O'Callaghan, you look wonderful," I said. "Thanks for coming." I gave her a brotherly kiss on the cheek. She returned the peck, then supervised her employees, who had their arms full with trays and covered platters. Cici didn't disappoint.

When the food was unloaded in the kitchen, Cici

dismissed her staff and joined us. She wore a white high-waisted baby doll dress with black shoulder straps, black trim across the low cut bosom, and a black bow tied in the middle. It would be easy to slip out of.

The sparkling wine was gone. I had bought a couple of dozen bistro glasses for the guests, and I circulated among the guests, pouring the first two wines. One was a petite sirah from the Spring Mountain area of Napa and the other pure Alicante Bouschet, from a low-rent district.

"Well, ladies and gents," I began, "let me welcome you all to our little noir evening." A siren wailed on a city street nearby, and I paused. Darkness was falling outside. I had the Venetian blinds open and as the streetlights came on, they shined in to my third floor walkup and cast long shadows across the room.

No one said anything. I probably should have invited a couple of hookers and an Episcopalian bishop, just to loosen things up. I cracked the blinds a little more. "I was thinking if we all got together again, we might shed a little light on the Thursby murder."

"Dreadful business," muttered Wolff. "But I see Miss Peregrino is amongst us once again. Does that mean you've cleared her name?"

"Not exactly, Marcus. Vera is only out on bail. I know she's innocent, though, and I plan to clear her once and for all when I name the real killer. But let's not jump around. I like to take things one step at a time, in a chronological order."

"*Linéaire.*" Joe drank from his glass of wine number one.

"Exactly," I said. "So let's go back to the train Friday night and imagine we're in the corridor of *Vieux Desirs* between five p.m. when we left Oakland and seven when we were all assembled for the tasting.

"It might have been fun to have been a fly on the wall. I imagine the corridor was like something out of a Max Fleischer cartoon, with doors opening, heads popping out, people scurrying from room to room. How do you like this first wine, Joe?"

"Not bad. Tastes a bit like a young Northern Rhone," he said.

"All California tonight," I said. "This is a petite sirah from Napa."

"It's very dark and inky," noted Sally. "Purple, peppery. I like it."

"Great. Compare it to the second wine if you wish." I tasted mine at this point. "At any rate, let's start shortly after we departed from Oakland. The way I figure it, Marcus Wolff was the first to step out of his compartment."

"That could be, sir. I'd arrived about fifteen minutes early, and as I said, those rooms, while nicely appointed, were a bit claustrophobic for a man of my size. I needed to step out."

"And so," I continued, "you slipped your Colt revolver

into your waistband and went to Thursby's room."

"Well, sir, I had my gun but it was not fired. You know that."

"Be that as it may, Wolff, you weren't just going out to take the air. You wanted to see the general about the Blackbird; isn't that so?"

"Well, yes." Wolff sighed. "Very well, this is a nasty business that won't bring credit to any of us, unless we're truthful. I boarded the train Friday intending to see General Thursby and to make him a new offer for the Blackbird wines in his cellar. You know I'm very—determined—about my wine collection. Friday, I did not intend to fail. Now, I always admired the late general."

Cicilia rolled her eyes, and drank.

"Oh, yes," Wolff continued. "We'd had our differences, indeed. But without some struggle, where is the pleasure in attaining your goal? If anyone could possess the Blackbird Noir, why should a collector like myself care about it? But it's the rare wine that drives my passions. I embarked on our journey expecting a challenge. However, my visit with the General was a surprising one. He agreed to sell me a vertical of six magnums, 1937 through 1942, to be specific. We concurred upon a price. Quite an outrageous price, but when a man is obsessed, well, what can he do? I paid him $400. But the wines are still in Thursby's cellar. I was to come round and pick them up this week."

"What do you say, Fenwick? The general did have

four new hundred-dollar bills with consecutive serial numbers. It fits with Wolff's story. If he comes around, will you give him the wine?"

I caught Fenwick in mid-sip, and he kept us waiting while he savored it and swallowed. "Are you saying Wolff's innocent?" he asked.

"I'm saying his story rings true."

"Yeah, sure, tell him to come by tomorrow. Er, come by tomorrow, Mr. Wolff," Fenwick told him himself. "I'll be in all afternoon."

"Thank you, Fenwick. That will be grand. At any rate, as a token of his good faith," Wolff continued, "General Thursby gave me a bottle of the 1945 Blackbird, the one we had the other night. Gave it to me, ladies and gentlemen, of his own free will. Isn't that how wine is? Something to be shared among friends."

Everyone drank and considered that. "This petite sirah is good," said Sally, "but the second wine is quite astringent on the finish."

"I know you said they're all from California, Swiver, but you know what this reminds me of? Algerian wine, cheap imported wine," said Joe.

"What a color, though," said Vera. "Bloody red. I'll bet it's staining my teeth."

"It's Alicante Bouschet, and it's from the San Joaquin Valley," I said. "Probably a bit like North Africa in the summer. But let's get back to Wolff's story. Marcus?"

"Uh, yes. To sum up, my meeting with Lloyd Thursby was cordial and productive for me. And when I left the general's compartment, around 5:20 p.m. with my bottle, he was quite well.

"That's all I know, and it's the truth, every word of it. Oh, yes, this too: just a bit before 6:50 p.m., I was about to step out into the corridor to go to the lounge. That's when I saw Madame DeBains in the hall, with a small revolver in her hand. I don't believe she saw me."

"Thanks, Marcus. Ladies and gents, I've talked to all of you, and no one has told me anything that doesn't fit with what Marcus has told us tonight. I believe he's telling the truth.

"The next party to visit the general isn't with us this evening. It was the critic, John McQuade. I'll speak for him tonight. But first, let me pour you the next pair. There's water if you want to rinse out your glasses." I showed them the bottles we'd started with, a petite sirah from Devil's Hill in Napa, and an Alicante Bouschet from an old vineyard owned by an Italian immigrant named Pagnani in Madera County. "The Alicante just says 'Burgundy Wine' on the label, like so many of them. They don't sell it under its real name. You might drink a good deal of Alicante from California."

"I don't," said Cici.

"What would you serve with a wine like that, Mrs. O'Callaghan?" asked Wolff.

"The first thing that comes to my mind is a spicy tomato sauce, like *arrabbiata,* maybe with prosciutto in it. Even a creamy, meaty *arrabbiata* perhaps, on *strezzopreti* pasta.

"Ah, my mouth is watering," said Wolff. "Your cooking is so exquisite; all you have to do is talk about it."

"Mrs. O'Callaghan," I said, "perhaps our guests are ready for something to eat with this next pair. I'm serving grenache and mataro now."

"Mataro?" said Damas.

"Mourvedre, Joe. This one is from an old vineyard in Contra Costa. Bridgehead Vineyard."

Sally offered to help Cicilia serve. Aromatic steam poured into the sitting room from the *Chez Cici* chafing dish, and the two brought out a robust, spicy lamb curry over long grain brown rice. I circulated around with wines three and four. "Okay, folks. Here's what I think happened when Wolff headed back to his cabin with his magnum of '45 Blackbird. John McQuade was worried."

"Hah. He always had a bug up his ass about something," said Fenwick.

"But why last Friday? Here's what I think he'd tell you . . . He'd been receiving death threats in the mail. For all he knew, the threats could have been coming from one of you." I gave them each, except Vera, three seconds of eye contact. Cici looked away. "McQuade's criticism in the *Spitbucket*—criticism that had a harsher edge than that

Alicante Bouschet we just had—may have been getting under someone's skin. One of the targets of his criticism, featured in his final issue, was the Blackbird. McQuade knew Thursby, knew his tastings always featured the Blackbird. Most of you welcomed that, right Marcus?"

"Of course. It's a great wine."

"Ah, but that was not McQuade's impression," I said. "When McQuade had opened his invitation, he found with it a note inviting him—"

"Ordering him," said Fenwick.

"Thank you, Nick—ordering him—to see the General in his compartment. McQuade associated the threats with Thursby, and he was carrying a gun—his Luger. We checked it out Friday. It had not been fired. At any rate, he opened his door to call on Thursby at about 5:20 p.m., and he saw Marcus here in the corridor with his bottle. That much he told us Friday evening.

"It turns out Thursby had a copy of the proofs for McQuade's next *Spitbucket*," I said. "How he got them I don't know. But Lloyd Thursby was a man of influence. Anyhow, the general flew into a rage. He owned Ravensridge and the Blackbird vineyard. He was thinking of making a change in his marketing plan, going to direct sales, and he didn't want this sort of criticism of his product coming out now."

The guests were eating their curry and drinking wines three and four. It was a tense moment for me. I remembered Conan Doyle's "Silver Blaze." If Cici had decided to poison my guests, the smart money was on the curry.

I continued, "It was completely unexpected by McQuade. How should he have known that Thursby owned Ravensridge? Not that it would have made any difference to McQuade. He would have written the same critique. He was totally uncaring about how his opinions would affect others.

"They argued. Well, McQuade grabbed the pages that Thursby was holding. They tore, and McQuade ran out with the bottom part. Thursby was left holding the smaller piece, just the masthead. General Thursby was alive and well when McQuade left."

"How do you know that, Frank?" asked Cici.

"A couple reasons, Mrs. O'Callaghan. For one thing, the torn copy of the new *Spitbucket* — the part in Thursby's room had blood or wine on it, whereas the part Joe found in McQuade's room was clean and dry. And McQuade verified for me he saw two bottles of '45 DeBains Pinot Noir. Joe admitted he broke one. Yes, someone else visited the general after Spitbucket McQuade. And the way I see it, the next person in cabin number nine was our friend Joe Damas. And the general was alive when he got there. Joe?"

"I like the mourvedre," said Damas, "but this other one, the grenache, it is hot, alcoholic, and coarse. In my country, this happens with grenache, when it's over cropped. In France it might be a basic Côtes-du-Rhone say from a cooperative, not a Côtes-du-Rhone Villages, or an estate wine."

"I was hoping you might tell us the next part of the story, Joe. It's your turn."

"Well, actually, Swiver, when I first opened my door, I saw someone else in the corridor. Perhaps she should go next."

"She?" I said.

"*Oui*," said Joe. "Miss Peregrino. I watched her coming from the direction of the lounge and go to compartment number seven. *Linéaire*, right, Mr. Swiver?"

"There's no need for that, Damas. Vera didn't go to Thursby's cabin."

"Let's let the young lady speak, Mr. Swiver," said Wolff.

"I don't mind," said Vera. "Nobody's listened to my story yet."

"We're listening now, dear," said Sally.

"Thank you." Vera wet her whistle with a drink of wine and launched into her story. "I've been working for Frank since 1945. I used to like the big lug. He seemed to be a good guy, a good friend. We did things together. In fact, I thought I loved him. But I guess that's what got me into this mess." She was right. My actions had positioned her behind the eight ball. Now I'm going to get you out from behind it. Don't stop loving me now, sweetheart.

"I went to see Nick Fenwick to get an empty bottle to put my flowers in. Maybe it was five forty-five or close to six. When I headed back to my room, I saw John McQuade going into number nine." You know how sometimes an object can have a sentimental meaning? When Vera mentioned that empty bottle, I remembered it in her room with the calla lily in it. I remembered how Vera and I were, our excitement boarding the train Friday. I remembered buying those calla lilies for her. What was I thinking then? I was feeling it again, tonight.

"McQuade must have entered Thursby's room before I poked my head out. I didn't see him, but I saw Miss Peregrino," said Joe.

"I saw McQuade, but I didn't see you."

"I ducked back in when I saw you coming," said Joe.

"Well, to go on," said Vera, "I wasn't back in my compartment too long. I was feeling happy, excited to be at a wine tasting with all these swell folks. About six thirty or so, I returned to number one to get Frank and go to the tasting. And what do you think I saw? Him and the O'Callaghan dame, that Lucretia Borgia, in there. They were really going at it, let me tell you. They didn't even hear me open the door. Frank had his hat on. The bum didn't even look up.

"Anyhow, that's what I know. I don't carry a gun. The murderer must have slipped it in with my undies when

I was out the second time, after six thirty. I know it must have been the second time, because when I changed my underwear after getting the empty bottle, there had been no gun in my drawer." Vera pointed a lean, bare arm at Cici and me. "I wouldn't trust either of those two, and they're the pair who searched my room and produced the gun. That Swiver's a no-account—he hasn't paid me for months."

"Vera, whenever a client pays, I give you at least a third, sometimes half, even if it means I don't pay the light bill."

She didn't argue it. She just said, "You owe me so much back pay, I couldn't afford to quit . . . until this happened. Now I don't care. And the O'Callaghan dame, well, she poisoned her husband didn't she?"

"Maybe I should of poisoned your curry, blondie," said Cicilia. Fenwick dropped his fork. Even Wolff paused and studied his food.

"I just don't understand why they'd want to set me up," Vera said. "I never did nothing to hurt them. Maybe they killed Thursby and needed somebody to take the rap."

"I hope you don't believe that, Vera," I began, but Cicilia was on her feet and steaming. Vera had at least four inches and maybe fifteen pounds on her. I didn't want a catfight.

33

Cabernet Frank

Easy, doll." I stepped in front of Cici with the bottle of Bridgehead Mataro. "Let me refresh your glass."

"I'm sick of everyone saying I killed Rusty," said Cici. "Now she's accusing us of killing Thursby too." But she held out a glass, and I poured.

"Vera knows we didn't kill Thursby, Cici," I said. "She's just a little upset. She had a tough weekend in the cooler up in Chico."

"Yeah, and then I come back to a dead cat," said Vera.

"You trying to blame me for that too?" Cici blazed.

"No, I told Vera the cat was my fault." I didn't exactly buy the chicken-bone-in-the-throat story, but lacking the money for a cat autopsy, I played along with Cici's story, for now. And lacking proof to the contrary, I could convince myself I was safe with Cici. I steered Cicilia back to her chair and pushed her down by the shoulders. "Cici, maybe you'd like to tell your story, now that Vera's done.

Joe, could you help me get the next couple bottles and some food?"

I lifted the lids on *Chez Cici's* dishes until I found some nice thick porterhouse steak sauced in brandy and smothered in shiitake mushrooms. I placed some Louis Martini wines from the old Monte Rosso vineyard in paper bags. One was a cabernet sauvignon, and the other was zinfandel. I gave them to Joe and we brought out the steak and wine.

"Go ahead, Cici," I said.

"Okay, Frank, I may as well get it off my chest.

"Thursby was a friend of Rusty's, so it was only natural that I'd go to the general when I needed help. Rusty left me with nothing when he died. I needed cash to open a second *Chez Cici*—I still *need* cash, dammit, and I'll find a way to get it.

"I called on Thursby last week to ask for a loan— $25,000. I offered to put up the cellar at my restaurant as collateral. Do you know what my wine is worth? A damn sight more than $25,000!

"But Thursby had some other stupid ideas. He thought I poisoned Rusty. Imagine! If anyone thinks I killed the dumb Irishman, they should try raising two children alone and working twelve hours a day."

"Mmm, these wines are excellent, Mr. Swiver," said Wolff.

"So is your steak, Mrs. O'Callaghan," said Sally.

"Thank you, dear," Cici accepted the compliment with a wave of her cabernet glass. "Rusty's death was an accident, pure and simple. Not that he was any good. He was broke. He had no income since Prohibition ended. Every cent we made at the restaurant, he used for gambling money. When he wasn't gambling, he was drunk. And when he was drunk, there was no telling what he would do. God knows how poor Brigid will turn out after all she's been through.

"Thursby refused to loan me the money. But he invited me to the tasting Friday, so I came. I thought I could talk with him during the weekend and try again. I'd beg him. I'd do anything — anything within reason."

I relieved Joe of the cabernet and strolled around the room pouring for the guests.

"I was in compartment two, and Frank was in one. I used to know Frank when I was a waitress at John's Grill. That was back in '33 and '34." She smiled for the first time. She was smiling at me. "I wish now I'd stuck with him, instead of latching on to Rusty. I wouldn't have been any worse off than I am now, that's for damn sure." Oh, Cici. That sounded exactly like what I'd wanted.

"I was right next door, so I slipped in to see Frank, to ask him to help me get my money from Thursby. I admit it, I was a little afraid of Thursby after the reception I'd had at his house. And I don't trust his goon." She pointed at Fenwick.

"You're a tramp," Vera said. "You seduced Frank to get him wrapped around your little finger."

"Okay, maybe we went too far, but I'm not a tramp. I'm still young, and I've been alone since Rusty died. What's a girl supposed to do? I'm in my prime.

"At any rate, as far as Thursby's murder goes, Frank's my alibi. I was with him from about five forty-five until nearly seven, when we all met for the tasting. And I don't have a gun. I don't know who killed Thursby, but it wasn't me. It wasn't Frank either, sweetie," she said to Vera. "I don't think he ever left his room. We had no reason to set you up. Listen, Frank found that gun in your drawer just like he said, and if I hadn't been there, he probably would have tried to cover it up. He didn't want to put you on the spot."

Vera had nothing else to say to that. The room grew quiet. "Vera," I said, "don't worry about it. All that means is that the real killer got into your room and left the murder weapon in there. But we still have to take it step by step. Linear. Now it's time to hear Joe's story."

"I'm next?" said Joe. "Okay. You know, I feel terrible about General Thursby's death. I can hardly believe that one of us must be the murderer." Joe had poured the zinfandel while Cici was telling her story and now settled back in his chair with his own glass.

"I boarded the train last Friday with a troubled mind," he continued. "As the distributor for Ravensridge Wines,

I knew that the owner of the winery and the Blackbird Vineyard, and the principal in Wine Partners Trust was General Thursby. We met after I came to America in 1943, and started doing business in '44. The general gave me a great deal of responsibility for managing sales and distribution during the war. I wasn't eligible for the draft, you see, for, umm, medical reasons."

"He means he's a fairy," said Sally DeBains.

"You know, someday, someone will cut out that sharp tongue for you, Mrs. DeBains," Joe snarled.

"Sally, would you get one bottle of the '45 Noir Côtes DeBains Pinot Noir I asked you to bring? Hang on, Joe, we'll be right back." I got up and guided Sally by the elbow to the kitchen. We each came back in with a bottle. "You'll need two clean glasses here," I announced as we walked around pouring. "These both say '45 DeBains, but one is from General Thursby's collection and the other is direct from the winery."

"But they're the same wine," said Wolff.

"Keep an open mind, Marcus," I said. "You know what your boy Nietzsche says: 'The irrationality of a thing is no argument against its existence, rather a condition of it.' Go on, Joe."

Joe shifted in his seat and his eyes darted from Sally to me and back again as we circled the room pouring the two wines. "Very well. I arrived early, about 4:40 p.m. or so, and Mr. Fenwick here assigns me to compartment four. It is small, but a functional, attractive cabin. I am comfortable there. I have to talk to General Thursby. He had sent me word that with this vintage, the 1946s, which are coming out in the fall, he is canceling our distribution agreement. He has this idea about establishing a mailing list and selling direct to the wine consumer. Well, I'm sure you can all see it is disastrous for me. So I plan to talk to him about it." He slipped his pocket handkerchief out and wiped his brow, then the back of his neck.

"I unpack and refresh myself and relax a bit. I want to get business with Thursby out of the way before the tasting begins. But when I open the door, I see Miss Peregrino in the corridor coming from the lounge end of the car. Not wishing to be indiscreet, shall we say, I slip back into my room. That is sometime before six. I smoke a cigarette and give her some time to clear the hall." That seemed to remind him he didn't have a Gauloises drooping from his lip so he picked one out, tapped it on the blue box, and lit up.

"Then I step out. I'm going to say it is now after six, maybe half-past. I have my Beretta with me, but that means nothing. Everyone knows I carry a heater. You verified, Mr. Swiver, that it had not been fired." I nodded.

"My visit with the general goes badly," said Joe. "He is not in the right frame of mind to discuss business. In fact, he is not at all reasonable, but insists on allowing other interests to interfere with what could have been a mutually profitable business arrangement."

"I say, Mr. Swiver, how can these wines both be '45 Noir Côtes DeBains?" said Wolff. "They don't taste alike."

"Interesting isn't it?" I answered. "Cici, what did you bring to serve with the pinot noir?"

"Salmon, baked on cedar planks with rosemary in a hot oven. I'll get it." She got up. She had kicked off her heels and was in her hose. "Marcus is right," she said. "These aren't the same wine."

"You know," said Vera, "this one tastes like my dad made it."

"Which one, sweetheart? The one I poured? Or the one Sally poured?"

"I'm not sure," said Vera. "But it's this glass. Could be Peregrine Burgundy."

"General Thursby had two bottles of 1945 Noir Côtes DeBains Pinot Noir on his table Friday night. Didn't he, Joe?" I said.

Joe sighed. "*Sacre bleu*. Yes, all right? He did. I make him my offer, which is a three-year deal, to continue to buy his entire stock at wholesale, with a handsome increase of twenty percent to him this year, another ten percent for the '47s, and five percent more for the '48s. I will handle transportation to my warehouse in San Francisco and then set up and maintain the subscription or mailing list and arrange shipping."

This was not the same deal that Joe had told me about

at his place, about trading off Wolff's head for continued distribution rights, but it seemed as good for our purposes tonight, just more discreet.

"It is a great deal for him, and it will keep me in business," said Joe. "But Thursby won't hear of it. He is agitated and accuses me of dishonest handling of wines. He said one of his bottles of Noir Côtes DeBains was counterfeit, the other was real, and that he is going to serve them at the dinner. He plans to have Spitbucket McQuade with his unquestioned palate, expose the fraud, and let the opinions of the whole group confirm it. Well, I simply cannot allow this. There is a certain variation from bottle to bottle in a production as big as Sally's, you know. I pull out my Beretta and smash one of the bottles. Clumsy fool that I am, I receive lacerations to my hand. It is quite painful. I am bleeding, and so I terminate our interview immediately to return to my compartment and see to my wound. I am only in Thursby's room a short time. It is all quite unpleasant, but General Thursby is alive when I leave him."

"Joe smashed one of those bottles," I said, "so we never had the tasting that Lloyd Thursby had planned the other night. But I picked up the other bottle, the one that was rolling around in Thursby's room. Tonight we're having one bottle from the general's cellar, and one that Sally DeBains brought from her winery."

"It's amazing," said Wolff.

"Yeah, it's two different wines," said Fenwick.

"*Merde*," said Joe. "How do you know which one I broke? It could have been the alleged counterfeit, and the bottle that survived could have been Sally's true wine."

"I thought of that, Joe. I said 'one bottle was from the general's cellar.' And that's true. I got a bottle of Noir Côtes DeBains '45 Pinot Noir from the floor of cabin nine on the train, but just in case, I also picked one up Tuesday morning from your pantry, Fenwick. I saw that the general had purchased about a half dozen, probably with this test in mind."

"How could you get one from our pantry? You didn't ask me," said Fenwick.

"You weren't exactly home at the time, Nick," I said. "Just to be sure, let's get another of Sally's bottles and the one I lifted from Thursby's cellar, and I'll open the two out here in front of you. It'll only take a minute. And while I'm doing that, Sally, you can start your portion of the story."

Sally started telling her story, and I was back with the two bottles in a jiffy. I marked an "X" on the one from Thursby's place with a grease pencil and poured a little from each bottle into each guest's two glasses while she spoke.

"All right. I joined Lloyd Thursby's little private train car expedition for one purpose Friday night, and it was not to get sloshed with a bunch of losers. I wanted to buy the Blackbird Vineyard. I planned to make it the crown jewel in Domaines Sally DeBains.

"I arrived comfortably before five," Sally said. "I told Fenwick I wished to see the general immediately, but he was a stubborn gatekeeper, so I had to wait. I decided I'd have to slip out of my room later and see Thursby when Fenwick was busy and couldn't interfere.

"So I tucked my little revolver into a special holster I have at the top of my hose. Yeah, I carry a shooter, see?" She hoisted her skirt and flashed some thigh. "I've carried it since the war.

"Some time after we had left Oakland, I looked into the corridor," she continued. "I wanted to slip down to Lloyd's room and make him an offer for the Blackbird. My intention was to make it an offer he couldn't refuse. But I saw Fenwick out there having a smoke. I figured he'd stop me, so I returned to my room and bided my time. Later—I'm not sure exactly when—I don't wear a watch . . ."

"Just a gun," said Joe.

Sally had a drink of her wine. "As I was saying, later, I tried again. This time no one was in the corridor. I knocked on Thursby's door, but there was no answer, so I tried the handle. It was unlocked.

"Well, I saw Thursby all right, but we didn't have much of a business discussion. He was quite dead when I entered," she said. "I was only in there a few seconds— long enough to check the body for signs of life, draw my gun, and take a quick glance around the room."

"Mrs. DeBains, if you found a dead body, why didn't you tell anyone?" asked Vera.

"Call me Sally, dear. We're practically neighbors. Why didn't I tell anyone about the body? Well, I hadn't wanted anyone to know about my business with the general. He was dead, and someone would find him soon enough, so I figured what difference did it make. Besides, I still want the Blackbird Vineyard, and I said to myself, with Thursby out of the picture, what do I have to do to get it? I was thinking about the general's partner, V. Thursby. Who is 'V. Thursby?'"

It was quiet for a few moments. Some folks sipped one or the other of the Noir Côtes DeBains and compared. Wolff tried both during the pause, but Joe ignored his glasses.

"If we're going *linéaire*," said Joe, "somebody's lying. I mean we've heard all the stories. No one killed General Thursby. I was the last visitor before Sally, and the old man's alive; then Sally goes in and he's dead. I'm not taking the fall for this, Swiver. I'm not a murderer."

"Have we heard all the stories?" I said.

"Well, we heard from Wolff," said Vera, "then McQuade, me, Mrs. O'Callaghan, then Joe, and finally Sally. The only other ones on board were you and General Thursby."

"Thursby didn't kill himself, not with two to the heart. And it wasn't me. Cicilia O'Callaghan is correct. I didn't leave my room from the time we boarded until everyone else was already in the lounge for the tasting," I said.

We'd been building up to this all night. I moved around my living room. I'd never had a case like this, where I had all the suspects together and got to name the killer. I was going to savor the drama. "You've all given your accounts of what you saw and did, and it seems to me every one of you could be telling the truth. Let's open the Blackbird, shall we, and I'll tell you what I know, and what I think happened." I brought out an old magnum of Blackbird and set to work opening it.

"You see, Thursby was working in his retirement on an assignment for the OSS, helping to track down Nazi agents," I said.

"What's the OSS?" asked Vera.

"Office of Strategic Services," said Fenwick. "It was formed from a military intelligence unit. Actually, since the National Security Act last year, it's the CIA — Central Intelligence Agency."

"Thursby was after Wolff," I continued, "but I don't think he had anything on him. Maybe that's why he finally decided to sell the Blackbird to the philosopher. The general probably had a surprise lined up for Wolff when he came over to pick up his case." Now I had opened my Blackbird, the one I'd purchased from Fenwick, and began to circulate with it. "Between Wolff's and Damas's visits, Thursby called John McQuade in. As Joe said,

Thursby had planned to enlist McQuade as an ally to expose the counterfeit DeBains Pinot Noir when he sent the invitations. But since then, Thursby had somehow obtained the galleys of next month's Spitbucket, and he flew into a rage when McQuade came in. McQuade panicked. He grabbed the draft of the next *Spitbucket* and ran."

Everyone now had a glass of the Blackbird that I'd poured. I thought I was weaving a good yarn, but all these winos were swirling their glasses, gazing at the opaque wine, sniffing.

Oh, well. I guess even a murder can't compete with a wine like that. I forged on. "Our friend Joe Damas is a scratcher, and a good one. Having stumbled upon the DeBains forgery, Thursby decided to end his distribution agreement with Joe before the same thing happened to him. Thursby intended to expose Joe at the tasting on the train. Joe carries a rod, but he didn't want gunplay, so he simply smashed the evidence. It didn't matter which one he broke, the real one or his counterfeit. Without two bottles to compare, how would you know one is fake? By the way, Vera, I'm pretty sure you're right. Your dad probably did make that wine. Your parents claim they don't know Joe Damas, but that's what Joe told them to say. I saw Joe at the Peregrine ranch Monday evening. They've probably been doing business since the war."

"I like your folks, Vera," said Joe. "Your dad is always

struggling. I can help them with their business." Vera frowned, uncertain how to feel about that.

"Thursby also clashed with Cicilia O'Callaghan," I said. "I knew her when she was Cicilia Ricci, see, a seventeen-year-old waitress at John's Grill. I got a visit Friday on the train from Cicilia. She had found out I was coming and probably guessed that Thursby wanted to hire me to investigate Rusty O'Callaghan's 'accidental' death. The general liked Rusty. Did O'Callaghan die accidentally?" I shrugged.

"Oh, come on, Frank," said Vera.

"Vera, tonight let's focus on who killed General Thursby. That's the murder you're on the hook for. How does everyone like the Blackbird, by the way?"

"It is perfection, as always," said Wolff. "It sings to me, like opera."

"Sounds like Edith Piaf to me," said Joe Damas. "It sings with passion."

"Sinatra," said Sally DeBains. "It fills me with desire."

"To General Thursby. He made good wine." I studied the room over the rim of my glass. Fenwick wasn't drinking, just staring at me. "Nick, would you help me get another dish? What did you bring to go with the Blackbird, Cici?"

"Just a simple roast pork loin," she said. Fenwick carved the "simple" pork loin, which was stuffed with slices of California plums, and crusted with Dijon mustard and chopped pecans. I brought the little plates out, a couple at a time, and returned to my narrative.

"Now Cicilia didn't want Thursby dead. She wanted his money, and needed him alive for that. She came to my compartment and made up a story that Thursby owed Rusty more than $25,000 in gambling debts. She showed me some IOUs. Maybe they were real, and maybe Christmas comes in July—but I didn't buy it. They were phony, but they were damned good. We can ask Joe about that too." Joe tugged at his collar then drank some of his Blackbird. His eyes bored into me.

"At any rate, I didn't want any part of it, but I smelled the honeysuckles in Cicilia's hair. I knew she was trouble, but I pretended to believe her, for old time's sake. I'm sorry, Vera, but Cici meant a lot to me, back before I'd ever met you." Vera didn't lash out at me like before, but she didn't show me any sympathy, either.

"We've all heard Sally's story. She was determined to get her way with Thursby and probably would have held a gun to his head if that would have helped her get what she wanted. But she didn't knock him off. Madame DeBains is tough all right, but her business is wine, not murder.

"Murder is my business—mine and Vera's. Vera Peregrino grew up in the shadows of Blackbird Hill. She always wanted to make wine, good wine. Just like Sally, Vera would like to have the Blackbird Vineyard, wouldn't you, sweetheart?"

"Damn you, Frank. Hell, yes!" said Vera.

"Well it turns out Vera doesn't have to kill for it. You see, General Thursby left it to her in his will."

Vera's hands clenched the arms of her chair. "Is this one of your jokes, Frank?"

"What?" said Sally. "Why? You mean Vera Peregrino is 'V. Thursby?'"

"If I'm figuring it right, yes. You see, it appears Lloyd Thursby was stationed at the Presidio after World War I and spent a great deal of his free time in Sonoma. In 1919, when Angelo Peregrino took his wines to the county fair, Thursby had a fling with Louisa Peregrino. When Thursby bought the Blackbird vineyard in 1931, he saw the young Vera and realized she was his daughter."

Vera gasped. "Frank, what are you saying?" she asked.

"I'm sorry, sweetheart, I don't want you to hear it like this in front of everyone, but I've got a killer to catch. You're not all Peregrino. That's why your dad's always been so cold. You should talk to your ma."

Well, that had been the easy part. Now I sipped a mouthful of the Blackbird, swallowed it, and gulped another to stiffen my spine for what came next.

"All very interesting, Swiver, but you don't say nothing about who the killer was," said Joe.

"I'm coming to that now, Joe."

"Yes," said Wolff, "Who visited Thursby after Joe but

before Sally?"

"Yeah," said Sally. "I'm telling the truth. Thursby was dead when I entered his compartment."

"Well it was the only other person on the train that night," I said. "He saw Thursby between the time Joe left and you arrived."

"Who?" said Vera.

"Niccolò Fenucchi," I said.

34

Niccolò Fenucchi

N iccolò! Oh, Frank." Vera extended her arm and pointed at Nick Fenwick. "I knew it when I got on the train. I knew you seemed familiar, Nick, but things have been happening so fast, and it's been fifteen years since I've seen you. I didn't recognize you. Niccolò Fenucchi, that's who he is," she said to everyone, "the boy next door. Hey, Nick." Vera gave a little wave.

I had been walking around pontificating, weaving my yarn, while the other guests were perched in the living room on the davenport and a couple of easy chairs, wine glasses on the cocktail table and plates of Cici's cooking balanced on their knees or the arms of the furniture. Nick sat alone at my desk, a glass of the Blackbird in his left hand, his right arm down out of sight. A smirk broke across his face.

"Hey, Vera," he said. "I recognized you right away. I always knew you were going to be beautiful someday.

Remember that summer, kid, when we were skinny dipping in Green Valley Creek?"

"Oh, God." Vera shivered. "You weren't so hairy fifteen years ago. Maybe I'm wrong."

The happy memories were over for Fenwick. "You're right, Swiver," he said, "I plugged Thursby."

Bien pensé. Well planned, Swiver, I told myself. I'd hoped my dramatic presentation would elicit a confession.

"I'd been thinking about doing it for years," Nick continued. "We'd had it rough, with the price of grapes so low, and thieves like Peregrino, Thursby, and DeBains after our land. Then with Prohibition, sometimes we didn't even have enough to eat. Pa wasn't a farmer; he was a winegrower. Thursby robbed the Fenucchis of our land, and that was the most important thing to my father—his land. When Thursby acquired the Blackbird Vineyard, he took Pa's reason for living. Pa lost his mind, his health, and in eighteen months, we buried him. Just to stay alive, we sold off the great vintages of our private cellars as sacramental wine."

"The Vatican should send a monsignor to investigate sacramental wine like this," I said. "It's a miracle. This isn't one of Thursby's Blackbirds you're drinking. It's the 1920 vintage, a rare Prohibition-era Fenucchi Blackbird. To your father, Nick, to St. Vito." I showed them the bottle. It was etched with gold leaf, "Vera's Vintage." Who had done that? Thursby, for his daughter? Or did Vito do it for his neighbors? While the crowd eyed the bottle, I eased myself between Fenucchi and the others.

"No kiddin'?" said Niccolò. "You're all right, Swiver, serving a bottle of my dad's juice like this. But that don't change nothing. I'm not sticking around to step off for the killing." He showed his right hand now, and it was filled with an Army Colt. It was the twin to the Thursby murder weapon and in a room the size of my parlor, it was deadly. "Sit back down," he growled.

Mal joué. Badly played. I had the confession I'd wanted. Now I had to live long enough to use it. I plopped down on the davenport next to Cicilia.

"We sold that wine at a tenth of what it would be worth to collectors — people like Thursby, Wolff, and McQuade," said Fenucchi. "We lived like dogs with nothing but the scraps of charity we could get from the church. Eventually, I had to join the Army, to send money to Ma.

"All the time I was in the service," he continued, "I never forgot the man who killed my father. I never forgot about getting even with Thursby, and when the war was over, I looked him up. Niccolò Fenucchi disappeared in the Pacific. I called myself Nick Fenwick and got a job in Thursby's service, just to get close to him. Then I waited for my chance.

"Friday night, opportunity finally knocked. I had just finished preparing everything for the tasting and was going to see if the general was ready. I saw Damas stumble out, bleeding. When I entered, I found Thursby sitting there with wine, blood, and broken glass all over the table. 'Why not now?' I thought. After all, half of you were packing rods. Thursby was after Wolff as a Nazi, and the Blackbird was missing. Some kind of altercation had just happened with Damas. If I was quick and careful, I could get my vengeance, and I'd be so far down the list of suspects the cops would be sure to pin it on someone else.

"So I grabbed one of Thursby's pistols out of his drawer," he said, "and let him have it as the train rattled across some switches. I figure nobody even heard the shots. Then I peeked out into the corridor, and I seen Vera going down the hall to the shamus's room."

"That's when I went back to get Frank for the tasting." Vera was wide-eyed and held the back of one hand to her mouth.

"I couldn't go out in the hall, so I passed through the connecting door to my compartment, number eight," said Fenucchi. "Then I used my pass key to slip in to number seven. I ditched the rod in with Vera's clothes. No plan, no reason. I just wanted to get rid of it, and I knew you weren't in your room," he said to Vera. "Then I remembered I'd left Thursby's cabin open. I listened at the door on that side of my room, and I didn't hear anybody, so I returned to Thursby's room and locked up from the inside."

"I told you I wasn't in there long," said Sally.

"I didn't want anyone to see me come out of Thursby's,

so I exited through my room, into the corridor from there," said Fenucchi. "And that's all there is to say. Thursby's sleeping the big sleep, and I killed him. I figure he had it coming. Now Vera's going to own the Blackbird Vineyard. Justice works in mysterious ways."

"That ain't exactly the end of it," said Vera. "Thanks to your little trick, I'm still facing the gas chamber back in Chico for murder."

Nick snorted and nodded toward me. "Lover boy will get you off."

"You were far down on the list of suspects, Fenucchi," I said, "and as long as the Chico police had Vera on ice, you were safe. But I was trying to spring Vera, and if I did, they'd have to start searching again for a killer. So you came after me, to make sure she took the fall for Thursby. Sunday you followed me and made a play at the Biarritz. But that failed."

"My bad luck," Fenucchi said.

"Then Monday I don't know if you were following me again or just visiting your mom by coincidence. You fired a couple shots at me outside her house, then sped off down the coast."

"It don't matter," he said. "I won't miss again. I'm getting out of here." Standing, he grabbed Vera by the upper arm and waved the gun around the room. "Nobody try anything; I've got the blonde."

"Don't take her, Nick," I said.

"Call me Niccolò. I'm tired of 'Nick.' You can't stop me, shamus. I don't want any more gunplay, but I'm not taking the fall for this. If you interfere you'll be responsible for what happens to Vera." He started backing toward the door, dragging Vera along with his left arm wrapped around her shoulders, and his gun at her head.

"Frank," Vera pleaded, "Don't let him take me."

I was already responsible for what happened to Vera. I was not about to let it get any worse. "Go ahead, Nick," I said. "You can walk right out. But there's no need to take Vera. No one will stop you."

"Well if the dick isn't going to do anything, I will." Sally DeBains reached under her skirt and tried a quick draw from her thigh holster.

"Don't be a fool, Sally," shouted Joe Damas and lunged in front of her. Fenucchi fired once and the blast from the .45 in the little room paralyzed everyone. The bullet ripped into Joe, and dumped him across Sally's lap. Vera screamed.

"Just hold it, Fenucchi." I stood up and held my empty hands out to my sides. "You know I'm a peaceful man. Nobody's going to try to stop you."

"That's right," he said, "or Vera gets the next one."

I shook my head no. "There's no need. I'm not going to raise a finger. You don't need a hostage; you can go. Turn her loose."

"Forget that," he said. "You must think I'm pretty

dumb."

"All right then. Turn her loose; you can take me." I had a chance to save Vera and set things right. Nick could plug me, but I had to risk it. I stepped over close, kissed Vera on the cheek, and turned my back to Nick.

"You're serious? Okay, then." He must have shoved Vera away, as she was propelled into the room, and Fenucchi yanked my left arm into a hammerlock and clamped the gun to my head. "Take me out of here, Swiver."

"Just a second, Niccolò, and we'll go. How is he, Sally?"

Mrs. DeBains had turned Joe over on the floor and propped him up with his back to the cocktail table. "It's his shoulder, I think." She was opening his suit jacket.

Joe's head had been lolling on top of his torso but now he raised it up and opened his eyes. "Hurts like hell. But I'll be okay if you stop the bleeding. *Merde.*"

"Vera, call an ambulance after we go. Okay, Nick. Follow me." I stepped to the foyer. Fenucchi kept my left arm pinned, and I let him steer me. I opened the door to the third floor landing and led the way.

The hall light bulb was out. Lieutenant Overby stepped out of the shadows with his police special drawn. "Who the hell's this?" said Niccolò Fenucchi. I heard a swish, and Nick let go of my arm. Sergeant Snoots, from behind my open door, had sapped him down.

"Thanks, Overby. You boys were just in time."

"We heard the gunshot on our way up and were going to bust in. Then I heard the door opening, so we took cover instead," said Overby. Snoots bent over the fallen Fenucchi, snapped the bracelets on him, and heaved him into my foyer. I checked on Joe. Vera was kneeling on the floor next to him with one of my towels pressed on his shoulder.

"You're all right, Joe," I said. He managed a weak grin.

Sally was on the horn, calling for a meat wagon. "Well, Lieutenant," I said, "here's your man, Niccolò Fenucchi." In the corner, Fenucchi groaned. "He shot General Thursby Friday night on the Southern Pacific to Portland."

"We got him, Swiver," said Overby. "Are you saying he killed John McQuade too?"

"You could also charge him with attempted murder tonight," I said. "He fired at Sally DeBains, hit Joe Damas here."

"Fine, but you promised me McQuade's killer, and I want him — now."

"Well, that's going to be a little more difficult, Lieutenant," I said.

"That does it then," snapped Overby. "I'm taking you in for McQuade."

"Now hold on, Overby," I said. "I can name McQuade's killer for you." Cicilia sipped her wine and looked straight ahead. She was holding her breath. "I just can't produce him."

"Him?" Vera eyed me, and as I glanced around the room, at Wolff, Damas, and DeBains, I noticed I had everyone's attention.

"Lieutenant, Lloyd Thursby killed John McQuade. Thursby's funeral was today."

"Thursby? Oh, Frank." Vera rolled her eyes. Cicilia slumped back on the davenport and exhaled.

"Why would Thursby kill the critic?" asked Overby.

"We'll never know for sure, but we do know that Thursby was furious over McQuade's reviews of his Blackbird Vineyard wine. He wanted to put a stop to it. Thursby wanted McQuade dead, and he didn't want any comebacks. So he poisoned a bottle of wine, a Burgundy, one of the critic's favorites. Thursby knew it was only a matter of time until McQuade would open it and drink it."

Sergeant Snoots said, "Hey, I like burgundy too, Lieutenant."

"Shut it, Snoots," said Overby. "It ain't the same kind what you drink."

"Well, this one did have a cork in it," I said. "Thursby injected poison through the cork with a long hypodermic syringe. He gave the bottle to McQuade as a gift. Having a small apartment with limited storage, McQuade kept some wine in the cellar at the Black Lizard. The poor sap just happened to open that one for lunch Sunday."

"Frank, you don't believe that do you?" said Vera. "Who uses poison? Think. You know it wasn't—"

"Why not, sweetheart?" I said. "Thursby had means, motive, and opportunity. It fits."

"Lieutenant, this guy's coming around. We ought to get him over to the clubhouse," said Snoots.

"Okay, take him down to the car. I'll be there in a minute," said Overby.

"Well, I should be toddling along too," said Wolff, getting up. "'All credibility, all good conscience, all evidence of truth come only from the senses.'—Nietzsche. Officer, I'm sure Mr. Swiver understands this all better than I do. But you certainly have the right man for the Thursby killing. He confessed in front of all of us and then shot poor Joe. Um, if you need me, I'm at the Hotel Biarritz."

"All right. Don't leave town," said Overby.

"Don't leave town! Ha, ha. How droll. Well, not for another five days or so," said Wolff. "But then my ship sails for the canal and Buenos Aires. You see my friends, after all this excitement, I need a change of scenery. I think I shall visit Willi in Argentina. Besides, I now realize there is a serious hole in my wine collection—I have nothing from South America. Goodnight, ladies. Joe, I'll come see you in the hospital. Mr. Swiver, it's been a delightful evening. Thank you for the best Blackbird I've ever tasted."

"Goodnight, Wolff," I said. "'Be content to seem what

you really are.' Marcus Aurelius."

"The butler did it. Humph. Ha, ha. Droll indeed." And he squeezed out my front door, just as the ambulance men arrived with a rolled-up stretcher.

Overby glanced around quietly. "This Fenucchi guy," he said to Mrs. DeBains, "he shot at you?"

"Yes, he did, Lieutenant. He's just lucky I didn't get my gun out a little faster. I would have drilled him."

"Everything Swiver and the fat man said sound on the level to you?"

"Why, yes. He confessed, and then he grabbed Miss Peregrino as a shield. That's when I tried to draw my roscoe. Joe here jumped between us. I guess he saved my life."

Joe had a dressing on his shoulder now, and the crew prepared to lift him onto the stretcher. "I'll come with you, Joe," said Sally.

"You have your car, ma'am?" said the ambulance doctor.

"Yes."

"Meet us at San Francisco General. That'd be better."

The stretcher-bearers hoisted Joe up and trotted out, with Sally gathering her wrap and following. Cici waited quietly on the davenport. She hadn't said anything since the excitement started, nor for a while before that. Vera rose to her feet. "Well, I see how it is Frank. I'm leaving too."

"Vera, we wrapped up the Thursby murder. It's just a formality now, but they'll return the bond up in Chico and drop the charges against you."

"Yes, the bond . . . " she said.

"Your parents' ranch—"

"My parents . . . "

"Well, the Peregrine ranch," I said. "Your father's land is probably going to come to you."

"My . . . father . . .?" she said.

"Lloyd Thursby. It's a lot to think about. I'll call you in the morning," I said.

"No, Frank. Don't call me." She held up a hand, palm toward me. "You've made your choice." A sneer curled on Vera's lips.

"Vera, please. Friday, when you said you loved me—" I moved to touch her.

"Shut up, Frank. Where's my coat?" I retrieved her trench coat from the closet for her. She thrust a hand into a sleeve and continued to the door, yanking the coat from my hands. "Good night, Mrs. O'Callaghan. Goodnight, Lieutenant."

"Wait, Vera." But now she was out in the hall and had slammed the door. I followed and heard the clatter of her heels on the steps as she descended the first flight. My legs felt weak. It could have been the close call with Fenwick. My mouth was dry. It could have been the wine. It could have been love.

"I made mistakes," I called after her, "but I've learned a lot. I'll call you in the morning."

She shook her head. "I won't answer if I think it's you. You've made your choice." Vera Peregrino slipped away into the night. I deserved that.

And I still had Cicilia to deal with.

35

What Do You Do with a Girl like Cici?

Overby studied Cici. "Mrs. O'Callaghan? Now I recognize you. You're Rusty O'Callaghan's widow, ain't you?"

Cici gazed up at him. "Yes."

"I was out to your place a few months ago when your husband passed. What do you have to say about all this?"

"Frank is an amazing detective. I don't know how he did it, but he figured everything out. Poison through the cork with a hypo. That's the explanation. That bottle in McQuade's collection, it was like the loaded chamber of a revolver in a game of Russian roulette. McQuade spun the barrel and it came up. It was perfect. You can't trace it back to Thursby. There's no evidence left from the bottle — Beef Ballou probably threw that away before you even suspected homicide. And besides, Thursby's dead, case closed. Frank's a genius."

Overby contemplated her jewel-like green eyes until he couldn't hold their gaze anymore. Then he turned to me. "Maybe I underestimated you, Swiver. I thought you were an empty trench coat. Well, everyone seems satisfied. We'll talk to Fenwick or Fenucchi about it. He was Thursby's valet, wasn't he? Maybe he'll know something."

"Sure, Lieutenant," I said. "I don't know for sure that Thursby poisoned the bottle himself. Maybe the old general asked Fenucchi to do the job."

"Okay, I got to go," Overby said. "You two planning any trips?"

"No," said Cicilia.

"You know where to find me, Lieutenant," I said.

"Good. Thanks, Swiver. Good night." He tugged down on the brim of his hat, and disappeared into the night.

Both of us looked at the foyer and the closed door. Cicilia spoke first. "I'm tired, Frank."

I realized I was running on fumes, *nero misto* fumes. It was stuffy in the apartment, the steam from the *Chez Cici* chafing dishes, the smoke from Damas's Galousies, even a whiff from the gunshot hung in the air. I slipped out of my sport coat. The back of my shirt was sodden with sweat. "We should talk a little, Cici." I opened the kitchen window, and brought out two big balloon goblets with real stems. I came out and sat close to Cici on the davenport and poured each of us a generous glass of the 1920 Fenucchi Blackbird. Then I leaned back and considered her. "Think it'll hold up?"

"Why not?" she said. "Fenwick's going down for Thursby's murder, and Thursby's not talking. I don't think the others care. Except maybe Vera. Thank you, Frank. Why'd you do it?"

"Whose sins you shall forgive, they are forgiven them; and whose sins you shall retain, they are retained."

"What are you talking about, Frank?" She tasted her Blackbird.

"You were raised Catholic, weren't you, Miss Ricci? You remember the gospel reading that's from? Ah, never mind. You admit it then, doll? You poisoned the wine you gave McQuade?"

"Yes. I admit I have a dark side. I knew it was wrong but I couldn't stop myself."

"I forgive you. And that mushroom omelet you fed Rusty. You knew it was poisoned too." I slurped a mouthful and aerated it over my palate.

"I thought they were chanterelles. Let's not talk about that. I love you, Frank. That's what matters."

"How can I trust you? I'm like Didymus, the twin, two personalities in one person," I said. "One side of me believes you; the other side of me has doubts. The mushrooms probably *were* chanterelles, doll, but they were just a cover. Vera tells me even the deadliest mushrooms, amanita, 'death-caps,' take twenty-four to forty-eight hours to act. What did you use, Cici? Arsenic? Or maybe the mixture you killed McQuade with?"

"That's crazy, Frank. How can you keep accusing me of something like that? Look at me." Her long dark eyelashes shaded her bright green eyes. Her words were starting to slur. "Now that we've found each other again, let's stay together. You won't have to work for twenty-five dollars a day. The restaurant business is a tough one, but together, we don't have to be poor."

"Stop it, Cici. These poisonings aren't crimes in a moment of passion. These are planned murders in the first degree. You'd get the gas chamber for them."

"If you don't like it the way you're telling it, why didn't you give me to Overby? Vera would have been happy." She pouted and drank. "Frank, is the fire still lit under that chafing dish?"

I turned to look where she was pointing. I had to stand up to peer into the kitchen.

"No, it's out." When I sat back down the wine in my glass was rocking. "Maybe the poison was something from your garden, Cici. I saw your kitchen garden the other day. I had my coffee out there. You have some unusual herbs. What do you grow?"

"Fennel, parsley, carrots . . ." Cici grinned a little.

"And hemlock, laurel, foxglove, nightshade, yew? What did you lace the chicken with that killed the cat? I'm no expert on herbs Cicilia, but . . ."

"This Blackbird is fantastic, Frank," she interrupted. "Old man Fenucchi made even better wine than Thursby." Her lips left no lipstick where they touched the glass. It had worn off through the long evening of food, napkins, and other glasses.

"Cici, would you get that light? It's still too warm in here." She turned and yanked the chain on my reading lamp behind her. While she was looking the other way, I switched the glasses on the cocktail table.

I selected the glass Cici had started and drank from it. I carried it over to the sitting room window, and I opened that too. "So why'd I do it? Why'd I give Thursby to Overby for the McQuade killing? Two reasons, first, Thursby was no innocent. He had enough money to pay Vito Fenucchi a fair price for the Blackbird Vineyard. He could have afforded it. The money could have helped the Fenucchis get through the Depression and Prohibition. But it wasn't enough for Lloyd Thursby to get a great piece of vineyard land. He had to take advantage of the Fenucchis when they were down. He had to screw them out of their land. And for what? His sin I retained." I moved back to the couch and Cici.

"Kiss me, Frank." That was all right with me. I set my glass down on the cocktail table, leaned across, and kissed her. We held that for a while, and then we moved it around a little. When I leaned back again, it seemed to me that my glass was closer to Cici than it had been when

I put it down. She drank from her glass.

"Pour me a little more, Frank. I have to go powder my nose." While she was using my bathroom, I filled her glass so that both were the same level, and switched them again. When she came back in I was sipping from a goblet, the one she had just drunk from. But I realized I hadn't peed since about 6:30, before the guests arrived. I had to go too.

"'Scuse me." I went to the bathroom.

When I came back, Cici was drinking. Had she switched glasses? She asked, "So, what's the second reason?"

"That I didn't give you to Overby? McQuade was a bastard. What harm did you do by killing him?"

Cicilia stood up and undid the bow on her dress. The straps slipped off her shoulders, and she slipped out of the dress. I was right when I first saw it. Taking it off was quick and easy.

Now she stood in front of me in her half-slip and lacy black bra. Beautiful raven-colored hair, deep-green eyes, Night of the Honeysuckles scent. "Mmm," I said. "There's a third reason."

Fumbling behind her back, Cici undid the clasp on the black bra, slid her arms out of the straps, and held her shoulders back. Then she dropped her slip. Now she wore only her garter belt and hose. She straddled me on the couch. "I have something to tell you, Frank."

Hugging her and nibbling around her neck, I reached

behind her to the table and switched the glasses again. Instead of taking a drink though, I kissed her breast. It was hot, and the nipple tasted salty. The softness above her sternum glistened in a sheen of perspiration.

"Yes, Frank, oh, yes." As I worked the nipple in my mouth, I was conscious Cici was leaning back. Reaching for the wine? Was she having a drink? Or just switching glasses again? But things were heating up, and I forgot about the two-glass monty for a while.

Afterward, we found ourselves on the carpet, next to the table. I checked my watch. It was almost midnight. Both wineglasses were at about the same level-half full. Or were they half empty?

"What now, Cici?"

"Come live with me, Frank. No matter what I've done, you know that I love you. In your heart, you know we love each other. At last we can be together."

"For how long?" I said.

"The rest of our lives?"

"That's what I was afraid of. I want to, Cici. It's all I ever wanted, all these years. But how long will the rest of my life be? How can I believe in you? I don't want to end up like McQuade . . . and Rusty. As long as I know you killed Rusty, I could never feel safe that you won't try to silence me." I shook my head. I was trying to find a way to tell her good-bye. "What was it you wanted to tell me, Cici?"

"Brigid is our daughter. I was pregnant before I married Rusty."

"What?"

"You're Brigid's father."

I was so stunned I almost drank. "Me? A father?"

"Yes, Frank. I wanted to tell you, but I've kept it secret for all these years. I was pregnant by you before I ever let Rusty touch me."

"When was she born?"

"June 16, 1934."

"Let me think . . . you didn't start going with Rusty —"

"Until November of '33. He thought she was premature. That and he couldn't count very well."

"I'll be damned. Me, a dad."

"Oh, God, Frank. Look!" She flung out her arm and pointed at the window I'd opened.

"Sorry, Cici. I'm not falling for that old routine."

"What are you talking about?" She had a frantic note in her voice. "It's the black bird."

I was ready to kick myself, but I heard a tapping, and even if it gave her the opportunity to switch glasses, I had to turn to the window. There, sitting on the sill, folding a pair of long, tapered wings that must have spanned four feet was an enormous black falcon. It was a slender bird with a powerful chest, a golden cere over a black beak, and shining black eyes.

The night sky behind the falcon was black. I blinked but

it was still there. The black bird moved its head and gave its call, almost a mocking sound, then remained perfectly still, ruling the night from its perch in my window.

I laid my hands on Cici's shoulders and looked into her eyes. "I don't know that someday you won't decide to poison me, Cici, but I know what I want, what I've always wanted. The third reason I didn't give you to Overby — I'm nuts about you, Cici. I've wanted you for fourteen years. I still want you. Why should I hand you over for McQuade when all of my soul, all of my being says, 'You can save her from her darkness. You can have her.' Yes, Cici. I love you." I smiled and kissed her. Oh, yeah. I was nuts about her. She was a religious experience. I believed her ass in the sack. Yeah, I'd been planning to dump her until — until she'd mentioned Brigid. Knowing Cici and I had a daughter, a thirteen-year-old, changed my thinking. I was ready to forgive her everything, even if it meant risking my life.

"Oh, yes, Frank. With you in my life, with what we have together, I can bury my dark side in the past. You can help keep me out of the dark." She stared into my soul with her green eyes, and before I realized what was happening, she picked up her glass. I wanted to stop her. I had to stop her, but in an instant, she drank it down. I kissed her again.

I was horrified. "Then I'm in too," I said. I drained the other glass to the dregs. I guess in my half-drunken mind,

I thought it was a grand gesture—my love was so strong I'd take the risk for her.

I hadn't thought it through, but Cici's expression told me what I needed to know. Her eyes widened, appalled at what I was doing. "No, Frank, stop!" Now I knew she'd used poison. I might be a dead man, but it was good to know she had a change of heart. She wanted me to live.

The falcon pivoted on one foot, extended its wings, and flapped away.

Cici's green eyes filled with tears. "I've got to go," She slipped her dress over her head, stepped into her heels, and wobbled toward the hall closet.

"Wait, Cici," I called, but she grabbed her mink jacket and was out the door. Was her last word to me, "Nevermore," or had I just had too much to drink?

Epilogue

The wine of life is drawn, and the mere lees
Is left this vault to brag of. —Shakespeare

Cici never made it home. I found out later (when I didn't die from my wine) that she'd set off on foot, leaving her Cadillac parked outside my place. Maybe she was feeling too lit up to drive safely. Maybe she wanted some fresh air. Or maybe she was looking for hack. She got as far as Geary and stepped out in front of a streetcar.

It seemed clear enough to the medical examiner that the cause of death was being run over by a tram, so case closed. Did Cici drink poison and become weak, disoriented? Was it a drunken accident? Or knowing she'd drunk poison, did she decide to kill herself? I took the wineglasses we'd used to a friend of mine who had a chemistry hobby. He said the glasses contained no arsenic, cyanide, or strychnine residue, but he didn't have the means or a big enough sample to test for every toxic garden plant.

My guess was hemlock. But I preferred not to know for sure. If I did, I might have to live with the knowledge that I had killed the love of my life.

I visited Joe Damas in the hospital. Sally DeBains was sitting on one side of his bed. The young man I'd seen in the hallway at Joe's place on Magnolia was on the other side. Joe was upbeat and had the customary Gauloises hanging from his lips, filling the hospital room with blue-black smoke. "The bullet tore the flesh from the top of my shoulder, but it didn't hit a bone," he told me. "I'll be out of here by Monday, I think."

"He's so brave," said Sally. Joe gave his usual shrug and then winced at the pain. Everyone laughed.

Joe told me Cicilia O'Callaghan had visited him the week before the train trip and asked him to forge General Thursby's signature to the promissory notes she had shown me. He did the job and for $250, gave her roughly $25,000 of authentic-looking IOUs. I tore them in half and gave them back to him.

Vera wouldn't give me the time of day, but she did agree to come to the opening of Lloyd Thursby's will at the offices of Lamm, Agnello, and Wolfowitz the following week. We brought Louisa Peregrino with us. Wolfowitz was an old-fashioned gentleman, and Louisa didn't have to say anything. Wolfie was satisfied from Thursby's notes that Vera was the "Vera Thursby" of the will. He drew up papers transferring to her sole ownership of the Blackbird Vineyard, four acres of the finest old-vine mixed black in the county. She's giving up her apartment in town, and moving up to Sonoma to work the vineyard. "I'll stay at Mom's for now," she said, "until I can get my own place up there." I have a hunch she'll make out good, and probably be a better winemaker than General Thursby was.

I had to go hear another testament opened in May — Cicilia O'Callaghan's. After Rusty had died, Cici had her lawyer draw up a new will. She left everything to the girls, Brigid and Meaghan. But until they turned twenty-one, the estate was in the hands of the executor. The O'Callaghan estate comprised the house on the north side of Lafayette Park and a '41 Cadillac; Rusty had paid cash for both purchases. The restaurant, *Chez Cici*, was in a leased property, but it had some liquid assets, mainly the wine collection. Other than that, Cici had been broke, living on the cash flow from the restaurant.

Cici mentioned in the new will that I was the father of Brigid. She had named me executor of the estate too. Most likely, when she wrote the will, she hadn't expected she'd try to kill me.

I'm adjusting to my new life. I let my apartment in the Haight go to save money and moved into the big house with Brigid and Meaghan. I'm trying to learn how to be a dad. That's not all silk so far, but I'll pick it up. Chasing bad guys for twenty-five dollars a day gets depressing sometimes. I get lonely. I think the girls will be good for me.

So, yeah, I'm still working at the private dick trade to keep myself in gas money and the occasional pack of butts. And we're struggling to keep the restaurant open with a new cook, to keep Meaghan and Brigid in shoes.

I haven't seen Vera since that day in the law office, but I haven't forgotten about her either. I remember her holding those calla lilies in front of that scarlet dress, a bit of thigh peeking out as she climbed aboard *Vieux Desirs*. I'll never forget how she winked back at me.

About the Author

Harley Mazuk was born in Cleveland, the son of a blue-collar worker, and majored in English literature at Hiram College in Ohio and Elphinstone College, Bombay U.

Harley worked as a record salesman (vinyl) and later toiled for the US Government in computer programming and in communications, where he honed his writing style as an editor and content provider for official web sites.

He began writing the Frank Swiver series of private eye stories in 2010 and has published four stories in *Ellery Queen Mystery Magazine*. His novelettes and flash fiction have appeared in Dead Guns Press and Shotgun Honey.

Harley's passions are writing, reading, his family, peace, Italian cars, and California wine. He and his wife Anastasia live in Maryland, where they have raised two children.

Find Harley at: www.harleymazuk.com